Selara's Rules

James L Baron

OCEAN HOUSE COMMUNICATIONS CANADA

ACKNOWLEDGEMENTS

Thank you to Peers Anthony for your stories, encouragement,
and advice — giving me the courage to complete this book.

Many thanks to the students and teachers of Captain Meares
Elementary Secondary School and the folks at School District 84
for their support and encouragement.

A special thank you to Pieta Woolley, my first draft editor,
who encouraged me to build a bigger story.

Thank you Ann Mander, my final draft editor, for helping me craft
a complete and wonderful novel.

Thank you Robert Dufour for his creativity and technical expertise
bringing this fairy tale to a much larger audience.

DEDICATION

I would like to dedicate this book to my wife and family; especially my children for encouraging me to weave my own bedtime stories to share with the world.

A Note to Travelers in Selara's Kingdom

Selara's Kingdom is one of ten kingdoms spread out over a vast region. The kingdoms are separated by steep mountain ranges and dense forest. There has been unrest in Selara's kingdom since the emergence of Dark and Elemental Majik over two hundred years ago.

Dark Majik (spelt in the old way) has always co-existed with Elemental Majik. The two types of majik are on opposite ends of the majik spectrum. Dark Majik abilities run in families in Selara's Kingdom. As with all talents, some children are more gifted in the ways of Dark Majik than others. The practitioners of Dark Majik can impose their will on weak minds, use Dark Majik energy as a weapon, create illusions, and manipulate the laws of the natural world to suit their own ends. It is best not to become too friendly with those who practise Dark Majik.

To enhance their abilities, Dark Majik practitioners often use spoken spells accessing Neutral Majik, written long before Dark and Elemental Majik manifested in the kingdom. These spells are used by both Dark and Elemental humans.

Natural creatures abound in the kingdom: Valerian boars, deer, bears, mountain cats, timber wolves, crows, and common birds. Some animals, birds, and even insects, have evolved with special abilities due to constant exposure to Dark Majik. Some non-majik humans — referred to as the Nomaji (due to their lack of Elemental or Dark Majik), have developed an immunity to many of the spells and powers associated with Dark Majik. The Nomaji are not fooled by Dark Majik illusions and mostly unharmed by Dark Majik attacks.

Dark Majik in itself is not evil, but its power is seductive and highly addictive. Some individuals find that certain emotions, like greed and the need to dominate, are magnified by Dark Majik. These individuals need to be careful they're not overcome by these types of intrusive thoughts and emotions that fuel the ego. The use of Dark Majik is associated with the colour green in this kingdom. The energy produced by Dark Majik manifests as different shades of green. If you see a human with a green aura, or manipulating green fire, they have Dark Majik powers.

Dark Majik practitioners and Elementals use majik creatures associated with their abilities. They use these incarnations to protect and serve them. Dark Majik practitioners use green fire creatures, their most dangerous weapon. Because Dark Majik practitioners are not like Elementals, they can only manipulate and conjure creatures from the energy of green fire rather than water, air, and earth.

Various races in the kingdom have been spawned through Dark Majik, such as Ogres, Dark Creatures, Daemon Wolves, Thought Listeners, and Night Birds. These races evolved through intentional or unintentional exposure to Dark Majik.

Elemental Majik manifests itself in human families. Just like Dark Majik, the Majik abilities vary depending on the individual. Some Elemental abilities are more common in males or females. For example, in the time of Selara, Fire Elementals are almost exclusively female and Wind Elementals almost exclusively male. Both Water Elementals and Earth Elementals are commonly male or female.

Humans can only manifest one Elemental ability in their lifetime, the elements are: water, wind, fire, or earth. Some Elemental humans can completely transform into aspects of their "Element" while others can only partially transform. When the natural majik is stronger in them, anything the person wears transforms with them, while in others, only their bodies will transform. Some humans have limited Elemental abilities. These individuals are referred to as Lesser Elementals. It should be noted that Elemental Fire manifests in orange, red, white, or yellow. If you are lucky, a Fire Elemental may do the "fire trick" for you.

Just as Dark Majik practitioners use majik creatures, some Elementals can conjure serpents, dragons, or hydras from the majik of their Element. Elemental creatures are mostly used for protection. Elementals who are well practised in the majik art of their Element can conjure weapons. Elementals are normally friendly. You should not be concerned if you encounter one. Unfortunately, most Elementals are in hiding at the writing of this book. The tyrant Daemon is attempting to wipe out all traces of Elemental Majik from the kingdom.

It is very important to note that both Elementals and Dark Majik practitioners are vulnerable when they are not using their powers or abilities. Assassins can kill even the most powerful Elemental or Dark Magician in their sleep or in a surprise attack. There is only one spell that can make a human impervious to death, but the price of immortality is steep and the spell is strictly forbidden.

If you see a Dark Majik-Elemental couple, remind them that they can only be friends—nothing more! The offspring of these unions are called Dark Elementals. These unfortunate humans are blessed and cursed. They are extremely powerful and can manipulate Majik in new and creative ways, but the constant struggle between Dark and Elemental Majik inside their bodies destroys them mentally and physically. They go mad or become extremely dangerous as the internal battle tears them apart. At the writing of this manuscript, there is no known way to balance this Majik.

Wizards are Nomaji, humans who have studied and memorised many of the ancient spells created before the emergence of Dark and Elemental Majik. These Wizards always seek a balance of peace in the kingdom. They are largely aligned with Elemental Majik, which they view as being pure and occurring in accordance with the basic laws of nature. They are the keepers of knowledge and are often called upon when problems occur in the kingdom. The Wizards believe that Dark Elementals can be taught to balance the warring majik inside them. If you have any questions or concerns in your quest, you can always ask a Wizard for help.

The Nomaji (No-Majik) are humans who have no majik powers. Like you and me, they may be curious but are largely suspicious of those who possess majik powers. The Nomaji make up for their lack of majik using the basic physical laws of their world. They use gravity, metallurgy, chemistry, mathematics, and rudimentary science to create ingenious weapons and inventions that are a type of majik in their own right. Their work is not taken seriously by majik practitioners. The Nomaji routinely banish humans in their villages who begin to display majik powers. The Nomaji villages use running water, plumbing, and advanced construction. If you are fortunate to stay in a Nomaji village, you will find that you will feel right at home.

The Night Birds evolved through constant exposure to Dark Majik. They are largely feared by humans because of their vicious nature and unpredictability. They can snap broomsticks with their beaks, and their claws are razor sharp. Through their evolution, the Night Birds have become exceedingly creative and innovative. Their nests have become elaborate weavings. The Clan (as they refer to themselves as a group) live in ornate basket cities unseen and untouched by Hu-mans. (spelled and pronounced this way in their thoughts and in their language). If you are fortunate enough, you may be able to purchase an old Night Bird basket woven before the Night Birds went into isolation.

The Night Birds have very strict Clan Laws and they live by codes of honour. The Night Birds have the majik ability to bond psychically with humans. When a bonding takes place, they can communicate telepathically over great distances with their Hu-man and share thoughts and memories. A bond lasts for life and can never be undone until one of the bond-mates dies. In the early years, bonding was a common practice, but as wars and conflicts grew, the practice became strictly prohibited. Any Night Birds who bonded with humans were killed or banished from the Clan. Certain gifted Elder Birds could sense when bonding majik occurred, and would send warrior birds out to kill the offending Night Bird and sometimes their human bond-mates.

The Night Birds are very sensitive to all types of majik. They can sense and see majik auras around other creatures. The Night Birds cannot use spells or speak human languages, but when bonded with humans, they can communicate easily and interpret language through the thought images of their bond-mates. When visiting the kingdom, stay far away from the Clan Trees as no human visiting them has lived to tell the tale. If you encounter a Night Bird, be very cautious and respectful. It would be wise to learn the Holy Sign of the Night Bird and visit one of the many chapels dedicated to the Princess of Peace. Do not let a Night Bird bond with you!

Thought Listeners are a special and rare form of Dark Creature (they know what you are thinking right now). The Thought Listeners were created by an ancient form of majik that has been long forgotten. Even the Wizards cannot find the original creation spells for Thought Listeners. At the time of this writing, only one Thought Listener is still living. A Thought Listener can see thoughts laid out like a tapestry before them. A Thought Listener reads this tapestry of thoughts like one would read this book. But you don't have to be concerned unless you are plotting to overthrow the Thought Listener's master. Make sure you avoid looking in a mirror while visiting the kingdom. A Thought Listener cannot only read your thoughts, but they can see you and locate you when you see your own reflection.

Daemon-Wolves are unnatural creatures spawned from the common timber wolf. They have a sensitive sense of smell and a voracious appetite. They are difficult to kill, travel in packs, grow up to seven feet tall, and are led by an alpha male. Their claws and fangs are razor sharp, and they are physically strong. You will smell a Daemon-Wolf before you see it. The smell is distinctive and repulsive. If you smell the stench of a Daemon-Wolf, you may have just enough time to seek safety in a shelter while it passes by. They are similar to Were-Wolves, but Daemon-Wolves are an entirely separate race that never transform back into their original form. They were created by Daemon, a very gifted Dark Majik practitioner, by accident. He decided to create more of them when he realised what deadly and powerful servants they could be. The Daemon-Wolves are the ultimate killing machine in the kingdom and should be avoided at all costs.

Dark Creatures can be found in various forms. Many of the Dark Creatures were "mistakes," created through flaws in Dark Majik spells.

Some of these creatures have wings while others may have several arms. The Dark Creatures always seek a purpose for their existence and will often gravitate to serving a Dark Master. Although many of them appear dangerous, they are largely harmless unless they are at war. If you encounter one of these creatures, try not to stare.

Ogres are largely misunderstood creatures spawned originally as the servants of Dark Majik practitioners. They are large, powerful, and single-minded. As years went by, the race of Ogres sought their independence. They retreated to the deep forest and created a small kingdom of their own. The Ogre society consists of an elected queen and court officials. Many Ogres still practise their warrior traditions. Ogres are rarely seen by humans, but if you see one, give them a friendly wave and be on your way.

Marauders are part of a hired army. They are made up of thieves, murderers, and bandits. Their Dark Majik master keeps them in check through a combination of fear and rewards. Marauders are almost always Nomaji (Non-Majik humans) who have learned to survive by forming an alliance with a powerful leader. Marauders are skilled in hand-to-hand combat and archery. They attack in small groups, often in the company of Daemon-Wolves, who are used for tracking and killing. The Marauders are heavily armed and travel mostly on horseback. Their job is to collect taxes, intimidate, guard, and hunt Elementals. At the time of this writing, many Elementals have been murdered by Marauders. If you are unfortunate enough to come in contact with Marauders, make sure you are carrying a few gold coins to bribe them.

The Wraiths do not actually dwell in Selara's kingdom. They are a majik race that exist between worlds. They often communicate in dreams and do not normally seek to interfere in the politics of the kingdom. Wraiths are skilled artisans with the ability to create majik artefacts for a specific purpose. These objects defy the natural laws of the kingdom and are virtually indestructible outside of the world of the Wraiths. The circlet, for example, was created by the Wraiths to give additional power to a worthy ruler in the kingdom. It was sent into the physical world of the kingdom at great cost to help with the balance of conflict in Selara's kingdom.

You may hear the people of the villages refer to the Second Realm. The Second Realm is the next world where the soul passes after death in the kingdom. It is expansive without a physical dimension where all sentient creatures go when they pass on. If you find yourself looking at the purple skies of the Second Realm, something has gone dreadfully wrong with your visit to Selara's kingdom.

In your travels, you may encounter one of the Brethren. Very little is known about the Brethren. It is a mysterious Night Bird cult composed of Nomaji, Elementals, and Dark Majik practitioners. It is said that every one of them is bonded to a Night Bird. They are fanatically dedicated to the doctrine and the rise of the Peace Princess. Sometimes they are seen in the Chapel of the Peace Princess in prayer. It is best to avoid the members of The Brethren.

chapter i

Rule 1: Never curse

Selara was a seven-year-old girl with shocking red hair and piercing green eyes. She felt the world was created for her, and she had no fear of it. But this was not her world, and this was not her time. Her presence here defied all natural laws, bent and broken by a dangerous and forbidden majik. In this world, she was a motherless waif, and strangely, her long forgotten mother was not even born yet.

The mist danced and swirled across the weary landscape and gently caressed the twisted trees with sleepy hands. The years of war left the valley listless, almost too tired for green fields and flowers. A few Night Birds floated silently in and out of the mist to perch on black blasted trees standing like weary soldiers on the edges of the grassy moor.

In the darkness of her room, Selara tossed and turned. Strands of hair stuck to her face. It was the talking book again. Squiggles and lines made sounds in her dreams. Her mouth moved involuntarily, forming its words in her troubled sleep.

In her nightmare, the air sizzled, encircling her window with green fire. Selara saw a tall woman sitting on a marble bench with her shoulders slumped. A few tears wandered down her cheeks as she sat in her green world of swimming stars. Suddenly, she turned and stared at Selara.

The girl screamed and woke up, shivering. *It was only a dream*, she thought, pulling her homemade doll close and falling back to sleep.

Selara awoke to the familiar clatter of dishes and smells of breakfast. Her grandmother and grandfather were the only parents that she could remember. They were mostly kind to her, yet secretive and suspicious of others. They were fiercely protective and constantly fought a losing battle to keep her out of harm's way.

Despite her young age, Selara was a force to be reckoned with and almost impossible to contain. Her knees and elbows were a road map of scrapes and scars. Her grimy skin was porcelain, scrubbed and polished by her grandmother nightly after a day of adventures. Grandmother tried desperately to establish rules to keep her safe from all things, seen and unseen.

Selara bounced down the stairs to morning hugs and a quick breakfast before bursting into the summer morning. She was a wisp of red hair, bouncing and weaving through the waving grass. Her piercing emerald eyes surveyed the misty moor, scanning the horizon. They narrowed as they spotted a distant, discarded trunk partially submerged in the mud, its lid broken and cracked open.

Nice try! she thought. As silent as a cat, her muddy bare feet closed in on the gaping maw. Suddenly, her fingers closed around oily black feathers. "Got you!" she said. The frightened, little bird croaked in alarm before relaxing and letting Selara's hands lift him from his hiding place. Selara giggled as she released the bird, letting him flap his wings indignantly.

"I win!" she shouted, doing a short victory dance before scooping up the flapping bird and placing him on her shoulder. From high on a twisted branch beyond their sight, a larger Night Bird shook his head in disapproval. He spread his powerful wings and lifted off into the grey sky.

"Grandfather said he would teach me how to make fire serpents," Selara said as she wound her way through the roots and clumps of grass. "But it's a secret, so we have to keep quiet about it." She stopped, looking sternly at the bird. "Do you understand? Grandfather tells me lots of things, but I'm not supposed to talk about them. Right?"

The bird gazed at her knowingly. He bobbed his head, looking as if he comprehended her incomprehensible language.

The two came to the edge of a clearing where she could see her grandparents' place. The ramshackle farmhouse and a few sorry-looking buildings leaned together in silhouette. The cows grazed contentedly, ignoring her.

"Nobody knows this yet, but the words in Grandfather's book can talk to me!" She looked around as if the trees might be listening. The black bird croaked in response.

Wading through the grass, she sifted through her favourite collection of memories. She found a good one: Grandfather carrying her on his back for miles, telling her stories of Dark Creatures, majik, and epic battles. When he told a story, Selara was right there, seeing all of the action and feeling all of the excitement. She was sworn to secrecy, promising never to tell Grandmother.

Selara's grandfather was a man who betrayed his age. He was slightly hunched from the weight of many hardships, yet he always had a never-ending zest for life. Once a week, Grandfather walked around the farm, sprinkling white powder in a huge circle around the buildings. Grandfather told Selara it was for luck and good fortune. He hummed some silly words and winked at his granddaughter. She laughed at his game. She found out later that it was much more than a game.

Some days, Grandfather looked around to make certain they were alone. Then he performed the fire trick for her. They made a firehouse out of a pile of dead wood and grass. Selara closed her eyes and counted. When she reached five, she opened her eyes, and a pretty orange fire serpent wrapped itself around the firehouse and chewed it hungrily. In its place, a bright cheery fire sprang up to keep them warm on the chilly mornings while they talked.

Today Selara crept tentatively into the shadows of the smaller building. Bird rested contentedly on her shoulder. The door complained, screeching as she pushed into the musty silence. "The book is here," she whispered as if they were entering a shrine. She smelled the incense of worn leather and drying herbs. She tapped the not-so-secret wooden drawer, and it slid open. There lay a book. Selara stroked the ornate spiral designs on its cover. She lifted the book from its hiding place and sat cross-legged on the dusty floor. Bird flew down beside her. Randomly flipping to a page, Selara peered at the intricate markings. She ran her index finger along the colourful script and smiled at Bird. "Do you hear them?" Bird was eyeing a nearby cricket, oblivious to her. "The words say we can fly. I want to fly just like you!" she said, clapping her hands. Selara stood up and placed Bird back on his perch. She spoke the incantations that filled her mind. *Nothing is happening*, she thought, frustrated. She held the book in one hand and flapped her arms like wings, repeating the words. Without warning, the walls around her melted. The whole world spun. Selara, the book, and the bird disappeared. Only their footprints remained on the dusty floor.

Selara found herself standing in an open meadow ten years in the past. Her hair fluttered like red banners in the dry wind. Bird trembled in shock. Chorusing crickets and chanting birds greeted them.

"Where the firk are we?" she asked, her voice a hoarse whisper. She remembered that she was not supposed to use that word. Grandmother's rule: no cursing. Bird let out a worried croak in response. She spun around. They were in the centre of a meadow under blue summer skies. Selara scanned the far edges of the waving grass and the rolling mountains beyond. The two stood in silence.

From the far end of the field, a growing wave of words, grunts, and guttural screams advanced. Bird flapped his wings in alarm. It sounded like every tree in the distant forest had a voice. Metallic sounds of clanging armour punctuated the marching. Eruptions of green fire exploded like thunder. On the other side of the field, the opposing army responded to commands. Sheets of orange flame reached out, blackening trees while small fires licked the grass.

Selara froze in icy panic as dark shapes advanced onto the meadow from either side. Horrible half-human monsters sniffed the air and lumbered towards her. From the other side, strangers wavered, disappeared, and reappeared somewhere else. In the confusion, a shadow fell over the paralyzed Selara. Massive claws swung at the tiny target.

She screamed in pain, a thin red streak of blood slowly rolling down her cheek. Her grandfather's book fell from her hands. Bird fluttered instinctively, avoiding the second blow.

"Stop!" she screamed. "You're being a bully!" Anger replaced her fear.

The grass around her withered into an oily, black sludge, and a curtain of thick smoke blinded the threatening behemoth. Two tongues of fire exploded from the blackened ground, encircling Selara and Bird in a weaving of green and orange fire. A low hum filled the air, growing steadily louder. Perched at the end of each flame was the head of a sparkling serpent with a tongue of fire. Each glistening body writhed in the thickening smoke. The twin snakes moved menacingly toward the monster.

Selara stood up with Bird gripping tightly to her. Her body glowed while she mouthed a silent incantation. The green serpent moved like lightning. Searing fangs sank into the monstrous face, tearing and burning through its grey flesh like paper. The orange serpentine twin worked in concert, burning the monstrous legs to the bone. The two were a deadly tornado, leaving black ash blowing like feathers in the wind.

The armies ran in opposite directions. The opposing leaders stood dumbfounded as the green and orange fire serpents entwined triumphantly around the girl. The serpents surveyed the meadow, challenging anyone or anything to defy them. Selara bent down, picked up the book, shimmered, and vanished. The impact of her actions sent both armies into disarray. Not because of the girl or the serpents, but because the serpents worked together for a common purpose — to protect the girl at all costs.

A dark, sinister woman remained and watched intently. Her face twisted in disgust. *Firk! What should have been an easy victory was snatched away by a wizard's trick,* she pondered. *Elemental and Dark Majik do not exist together. Everyone knows that.* She turned her head just in time to catch a quick movement behind her. She teleported to avoid a blow.

Ten years later, Selara landed hard on the floor of the shed, dropping her grandfather's book. She was breathing hard. Warm, salty tears traced their way down her cheeks. The door swung open. Grandfather's boots shuffled into the room.

"What happened?" he asked. The colour drained from his face as he spotted her bleeding scratch and his book of spells upside down beside Selara. Bird escaped through the open door.

Selara looked into her grandfather's eyes. "There were monsters, and one was a bully, and I got hurt," sobbed Selara, wrapping her arms tightly around his neck as he crouched down beside her. Grandfather tightened his grip.

"You were very brave — and Bird too!" Grandfather said. He picked up the book and held it away from Selara as if it would burn her.

"Big fire serpents came to save me!" blurted Selara. "I was so mad at that mean monster. My big snakes ate it, and all the bad things ran away."

He gawked. No one had taught her how to read the old language. More astonishingly, she used the incantation without the use of a time talisman to find her way back.

"Tell me about the serpents. You said there were two serpents. Two, you're sure?"

"Yes, and one was pretty green. He's my favourite. I think I'll name him Greenwald. The other was orange like our campfires. I haven't thought of a name for him yet."

Grandfather felt as if the air was sucked out of the room. He stared into the corner of the shed. "Two serpents," he said absently. Not only had Selara teleported back in time, but she had unknowingly conjured up two fire serpents. By the colours of their fire, he knew that one was Elemental, but the other one was far more disturbing. It was the product of Dark Majik.

"Are you okay?" asked Selara.

"Two," said Grandfather in a daze.

"Yes, they wrapped around us and kept us safe. The bully monster died and died."

Grandfather shook himself. "You must never use this book again or speak to anyone about what happened to you. Do you understand me?"

Selara wasn't used to seeing her grandfather this upset. She nodded, seeing his concern.

"Let's get you to Grandmother to take care of that cut." He slid the book into his vest pocket and scooped up Selara.

A full moon cast eerie shadows ten years into the past. Sheltered under the boughs of massive evergreens, bonfires lit the faces of men in celebration. The wizards had their revenge on the Dark Queen. "Is there still a chance she can free herself?" asked Chalon, pulling his robes tightly around him.

"No, only if the source of her prison is revealed. And none of us can ever speak of it or even take credit for what we've done. Her disappearance must remain a mystery. There are those loyal to her, and if they knew how we trapped her, they may try to free her. No one would suspect a simple locomotion spell to hold such a powerful adversary," responded Parseth.

"It was inspired!" said Theseus.

"And you had no other choice! She enacted the impervious spell," said Clovis, his dark eyes sparkling.

"Yes, but at what cost?" said Chalon.

"That's between her and the Gods," said Parseth. "Why would anyone endanger their soul simply to possess earthly powers? She's mad."

"Immortality, maybe," said Cay wistfully. "But who would want to live forever? It's unnatural." The men nodded their agreement.

"Your teleportation idea was a work of genius," said Clovis, raising a mug of mead to toast Parseth. The other men did likewise.

"You timed it perfectly, knowing exactly what she would do!" said Theseus.

"But what of the girl? Was she a sign from the Gods?" asked Cay, leaning closer.

"More like *what* was she?" added Chalon. "The soldiers on both sides are calling her the Princess of Peace — the sign to end the war. Was the princess an illusion, or was she real? How did the illusion vaporise a Manolith?"

"The Queen was as confused as all of us!" chuckled Parseth. "If the girl was from the Gods, then the Gods had perfect timing. The Queen needed to be caught by surprise. We needed to force her into enacting the teleportation spell, so we could fold it into itself."

"The girl was definitely an Elemental. But how could she conjure a Dark Majik serpent at the same time as an Elemental serpent? She couldn't be older than seven moons, much too young to summon majik creatures. Why did the Night Bird just sit there on her shoulder without biting her or flying away?" said Parseth.

"Okay, you've had your jest! Which one of you conjured the illusion? It was amazing! Own up! I want to congratulate you personally." There was complete silence in the group while everyone looked at everyone else. "If none of you created the illusion, then maybe she truly is a sign from the Gods. To the miracle at Albright!" he shouted with his glass raised.

"To the miracle at Albright!" they intoned.

"And to the Princess of Peace!"

"To the Princess of Peace!"

Ten years later, not far from the original wizard encampment, Grandfather opened the door to their little cottage, carrying Selara. Grandmother eyed the two carefully and assessed the cut on Selara's cheek. "It was that Night Bird, wasn't it? They're wild and dangerous," Grandmother's voice trailed off when she saw the look of concern in Grandfather's eyes. "It wasn't the Night Bird, was it?"

"No," replied Grandfather. The two fell silent. Selara kept silent, sworn to secrecy.

It was happening, thought Grandmother, *and so young! Daemon was right. She will be the most dangerous one of them all. She will either rebuild everything that was destroyed or end everything as if it never was.*

The next morning Selara woke up, unfazed by her strange adventure the afternoon before. She hopped out of bed and peered out the window. The morning mist was just beginning to rise on the moor, forming ghostly shapes dancing for the rising sun. Selara dressed herself and padded down the stairs to the smells of Grandmother's cooking. Grandfather was at the table, finishing his porridge when Selara rushed across the floor to give him a huge hug. She then grabbed onto Grandmother's legs, paused, and scampered to the table to join Grandfather. When Grandfather turned to speak to Grandmother, Selara deftly snatched a bun from the breakfast table and slipped it under her apron. Grandfather smiled at Selara's secret ritual, knowing she shared her bread with the little Night Bird.

A small smile crept onto Grandmother's face but left quickly. She remembered that not long ago Selara had reached up onto this very table and accidentally spilled a pot of boiling soup. The soup splashed onto Selara's leg. Shock turned to pain, to hurt, and then to anger. When Grandmother returned to the kitchen, the offending pot was a molten puddle pooling on the floor mingled with the blackened soup. Selara ran to her, bursting into tears, and said, "It's not my fault! It was the green serpent." Grandmother remembered holding her close, tending to her blisters, and when the metal cooled, the two cleaned up the mess before Grandfather came home.

When Selara calmed, Grandmother said, "The serpent was just in your imagination. The pot was old, and sometimes they melted." She was determined to teach Selara her most important rule: Never get mad and lose control!

Dishes clattered in the washing sink as Selara disappeared into the morning mist in search of Bird. "That girl is special," said Grandfather, his eyes following the shock of red hair through the window, bobbing into the mist.

"She is also dangerous," warned Grandmother, still focused on her dishes.

Grandfather sighed. He had to admit that even at her young age, hints of what she would become were appearing. He did not share Selara's misadventure with his book of spells. *How could she teleport into the past without training or guidance? How could she read the words in the book, let alone activate a dangerous incantation? There are forces working around this child that are beyond my comprehension. She's indeed dangerous, but she's also our only hope for the future.*

Selara trotted beside the fence, banging the fence posts with a stick. "Good morning, pigs! Good morning, horse! Good morning, cows! Good morning, chickens…" Selara remembered that there were no more chickens. No matter what Grandfather did and no matter what kind of chicken house he built, the Night Birds always found a way to steal and eat them. "I'm not upset," he had said, "because the chickens are an offering to the Gods, so the Gods won't pass judgement upon us." Grandfather dropped to one knee and made a strange sign, his two thumbs together with the fingers spread apart like wings rising up. At Selara's confused expression, he said, "It's the Sign of the Holy Night Bird." How Grandmother scolded him for teaching Selara such superstitious nonsense.

Selara passed by the pigpen, holding her nose. She wove her way down pathways, over roots, around mud puddles, and towards a tall twisted tree. She decided to name it 'Bully Hand' because it reminded her of the monster from yesterday. She startled a deer causing it to bounce into the forest.

That was when Selara felt a tugging at her hair. She spun around. Whatever had a hold of her was now hiding behind her. She spun around again and caught a glimpse of a black feather. "Bird!" she shouted, half annoyed but at the same time glad to see him.

"If you don't let me go, you're not going to get your surprise!" Bird let go immediately, hoping the surprise was food. Selara pulled the bun from her apron and slumped down in the grass against a yawning tree. Bird hopped onto her shoulder, and Selara broke off pieces to feed Bird and herself. His beak nipped her finger.

"Careful!" she scolded. "Grandmother says you can snap sticks with that firkin' beak of yours!" Selara liked the feeling she got from using the forbidden word. She had heard Grandfather say it when he nicked himself with an axe. He tried in vain to make her forget it, but she couldn't unhear it. Selara experimented with different ways of saying the word: in disbelief, "F-f-f-irk"; in anger, "FIRK!"; in disappointment, "fi-rr-kkK"; in silliness, "Fir-dillery-irk."

Bird nodded sagely, never understanding her exact words. He watched her body movements and listened carefully to the tone of her voice. Bird knew when she was happy, sad, or mad. Beyond that, her words were just a pleasant, unintelligible song.

Further to the east, gnarled trees stood like grey shadows against the morning sky. Wrapped around the fingers of the twisted trees were large wooden baskets woven from thin branches, leaves, and bits of discarded rope. Each Night Bird family had a dwelling of its own, passed from generation to generation. The dwellings of esteemed birds were massive and complex, woven in decorative patterns and adorned with simple pictograms. They were tapestries honouring important moments in the history of the Clan. Sweeping braided branches framed these homes like a sea of basket waves meandering through the forest. The morning sun cast dark blue shadows while the basket mouths greeted the new day.

In one such dwelling, the parents of Bird were upset.

"Fletcher's spending too much time with that Hu-man! He should be with his own kind! The council rules are there for a reason," Flank droned. "They were established by the founding elders themselves."

Terra turned from her perch and nodded absently to her husband.

"When's she getting here?" asked Flank. He paced back and forth agitated, peering through the looking holes. Their massive globular home was perched high in an old oak tree.

"I told her when the sun is high," she replied.

The Elder Bird Ceeka, ancient and imposing, was both revered and feared by those of the Night Bird Clan. She could gaze into a bird's soul and know their thoughts.

Flank shuddered reflexively. "Why did you have to call on her? We could've handled things ourselves!" he stated emphatically, systematically checking each looking hole for any sign of Ceeka.

"We weren't handling it ourselves. Complaining is not handling it ourselves. That's why I called her. We need to address this before things get out of hand and the rumours begin." At that very moment, there was a fluttering of wings, and a large, ruffled, old bird appeared at the door opening. "Come in, please," offered Terra.

Ceeka's imposing presence filled their home, and Flank stopped pacing and stood perfectly still, his heart beating faster.

"We're having trouble with Fletcher," said Terra. "No matter what we say or do, he won't stop visiting the Hu-man girl. And what's worse — she's some sort of Elemental! Flank has seen the majik waver around her."

Flank chimed in, "We're afraid of what other birds will say, and what will happen if this problem reaches the Elder Circle."

Ceeka listened, weighing each word carefully. She was silent for a time. Then she spoke. "The rules were created to keep us all safe. Is this true?"

"Of course," said Terra and Flank together.

"Has the Hu-man girl harmed Fletcher in any way?"

"No," said Flank.

"Has Fletcher bonded with her?" asked Ceeka.

"Heavens no!" gasped Terra, shaking her head in disgust.

"But something must be done!" said Flank, pacing back and forth.

"Why?"

Perplexed, Flank and Terra looked at Ceeka as if she were crazy.

"Because of the rumours and the breaking of rules," Flank said.

Ceeka turned and stared out of a looking hole in silence. Flank and Terra waited patiently for her to speak. It felt like an eternity.

"I'll go and watch these two myself. And then I'll decide what needs to be done." At this, the Elder Bird turned and sprang out into the open air.

Flank watched her, fearing the neighbours saw her come and go.

Ceeka expertly rode up and down the air currents. Other birds gave her a wide berth as she flew beyond the Clan territories and over the muddy marshes of the moors. She had no trouble finding them. The little Elemental's majik aura was easy to see from high in the clouds. Ceeka descended slowly, perching amid the groaning branches of a blackened tree.

Just out of sight, she studied Fletcher and Selara. The northern wind ruffled Ceeka's feathers. Gnarled talons tethered her firmly to a thickened branch. She had lived for many seasons and through many troubled times, yet her mind was as clear as a silent pool and as sharp as the tip of a claw. She had insights and instincts that the Clan did not fathom. *The Night Birds are divided*, she thought. *The world's changing, and our leaders are too proud, too stubborn, or too frightened to embrace it.*

The wind whistled behind her. She surveyed the rolling ocean of leaves, deep in thought. *When creatures refuse to change and grow, the world leaves them behind, and they become a distant memory. Our Clan avoids Hu-mans, but there'll come a time when Hu-mans and Night Birds'll bond and work together. Dark Majik's brought fear and mistrust, but this'll change. These two are the spring for a new world. But will any of us see it?*

Ceeka watched the Elemental girl carefully. *There's something strange about her aura,* she thought. It was brighter than any Elemental Hu-man she had seen before. She saw a queer fluctuation. The aura was neither Dark nor Elemental. It was somewhere in between. At first, she thought she was mistaken, but then there was that flicker again. *It's impossible!*

In a temple prison between two worlds, stars spun in a never-ending green mist. A stone monolith surrounded by walls with stone benches faded in and out of the swirling fog. A tall figure paced endlessly. The Dark Queen reflected in her emerald purgatory. Sometimes in the stone portal she saw Selara perfectly, and sometimes she could not. At this moment, she saw her playing her little games with that *damn Night Bird.*

She thought back to the day she was imprisoned here. "Wizards!" she spat. "They knew I couldn't be killed like any Nomaji. I'd seen to that." She regarded her left hand with the missing ring finger. *Some spells required sacrifice,* she thought dispassionately. *Stupid, stupid, stupid. Losing concentration for only a moment gave them just enough time to exile me to this green hell. When freedom is once again mine, I'll kill every wizard I find … slowly. When that little brat comes of age, I'll inhabit her body and reclaim the life snatched from me.* Her eyes gleamed. The thought of revenge warmed her. She ran her fingers along the stone walls and then pounded them with her fist. Blood ran down her bruised knuckles before disappearing. *Imprisoned in this green purgatory with no need to eat or sleep is maddening.*

The Queen raised her hands above her head. A bright green ball grew, expanded and spun. The fireball rose up and exploded. It was instantly consumed. Thwarted, she slunk back to the portal and gazed at Selara.

Ceeka watched Fletcher and Selara. They played hide and seek and chasing games. Sometimes they just sat while Fletcher rested on the little girl's shoulder or in her lap. They were two innocents whose spirits had found each other. Ceeka sensed a deep caring between them, and she knew that the little girl would never harm Fletcher. She was about to return to the Clan Village when she saw a dark shape moving ominously towards the two.

From her vantage point, she saw they were oblivious to the approaching danger. A large Valerian boar was digging roots. Normally, the deadly brutes did not frequent these meadows, but this one had wandered. Ceeka was not concerned for Fletcher because he would fly away, but the little Elemental could not. She, most likely, would be killed. Although her aura was bright, she was too young to use or to control her powers.

Most Night Birds were unconcerned about a Hu-man death and would enjoy the fresh meat. Flesh was flesh. But Ceeka had grown in spirit far beyond animal instinct. She viewed every creature as unique with an important role to play, no matter how great or how small.

Selara and Bird were sharing their last piece of bread when they heard a faint rustling in the grass. Both of them stopped to listen.

"What's that smell?" she asked, scrunching up her nose. Bird bobbed his head concerned. Selara held her nose and looked around. She wondered if one of Grandfather's pigs had escaped. Directly in front of her, something snorted, and a nightmare of matted fur and bone tusks exploded through the grass, running headlong towards her. Selara screamed as the enormous hulk advanced. Bird bravely placed himself between the barreling animal and Selara, but even a fully-grown Night Bird was no match for a boar this size. Bird was dwarfed by this behemoth. He acted more out of love than any likelihood of defending her.

Without warning, a dark shadow descended upon the creature, tearing at its eyes with razor sharp claws. The boar was momentarily startled. It shook its massive head. Its eyes burned as sharp talons pierced into them. The boar heaved upwards to gore blindly at the assailant while Fletcher twisted and dodged at the last possible moment. The mysterious attacker, undaunted, continued to slash. Selara stood frozen. The animal stabbed at the bird and then lunged blindly, reorienting on Selara's scent. The boar raised its head, and Ceeka felt a fiery tusk tear through her body, sending her spinning and crashing to the ground.

From where Ceeka lay, the life draining from her torn side, she watched in awe as two sparkling fire serpents rose from the ground. They gracefully wrapped themselves around the little Hu-man, which explained the strange fluctuation in the little girl's aura. They were majestic and beautiful.

The massive fire serpents dwarfed the floundering, blinded boar. They attacked the beast in unison, reducing the creature to a smoking, charred wreck. The serpents vanished, leaving an oily curtain of grey smoke. Selara was in shock, but rushed to crouch down beside her wounded heroine. Bird waddled beside her, tilting his head and bobbing with concern.

A gentle, reassuring voice spoke inside Selara's head. *You're a child born of two rivers. You have a deep love in your heart for the whole world, even for me, a stranger. Take your love into our world and heal it. This is why you were born, and I'm proud to die protecting you.* For a moment, Selara felt dizzy and fought to sit up. Strange thoughts of flying filled her mind. The dying bird was sharing her thoughts. The bird lay still.

Selara did not understand the old ladybird's message. She didn't understand about the rivers or healing the world. Bird flapped beside Selara then rose into the air in the direction of the Clan trees. Selara looked helplessly at the beautiful old bird as tears ran down her cheeks. She and the bird had shared their thoughts. Selara'd never been to a funeral or seen anyone die, so she didn't really know what to do. She trotted into the marshy grass to collect bright lady-slippers and daisies to thank the brave bird. She could still hear her soft voice in her thoughts, and they filled her with a sense of calm. She arranged the flowers around the motionless bird. She wove some of the daisies together to make a small crown and placed it on the old bird's head. *There,* she thought.

By the time Selara finished the crown, ten Night Birds, led by her little friend, flew in formation just below the clouds, gliding towards her like a massive black dagger. Their wings blocked out the sun as they descended into the small clearing. Selara backed away slowly from the body of the elder and stood at a distance. With a rush of wind, the birds landed, cocking their heads curiously at the ring of flowers, the daisy crown, and the smouldering remains of the marsh boar. Their black shiny beaks clicked and let out a series of broken croaks and chitters. Selara fidgeted, not knowing whether to stay or run. She'd never been this close to so many fully-grown Night Birds before. She was frightened.

The lead bird swivelled his head and regarded Selara with what could only be interpreted as respect. Three of the other birds approached the body and locked talons, and lifted her lifeless form, leaving only Selara's ring of flowers. The formation grew smaller and smaller as they rose into the open skies back to the territory of the Clan Birds. The few remaining birds unceremoniously gorged themselves on the remains of the boar while Selara hurried down the path, not wanting to watch.

This strange bird came out of nowhere to save her, and she mourned her death. Selara plunked herself down like a rag doll, thinking about the monstrous boar. It frightened her and would probably have hurt her badly, but she was still sad that it had to die. She thought about the serpents. They were made of fire, but they didn't burn her. Her serpents were so big compared to Grandfather's little fire serpents. This was the second time they had come to her rescue. She wanted to see them again and thank them for saving her. *Especially Greenwald,* she thought. Selara concentrated. She imagined herself dropping the talking book. She relived her fear of the boar, but no matter how hard she tried, her serpents wouldn't come out and visit her.

Selara padded along the willow path, swinging a long strand of grass. Swallows darted and swooped ahead of her as a chorus of crickets sang. The sun was well up in the sky and gently warmed Selara's cheeks. She felt free here, coming and going as she pleased. *If I share what happened today with my grandparents, then everything might change,* she thought. Grandmother had so many rules. She didn't want her to add any more. Her grandparents may even keep her from seeing Bird. She decided that her dangerous adventure would remain a secret. Selara thought of a new rule: Don't tell Grandmother anything that might give her a reason to make more rules.

The solemn birds cut their way through the drifting clouds and passed over the gaping mouths of the Clan homes. They touched down in the Elder Circle, gently releasing Ceeka. There were short shrieks and croaks as several Night Birds poked their heads out of their looking holes to see what was happening. Terra and Flank glanced at each other in shock, having just spoken to Ceeka. Was Fletcher safe?

They watched quietly from their dwelling while the birds dispersed, and the body of Ceeka was laid out in state. The Clan leaders needed to investigate and make funeral arrangements.

A hush fell as Glider hopped to the centre of the massive woven circle to address the Clan. "Ceeka has always been a wise advisor and a respected bird," he said. He surveyed the sea of eyes. "But in the end, she must've lost her mind, for why would she risk her life to save a Hu-man?" Squawks and chitters of agreement sounded among the group. "Today, we've lost an important member of our Clan. The rites of passage will begin shortly." Glider looked down at the little daisy crown on Ceeka's head. "And take that thing off her!" he said, shaking his head in disgust.

The warrior bird who led the formation stepped forward. "No," he said, "the Hu-man female showed respect. Ceeka shall wear this token with honour for her sacrifice." Glider croaked his displeasure and stomped off, grumbling. The daisy crown remained.

Three older birds approached the body, solemnly. They placed themselves around her and began a slow droning dirge of long sympathetic vibrations unlike the normal croaks and chitters of Night Bird language. Some of the other birds joined in, and soon the Clan forest filled with the melancholy droning rising up from the forest into an ocean of sky.

Fletcher flew up and perched by his mother. Fletcher recounted the day's events. Flank had joined the birds near the inner circle.

Terra spoke softly to him, "You mustn't tell anyone about the bonding or the Hu-man's fire serpents. Do you understand?" Fletcher bobbed his head. "You said you've seen these serpents before?"

"Yes, Mother, when Girl is in danger, they come," said Fletcher.

Terra leaned in and whispered, "Did the fire snakes ever threaten you? Did you feel that you were in danger from them?"

"No, Mother. They protect the Girl, and then they disappear. They burned the ditch pig until it died and then they left," he said, still savouring the memory of the delicious smell of cooked meat.

Terra held Fletcher's eyes. "And you say she was speaking to Ceeka? You're sure?"

"Yes, Girl was listening to Ceeka speaking without sounds," said Fletcher.

Terra shook her head in wonder. *Ceeka's last act was to bond with the little Hu-man, but why?* She knew that Fletcher was not in any danger because he could have escaped easily. For some reason, Ceeka had felt that protecting Girl was important. Ceeka didn't lose her mind. She must have had a very good reason for keeping this Hu-man alive.

chapter ii

Rule 2: Never get mad and lose control

Grandmother's brush struggled through Selara's tangles. "What did you do today?" she asked.

"Bird and I played hide and seek, and I saw a deer!" she said (implementing her new rule).

"You shouldn't be spending so much time with that Night Bird. You can't trust those creatures!"

Selara knew better than to argue with Grandmother and simply nodded her head in response. *Just like Bird,* she thought.

The frustrated brush continued to trace a bumpy start-stop-start-stop path through her red hair.

"I'm sorry there are no other children here for you to play with. I really wish things could be different, but your dear mother wanted us to keep you safe."

Safe and bored, thought Selara. She wished she had a mirror to see how nice her hair looked. But no mirrors were allowed. *Rule number three: No mirrors.*

Grandmother knew that Thought Listeners used mirrors for spying. If a Thought Listener saw Selara through a mirror, he could determine her location. Then he'd tell those who wanted her dead, and they'd send out an assassin. Mirrors were a dangerous luxury. She and her husband knew first-hand the trouble reflections could bring. When she was very young, her family hid from a vicious overlord near Circle Village. She'd found a piece of a discarded mirror and kept it hidden. One night when she looked in the mirror, a monstrous face appeared and then disappeared. That was the night the overlord found her family. They narrowly escaped. She never looked at her reflection again.

Avoiding mirrors was easy for Selara, but never getting mad and losing control was not. If something happened to cause her to become angry or anxious, Grandmother would remind her about the rule. As tough and formidable as Grandmother was, when Selara was hurt or upset, she felt emotion she wasn't accustomed to: fear.

"Grandfather and I were talking and from now on you're not to wander in the marshes by yourself," said Grandmother.

"What? That's not fair!" erupted Selara, her cheeks bright red.

"It's for your own good. We've given you much too much freedom, and it has to stop before something really serious happens. Grandfather can go with you when you've both finished your chores." It was as if Grandmother read her mind and knew that she'd been lying.

"No!" she said, her heart beating faster. She grabbed and threw the hair brush, causing it to skitter across the floor.

"Stop!" said Grandmother, meeting her eyes directly. "Rule number two, Selara: Don't get mad and lose control!" She knew what would happen if Selara's anger went unchecked. *She could manifest that green fire serpent or worse.*

But Selara wasn't listening.

"Firk," she said, kicking the chair over.

"What did you say?" Grandmother looked at her sternly. "Stop it!"

"Firk, firk, firk!" she said, glaring at Grandmother. Selara stomped up the stairs and slammed her bedroom door.

Grandmother slumped down while Grandfather snored in his chair. *I'm getting too old to manage this child*, she thought.

She remembered the early days. There were periods of peace with laughter and joy when the normal flow of life continued before being cut off sharply by the dangers and machinations of war. Her son had had a brief affair when he was barely a teenager. The brief encounter resulted in the girl becoming pregnant. Her family was wealthy and vindictive and had prevented Talon from ever seeing his son or his first love again.

They'd travelled far away and hid Talon's would-be family with Dark Majik. It broke his heart. For years, he felt he'd never love again until he met Seanna. She was an Earth Elemental with limited majik. Everyone warned them that they should never marry — even if her majik was weak. It was too risky. If both Dark and Elemental Majik manifested together in their offspring, the child could go mad as the powers battled for dominance in the human heart. But Seanna had his heart, and even though their union was potentially dangerous, nothing could keep them apart.

In spite of all of this, Grandmother and her husband had enjoyed watching Talon and Seanna's courtship. Even though that vindictive M tried to break them up with her twisted plans and manipulations, Seanna was level-headed and smart enough to keep that little witch in her place. Then beautiful, little Selara came along. So innocent and trusting. Everyone loved her, even M. Seanna knew she shouldn't have children with Talon, but she did. Dark Majik and Elemental Majik would continue their struggles whether it be on the battlefield or in the soul.

Selara couldn't sleep. She stared out the window at the blanket of stars. She tried to think of her mother. It seemed so long ago, and for some reason, she couldn't remember her face. Selara's fingers ran absently through the yarn hair of her little doll Grandfather had made. Her grandparents told her that her mother died fighting to keep her safe. Sometimes Selara wished she'd died too so that she could be with her mother in the Second Realm. Grandfather said when people died in this world, they came alive in another world called the Second Realm where they continued their soul's journey. *I wonder if the old ladybird and that smelly boar are alive now in the Second Realm,* she thought. *I hope the smelly boar isn't still mad at me.*

Grandmother doesn't understand, she reflected. *She's a bully!* "I'm not a baby," she said, addressing the doll. "And besides, I have majik fire snakes to protect me. I have Greenwald. I'm going to run away to a place where there are no rules! I'm going to make my own rules!"

A tapping on the bedroom window broke her revere. She saw Bird's shadow in the moonlight. She tiptoed to the window and quietly opened it. Bird fluttered in and perched on her bed frame. "I'm glad you came," whispered Selara. "I'm going to run away, and you can come too." Bird nodded gravely, sensing her words were important. "My grandparents treat me like a baby, and I'm so tired of all their rules: Rules, rules, rules. They're making me crazy! I'm going to look in a mirror, and get mad if I want to, and say firk as many times as I like, and no one is going to stop me!" "I'm going to escape like the man in the story Grandfather told to me about — and you have to come too!"

Bird hopped onto Selara's lap. She absently stroked his feathers. He chittered softly, sounding very much like a cat purring. He saw the excitement in her eyes.

Selara reached under her bed and produced a little bag containing all her worldly possessions. Holding it close, she deposited the doll head first and cinched the drawstring. Padding down the stairs, she moved slowly and carefully. An old stair creaked. She froze. The house was still silent except for the soft snores of her grandparents. She took another step and another, followed closely by tiny clicks of Bird's talons as he hopped from stair to stair. "Shh," she whispered to Bird.

She climbed on the counter and quietly opened the cupboard, grabbing the leftover bread from supper. She dropped it in the bag. At the front door, she felt a little sliver of guilt as she reached for the latch — she held her breath, paused, and quietly opened the door. It creaked, but not loud enough to wake Grandmother and Grandfather. She closed the door slowly and stepped into the cool night air. She was free.

Selara had no trouble following her favourite paths even at night. Her feet had memorised them. She wound around trees and roots like muddy worms — sure-footed as if it were broad daylight. Bird glided beside her, enjoying her company. Bird was developing his night sight skills. He loved to sneak out of his tree home in the black of night and practice. Flying with his friend made it that much better.

Selara had no idea where she was going. She was just going. Her freedom to roam the marshes alone was like breathing for her, and no one was ever going to take that away. She made her own rules now. She spoke to herself, "Rule number one: Selara is making her own rules. Rule number two: Selara can do whatever she wants. Rule number three … Selara can say firk as many times as she wants." She travelled far along the old creek trail, over logs and cascading falls. She moved with practised ease. She was travelling in the opposite direction of the village and into the wild country on the edge of the Valley of the Skulls.

After some time, she stopped to rest on a dry log. The moon cast stark shadows around her. Bird landed on her shoulder. Selara took out a piece of bread and ate it, breaking off a smaller piece for Bird. A few pangs of guilt poked at her, but she squashed them down. "They can't stop me, you know! I'm trapped by all the rules, just like the doll in my bag!" Selara chewed harder, pushing down her nagging conscience that wouldn't stay squashed. She reached into her bag and felt for her doll — she stopped — *Big girls don't play with dolls*, she thought. *Maybe that should be one of my new rules, too?*

Bird's eyes sparkled in the moonlight, focusing on her word sounds.

Even though she was all alone, she wasn't scared. Her fire snakes now came to protect her when needed, and she was sure nothing could harm her. She ran a finger absently along her cheek where the big bully monster's claw had scratched her. Grandfather had hidden the talking book so well she couldn't find it anymore. *It's probably better this way,* she thought. She hadn't dreamed about the talking book since she'd used it to go to the battle-world. She still didn't understand how she got back. *What if I hadn't?* She shivered.

Bird looked up at her, hoping for more bread. The little Night Bird wasn't afraid of her like the rest of his flock who scattered when she walked and played in the moors. He had met her accidentally when she was playing picnic in the meadow one day. All of his family and friends were frightened of the majik that surrounded her like a soft, glowing curtain.

Night Birds were sensitive to all kinds of majik, having been exposed and transformed by it through the years. Because of this majik, the Night Birds grew into an intelligent creative species with unique abilities and began to distrust Hu-mans as they decimated forests and used their majik to manipulate the natural world.

For some unknown reason, Bird was not afraid. The Hu-man girl didn't seem threatening to him, and when he saw that she was offering him food from her picnic, he took it willingly. After a time, he became her trusted and constant companion. He always pressed his soft, shiny head into Selara's hand as if to say thank you when she fed him.

The young bird followed her awkwardly, flying from branch to branch as she skipped and played. His friendship with her was barely tolerated by his family and friends. Night Birds were fiercely protective of their territory and deathly afraid of showing loyalty to Hu-mans. In the past, many died because of their alliances with majik Hu-mans. These fears led to rules against bonding with Hu-mans or associating with them. The Night Bird Clan isolated themselves completely.

After walking for hours, the initial energy and excitement of her adventure gave way to complete exhaustion. Selara sat down and pulled a small folded blanket out. She nestled into the grassy bed and fell fast asleep.

Bird hopped down and cuddled close to her for warmth. He was used to this. He often snuck out at night and joined Selara in her bed where he listened to her chat in whispered tones until the two of them succumbed to sleep.

Selara woke up, covered in dew to the sounds of insects — many of them became breakfast for Bird. The sunrise painted the world red and gold. Selara stretched out her arms, yawned, and shivered. "Grandfather taught me a fire trick!" she muttered drowsily to Bird who executed a perfect roll. Lacy wings of a dragonfly disappeared into his beak. "Don't eat those!" scolded a yawning Selara. "Grandfather says they eat the blood suckers. Firk! I hate bloodsuckers."

Selara wandered around her campsite, gathering dry grass and twigs. She carefully built a little fire house like her grandfather taught her. She whispered the incantation. A tiny wisp of grey smoke rose from the firehouse floor. It expanded until a tiny flame in the shape of an earthworm appeared and consumed the structure. The welcoming flame rose up, dancing happily and warming her face. Selara blew into the coals and snapped more twigs and branches to feed the growing fire.

Bird took a break from hunting and imitated Selara, snapping more branches in half with his powerful beak and tossing them into the hungry flames.

Selara laughed at him. He seemed to be growing bigger every day. *And he's so smart!* she thought.

Far in the distance, keen eyes spotted the growing clouds of smoke. As the fire grew hotter, Selara warmed herself, wiggling her toes and sitting close to the fire — satisfied with what she accomplished. Bird continued to devour the growing number of bloodsuckers that were attempting to land on Selara for their nourishment. Then they heard rustling in the grass. The memory of the giant boar loomed in her mind, so she closed her eyes and braced herself.

Nothing happened, so she opened her eyes to see a small hill growing in front of her. Bits of grass and twigs were displaced and ran down the growing mound. Selara tried to make sense of what she was seeing. Bird stopped eating and landed softly on her shoulder, focussed on the growing pile. The mound grew as tall as Selara then fell apart revealing matted white hair and a grubby smiling face. The little figure stood in front of her and Bird, eyeing them curiously.

"Hello," said Selara, looking suspiciously at this strange, little boy.

"Hello," replied the boy, grinning.

Selara secretly hoped her fire snakes were watching and ready to save her if she needed them.

"My name is Selara, and this is my best friend, Bird," she said, not meeting the eyes of the boy. She wondered if she should mention there was mud between his teeth. "What's your name?"

"Whig," replied the boy, joining her by the fire, uninvited. He warmed his hands.

"How'd you come out of the ground?"

"I am earth and you are fire. I dig majik tunnels."

"What do you mean?"

"The ground opens for me as I walk through it. I talk to the earth and it listens. Can you hear it talking?"

Selara shook her head. "I used to hear a talking book," she offered.

"You talk to fire and it listens," Whig continued, pointing at the roaring fire.

"I can't talk to fire. I just learned how to make a fire snake from my grandfather," she corrected. *This kid's so dirty. Grandmother'd go crazy if I brought him home. At least, he doesn't smell bad.*

Whig raised his hand, and a group of rocks rolled around obediently, encircling Selara's fire.

"That's awesome! How'd you do that? Are you majik?"

"I guess so. My parents taught me there is majik in everything. You just have to look for it. How come I've never seen you before?"

"I've never been this far before. Bird and I're running away," she said, looking down shyly.

Bird continued to fly around the two of them, feasting on bloodsuckers.

"You've got a Night Bird! That's so cool! What's his name?"

"Bird."

"I have earthworms. They follow me around. There're too many of them for names, so I just call them Earth Mob."

"Really?" She wasn't sure if she should be interested or grossed out.

"Want to meet them?" asked Whig, leaping up.

Selara didn't think she did, but she wanted to be polite. After all, Whig was the first boy she'd ever met since coming to stay with her grandparents. "Sure," she gulped.

Whig sat back down and closed his eyes. He put two grimy hands palms down in front of him, barely touching the mud. Slowly the soil twisted and undulated. A writhing pink ball rose out of the ground. Whig reached down and picked it up — a glistening ball of hundreds of coiled earthworms. "Do you want to hold them?" he asked, putting the wriggling ball into her hands before she could protest.

Selara took a deep breath and closed her eyes. She didn't have time to be grossed out. She didn't know if she would faint, throw up, or possibly die. When nothing happened, she looked at the pink, swirling mass and said, "It tickles." She laughed, surprised.

"They like you!" exclaimed Whig.

She turned the ball over in her hands. "Good morning, Earth Mob." The slimy sensation was oddly satisfying. "Can I put them down now?"

"Sure, but not too close to the fire. They wouldn't like that."

Selara gently placed Earth Mob into the grass and watched the ball melt as the worms wriggled away. Selara bent down and wiped the slime off her hands.

"My grandmother would have never let me hold Earth Mob. She has too many rules. That's why I'm running away."

"I wish I had grandparents."

Guilt stuck in Selara's throat, and warm tears threatened to fall. She was reconsidering her decision to leave. "From now on, I'm making my own rules," she reminded herself.

They spent the morning talking by the fire. Bird was happy to show off his new feeding-the-fire skills much to the delight of Whig.

Whig told Selara that when he was very little, his parents taught him how to survive on his own and how to hone his Elemental powers.

"Where are your parents?"

"They're both dead. They were killed in the last war," replied Whig, looking into the fire.

"I think that Bird and I saw that war," said Selara.

"How? That was a long time ago!"

"I read from Grandfather's talking book, flapped my arms, and Bird and I went to a different place. There were soldiers, monsters and fire. That's when I met Greenwald and his friend. They ate the bully monster that tried to hurt me. I was so mad. They're like Earth Mob. Only there are two of them, and they're made out of fire."

"Can you show me them?" Whig was stunned. He wasn't sure he believed her.

"I'm sorry, they only come out if something wants to get me and I get really mad."

Whig was disappointed. "How did you get back from the war?"

"I don't know. I just picked up the book, and it brought me and Bird back to Grandfather's shed. Grandfather was so mad at me." Selara tossed another branch into the fire. Bird continued to eat the insects buzzing around the two Elementals. Selara broke her last piece of bread in half and gave the other half to Whig.

He chewed it, slowly. "I eat mostly plants and roots, but I really like this."

"I'm still hungry," said Selara. She jumped up and ran to the edge of the path where some berries were growing. "White berries for breakfast" she sang as she skipped away.

Whig warmed his hands in the fire, then stopped. "No wait!" he shouted, leaping up quickly. But the bobbing red hair was already over the hill. Whig ran as fast as he could. Selara already had a handful of berries and was tossing them into her mouth. "Spit those out!"

"My new rule is white berries for breakfast!" she said, chewing. She suddenly felt dizzy. Whig's face blurred. "I don't feel so good." The rest of the berries fell from her limp hand. Selara dropped to her knees before falling down unconscious. Everything went cold and black.

"No, no, no!" said Whig, tears running down his cheeks. He crouched down, tapping her cheek to wake her up.

But Selara lay on the ground with her eyes wide open. She stared into nothingness, her lips white and her skin a light blue. Her heart had stopped. She was dead.

Whig panicked. He was grieving for the little girl but trying to stay calm at the same time. He sat down and rocked back and forth on his knees, thinking. He had experimented with a dead bird and with a baby rabbit. *But would it work on a person?* he thought. *I have to try.* Whig carefully closed her eyelids — they were creeping him out. He knew what came next, and it would be better if her eyes were closed. He knelt down and began to hum. In his mind, he pictured roots springing from the ground and wrapping themselves around Selara. He felt the soil teeming with life around him. He used his sheer will to focus all of that life into his new little friend, lying cold and still before him.

Bird continued to eat insects until he noticed both Selara and Whig were gone. He flew over the edge of the hill to see Selara disappear slowly into the ground. He thought she was playing a game with her new friend, so he continued to fly around, amusing himself.

The rabbit took a whole day, but the bird only a few hours, Whig thought. He rocked back and forth, nervously. Moving on shaky legs, he re-built the fire in front of the mound. There was nothing he could do now but wait. *I've done everything right. I just have to be patient.*

His parents had been patient. They were patient while he struggled to learn so much at such an early age. They were patient while the King did his best to defend against the Dark Queen after she began her quest to erase all vestiges of Elemental Majik from the kingdom. They were patiently hiding until the war eventually found them. He fought back tears. He had tunnelled deep into the earth and was well hidden from the soldiers and Dark Creatures. His parents were not so lucky. They couldn't tunnel as he could. Their powers were limited. Just when they thought the danger had passed, they were found. The Dark Queen showed no mercy, and he became an orphan.

A piercing scream echoed through the halls of the stone temple. The Dark Queen was staring at the lifeless face of Selara disappearing into the ground. She hammered her fists on the stone. "Stupid, stupid, stupid, little girl!" the Dark Queen fumed, her voice bitter and cold. "What am I supposed to do now?" She could feel the physical link with Selara fading to a mere thread, threatening to break at any moment. Being trapped here for all eternity loomed heavily in her mind. She paced back and forth, then sprinted headlong into the mists. No matter which direction she ran, she always returned to the same place. The temple was a Mobius trap that folded into itself. Angry green fire flared from her fingertips as she screamed in frustration. Rage turned to panic and then to a faint hope.

"What have you gone and done, child? You aren't making your path any easier, are you?" asked Ceeka gently.

"Where am I?" asked Selara, suddenly, recognizing the old bird.

"You've crossed into the Second Realm. It's so nice to see you, but you won't be staying with me."

"Where's my mother? Can I see her?"

"She's not here. She hasn't been born yet."

"I don't understand," Selara whimpered.

"Don't worry. Your little friend's bringing you back into the world. He possesses a powerful majik. You're not supposed to be here because it's not your time. You died. But you still have so much to do. Rest for now, child. Rest for now."

Selara felt sleepy and lay her head on Ceeka's soft feathers. She had a dream that she was a tree, her roots reaching down deep into the soil and absorbing the life-giving water and food there. Her arms and legs were branches, and her fingers, twigs and leaves. She revelled in the sunlight streaming into her and energising her spirit.

The dream became a nightmare. She was drowning. She gasped for air. She pushed and scraped with her fingers, trying to claw her to the surface. Her hand broke through the water and her fingers felt the cold night air. She struggled until her head broke through. Her stomach wrenched, and she threw up. Millions of tiny roots fell from her skin, releasing her. She was weak. Strong arms grabbed her and pulled her out of the earth.

Whig held her tightly. *It worked,* he thought triumphantly, tears of joy running down his face.

As her mind cleared, Selara felt someone holding her, and the smoke from a campfire stung her eyes. She stared up at Whig in surprise.

"Never eat white berries!" scolded a relieved Whig.

"Firk! What happened?" Selara struggled to think.

Whig looked at her, overcome with emotion but without the energy to explain.

"I have a new rule," she murmured. "Never eat white berries and die."

Whig wrapped her in her blanket, and she fell asleep in his arms. Bird waddled close and cuddled against Selara's cheek. Whig smiled at them.

When Selara woke up, dawn was streaming through the broken clouds. "I just want to go home," she cried, whimpering.

"Let's get you home then," Whig suggested, helping her up.

Whig gestured with his hand, and the earth swallowed up the fire. Even the smoke was consumed, sucked into a hungry mouth. Bird fluttered beside Selara, blissfully unaware of what happened to his trusted companion. Whig and Selara walked slowly. Selara tightened her fingers around the blanket still covering her shoulders.

"I met the old lady bird," muttered Selara. "She said coming back from the dead was important. And then I was a tree."

She sounds a bit crazy, thought Whig. *I hope her brain's okay.*

As they came over the hill, they saw the cottage, fences, and outbuildings in the distance. The cows grazed in the open pasture.

"There's a majik border here, so I can't go any further. Take this stone, and if you ever need me, hold it tightly and think of me and I'll come if I can." With that, Whig disappeared into the ground as if he were never there.

Selara looked curiously at the pretty blue stone in her hand. It had a small hole for a leather lace to run through and make a necklace. *Maybe Grandfather'll do that for me*, she thought. She wandered slowly down the hill towards the cottage.

Her grandmother spotted her through the window and burst through the door. She grabbed her and held her tightly.

"What happened to you? Why'd you run off? she implored, her hands on Selara's shoulders, looking deeply into her eyes. "Grandfather is still out looking for you — you worried us sick."

Bird flew into the trees at the sight of Grandmother.

Selara was expecting a punishment, so Grandmother's behaviour was very confusing.

Grandmother hugged her tighter and brought her into the house. "Let's get you cleaned up. How'd you get so dirty?" she said.

"I died," said Selara, matter-of-factly, too tired to remember her own rule about not telling Grandmother anything that would lead to more rules.

"Don't be silly, Selara," said Grandmother, confused.

"A little, dirty boy brought me back to life. The old lady bird told me I couldn't stay in something she called the Realm." She corrected herself,

"The Second Realm. Where's that anyways? She told me I had to come back here. I asked about my mother, but she told me she wasn't born yet, so I couldn't see her. Then I turned into a tree and had to swim out of the ground."

Grandmother's expression changed from confusion to horror. "Did you say you were in the Second Realm?" Tears welled up in her eyes. She felt dizzy.

"Yes, I think that's what she called it. The little boy who brought me back to life gave me this," she said, proudly showing off the little blue stone in her hand. "I want Grandfather to make it into a necklace for me. He said his name's Whig."

There was a shock of recognition on Grandmother's face. "How'd you die?" she asked, suddenly needing to sit down.

"I ate some white berries. The Earth Boy with white hair tried to stop me, but I ate too fast. I was trying to make my own rules … ,"

Grandmother hugged her tightly and cried.

"Never eat white berries and die," Selara repeated to herself before turning to her grandmother. "It's okay, Grandmother, don't cry."

How could we've been so foolish? Grandmother thought. *We've been so concerned with protecting Selara from dangerous majik that we never even thought of warning her about the obvious danger of eating white berries. How could we be so stupid? Why didn't Grandfather warn her about them?* Tomorrow she would send Grandfather out to destroy every last white berry bush.

The last time she had met Whig he was over ninety years old. He was one of the Elementals that made it possible for them to escape to this time in the past. Selara will eventually return to the very stone he created to tether her path back to the future. How strange that this little boy would help save Selara's life twice: once as a boy to bring her back to life, and once as an old man to save her life. Her enemies believed she died as a child when she was sent into the past. Little did they know that she would return as a young woman ten years later—a force for hope. *Thank the Gods for Whig! How're we ever going to keep this girl safe until it's time for her to leave?*

chapter iii

Rule 3: Never look in a mirror

It was Selara's tenth and seventh moon when her quiet life ended. Selara was now a young woman, and the fire serpents were a distant memory. There were no more melted pots or scorched walls. Grandmother had taught her how to control her temper well enough that she convinced herself that she was normal. Her world was changing quickly, and she was changing too.

Even her little friend Bird had changed. He was barely recognizable. He was no longer little. He was a mature Night Bird with all of the amazing abilities of his kind. However, he was larger, stronger, and faster. When he perched on Selara's shoulder, he was an impressive specimen. His feathers were now a deep shiny black. His beak was like obsidian, strong enough to snap bones. He possessed talons that could pierce flesh like razors, yet he rested gently on Selara's shoulder without leaving a scratch. Although he still enjoyed the crusts of bread that Selara shared, he was a hunter who brought down small animals and left nothing but bones. He was also Selara's ever-vigilant protector. Even when he was not at Selara's side, he was always aware of her location and her activities, watching for perceived threats or physical dangers.

There were times when Selara desperately wished to communicate with Bird. She imagined asking him questions like "Who were you flying with today?" or "Are you happy?" or "Did you hunt anything interesting today?" She had to be content with their unspoken language. Selara noticed a special change in Bird. He was flying with what she believed to be a female Night Bird. *Good for him,* she thought, *but what about me?*

Selara stared out her bedroom window, hoping for something to happen. Anything! She felt restless and unsettled. She was jealous of Bird flying with female Night Birds. She knew it made no sense, but she couldn't help herself. Her grandparents kept her completely isolated from boys and girls her age. *They really didn't need to,* she thought. She was safe now. She wasn't going to hurt anyone because she didn't get mad. On the rare occasions when Grandfather travelled into the village for supplies, she wasn't allowed to join him. She had begged and pleaded over the years, but they insisted that she not talk or develop friendships with anyone outside their little family. Even when she tried to manipulate her grandparents by pitting one against the other, they were unified when it came to this rule. Her only friend was Bird, and the only other person she had ever met was Whig. She wondered what became of him.

Grandfather must have dug up and burned every white berry bush from one end of the valley to the other. She smiled to herself. She absently touched the smooth blue stone she always wore around her neck, pinching it between her thumb and pointer finger. She did try to call for Whig once when she was lonely, but he never came. She guessed the stone call didn't work.

She daydreamed about leaving the quiet comfort of her life with her grandparents and beginning a new and exciting life somewhere else in the kingdom. And then there were the dreams. In her dreams, she sat on a throne, wearing a crown of fire. In her dreams, strangers bowed when she entered. In her dreams, she was someone important. But they were only dreams. When she woke up, she was just a plain, poor girl living on a tiny isolated farm in the middle of nowhere.

One morning, when Selara was out for a walk, she paused by the edge of the moor. In a dark still pond, she caught a glimpse of a beautiful young woman, slim with wild scarlet hair and shocking green eyes, staring back at her. She let out an involuntary gasp. She forgot to look away from her reflection. Grandmother's rule: never look into a mirror! But she froze, unable to look away. How the years had transformed her. Suddenly, the image wavered and metamorphosed into a one-eyed monstrous face staring back at her before it disappeared. She was disturbed by the face and ran to tell her grandmother.

Grandmother smiled and told her it was just a trick of the light and she need not worry. When Selara left the room, Grandmother's smile faded.

Later, Selara heard her grandparents talking in hushed tones behind their bedroom door.

Selara's grandparents slowed down as the days went by. Sometimes they found it more and more difficult to keep up with the simple chores of running the farm. One day, an exhausted Grandfather asked Selara to spread the white powder around the property for him. He told her that Grandmother was too busy and she would be mad if she found out that Grandfather hadn't finished his chores. As usual, he swore Selara to secrecy. She thought it all nonsense and silly superstition, but humoured Grandfather.

Selara waded through the wet morning grass and opened the latch to her grandfather's shed. The comforting smells of leather, dried herbs, and split wood filled her with warm memories. She fiddled with the ornate box with carved golden spirals that sat on a high shelf and plucked out the leather bag of white powder. She carefully walked around the property, spreading the white powder, and speaking his nonsense words. As she spoke, she felt strange, like someone else was speaking them for her.

When she completed the wide arc around the buildings, she got her wish and something unexpected happened. As the ending of the circle touched the beginning of the circle, a droplet of green fire dripped from her hand and landed on the powder. It lit like a fuse. It burned quickly along the snowy line, retracing her steps. An orange fire joined the green one but burned in the opposite direction. When the two fires met they went out, leaving no trace of the white powder. Selara, was upset, fearing she'd have to do it over again. When she told Grandfather, he said she'd done well and not to worry. He drifted off to sleep with a broad smile on his face.

In his high tower room in the distant future, Oag sat staring at the wall with his singular eye, watching and listening. Voices. Hundreds of thousands of voices weaving into a complex tapestry of thoughts. Oag quietly examined each thread. He was an abomination: a half-human, half-underling created by Dark Majik. He was the last of his kind, and the level of majik that created him was no longer remembered. He sat on his low stool, watching intently. His skin was like an old leather glove, and he was short and rotund. Oag spent much of his time, pouring over the endless thoughts that filled the kingdom. Although the product of Dark Majik, he found the thoughts of love and sacrifice warmed him, temporarily filling his empty heart. There were no good or evil thoughts for Oag — however, some thoughts were unique, or interesting for him. Every secret and private thought was available to Oag. Nothing was impervious to him except the words of the ancient languages. They were magically hidden, a fail-safe to protect his creators' privacy, like twisted threads that he couldn't unravel.

Oag, so old, was one of the most intelligent creatures in the kingdom. He was like a thought librarian. Even though his main work was uncovering plots to overthrow Daemon, he knew everything about everything from baking a perfect loaf of bread to building a cathedral. He had access to every human talent and ability. He watched all, learned all, and knew all — in other words, omnipresent. Oag knew more about humanity than any creature in their world. In his own mind, he was a God.

Oag was created long before he worked under the service of Daemon, and long before the more powerful and resourceful Dark Queen. In many ways, Daemon was a spoiled child compared to the dignified and disciplined Dark Queen. He was simply a bastard, born out of wedlock, who seized his opportunity. After the Dark Queen mysteriously disappeared, no leader rose from the practitioners of Dark Majik. After years of disarray, Daemon usurped her lands and created his empire.

A faint fluttering at the window distracted Oag from his reverie. His large eye blinked. *Birds have such simple thoughts,* thought Oag. His long pink tongue lashed out and his mouth crunched absently on the bones and feathers. Suddenly, a single thread glimmered and caught his attention. A beautiful face filled the room, and terrified green eyes studied him. He had seen this face before, but it had been much younger. He recalled a strange time when his abilities had faltered. Old lives and young lives seemed to appear and reappear. Their thoughts were confusing and disjointed. Oag felt that he was losing his abilities to read coherent thoughts, but now he understood.

She still lives. Daemon'll be furious. But something isn't right…Very clever. She lives in the past, with a single glimmering thread of majik still attached to this time. Brilliant! She was a reflection within past reflections, past layers of time. No wonder she was presumed dead. Finding her was an accident. Oag began calculating the odds of finding this hidden thread. They were astronomical. If he told Daemon, his killing monsters would wait to ambush her. She would certainly return soon. She was of age. Her full powers would soon manifest. *Clever!*

Oag paused. He contemplated the beautiful face in the water. There were thoughts of fear and concern emanating from her. The feelings of fear and revulsion were also delicious, but something about her warmed him. Oag tried to brush the thought away, but he was experiencing something that was unique to him: a curiosity, an attraction. He found himself savouring the memory of her. He replayed the vision in his mind. He became lost in her eyes, and the contours of her face. Part of him didn't want to share this news with Daemon.

Oag wrestled with the idea of keeping the maiden a secret. He played out the implications of his decision, with possible future events — including his own self-preservation. After carefully weighing the odds, he decided to tell Daemon. He predicted his decision would cause a chain of events that would allow the young

Elemental to begin her work dismantling Daemon's plans. *Clever*, Oag thought.

Oag rose slowly and reluctantly. He didn't like Daemon. He especially didn't like communicating with him. Oag made his way slowly down the twisted stairs to the meeting room. Daemon's thoughts were veiled as usual. Sometimes, however, Oag saw just a glimpse of them, but it was like looking into the inky, black darkness of a deep, dark hole consuming everything around it. Oag would have shuddered if he were able. He had seen many things in his long life, but nothing compared to the blackness at the heart of Dark Majik. The opposite of this darkness was love. Love was his curiosity, and love was his addiction.

Oag was largely untouched by the millions of thoughts he experienced every day, but love read as a glimmering, beautiful thread. Although he was a creature of darkness, these threads of pure thought were like sitting by a cheery fire. His leather feet shuffled down the cold stone stairs. Almost there. As he rounded the corner, he saw the tall, gaunt form of Daemon, staring out the window. *He looks so much like Talon,* mused Oag.

Oag had followed the thoughts of Talon and Cercil when they were younger. *They were not ready for that kind of love,* he thought. They met secretly at night in the hayloft at his father's farm. Cercil hid the fact she was carrying Talon's child as long as she could, but she couldn't hide it from her mother, who blamed Talon's parents for allowing it to happen. They forbade Talon from ever seeing her again and moved their family to the far edges of the kingdom. Cercil's father used everything he knew about Dark Majik to make sure that Talon never found her. Raised by his grandparents, Daemon believed his father never cared for him or his mother. When Cercil died of a broken heart, the truth died with her.

Daemon turned abruptly as Oag approached.

"Oag! You, despicable creature. What brings you to me? Do you have any news?"

"Yes, Master," replied Oag, summoning his courage. "The young Elemental still lives! She was hidden in the past!"

"What did you say?" Daemon turned a whiter shade of pale.

"She still lives," Oag said, cringing inwardly. "She'll soon return to the Valley of the Skulls."

"What?" he asked, trembling. The greatest threat to his plans for Daemon Kingdom reappeared. Daemon's face darkened. His fingertips glowed a brilliant green. Without warning, he threw a ball of fire at the wall, leaving a black scar to join the countless others. "How could this happen?" Another fireball went flying. This time scorching the ceiling.

Oag cowered underneath the safety of a table.

"Send out the Wolves. Go to the Valley of the Skulls. Tell them to kill anything that moves. Riches to anyone who brings me that Elemental's head," he screamed at the creatures lurking by the door. Daemon vibrated with rage.

I can't believe I let this happen, thought Daemon. *Who'd imagine anyone risking that kind of dangerous majik? The smallest mistake would send the user to a living hell where they'd be hunted by monstrous creatures, or twist the fabric of time in such a way that the majik practitioner ceased to exist.* He sighed heavily and sat down. *His Daemon-Wolves'll kill her this time. I won't allow the rising of a Dark Elemental!*

At the far end of the kingdom, Jonrah lazily stirred leaves into tiny dust devils and watched them whirl slowly around the courtyard. He stared at the manicured trees forming a border around him, but he wasn't really seeing them. His thoughts were far, far away.

Many seasons had passed since the last Elemental battle, and it was time for Selara to return by his father's calculations. *If she still lived,* he thought, grimly. His parents were counting on him to retrieve her quickly and quietly so as not to alert Daemon. Jonrah held up the parchment in the dying light with the incantation carefully inscribed on it. He could repeat it in his sleep. If he said it incorrectly, he might wake up in a vacant field before the castle was built, or be attacked by ancient flying dragons before the kingdoms even existed. He shivered. *There're very good reasons this majik should stay forbidden,* he reflected.

He couldn't remember his big sister, Selara. She went away when he was still young. Sara was the only real sister he had ever really known.

When Selara was young, she must've been a lot like Sara: mischievous, full of energy, and laughter.

Tomorrow he would journey to the place of the last battle, and the words on this tiny parchment would send him down the very path his grandparents and sister took to the past. As dangerous as this was, he had to admit he was excited. He was asked by his parents to do this for the family, but he would have volunteered willingly. He knew he could be trapped in the past. There was also the possibility that his grandmother, grandfather and sister died years ago, the instant the time incantation was spoken. Enemies in the past might have found them and killed them. Jonrah tried not to think about it.

He reflected. Technically, Selara and his grandparents were dead the moment they vanished from the battle. That was why Daemon's hoards were called back. Daemon mistakenly sensed his step-sister had died. *The moment I returned to retrieve Selara, I too would be dead*, thought Jonrah. He looked wistfully over the Keep at the candle-lit windows glittering like happy stars safe inside these castle walls. Sometimes he wished his life were much simpler and he lived behind one of those comforting warm windows with a Nomaji family, ignorant of the coming danger, rather than carrying the weight of the entire kingdom on his shoulders.

This mission was important for all of them. He had to do and say everything perfectly. A time anchor only supported two adult travellers. *Our grandparents'll have to remain there*, he thought sadly. As much as he tried to squash the small worries, they kept creeping in. *Am I ready to die tomorrow or the next day? Will I arrive in the past only to find Selara and our grandparents never made it there?* He wished he had the courage and confidence of Alan. He wondered if Alan was still alive. Everyone loved and respected him. He had successfully used his powers to save the Elementals even though he was not much older than Jonrah at the time.. No one had heard from him in months. He reassured himself that soon his family would be together again, much stronger and much safer.

The sun sunk completely into the horizon by the time he climbed the stairs to his tower room and peered out the window. He wondered if

Selara were moody and unpredictable like his girlfriend, Tamara. He lay down and dosed off. He dreamed of impossible nightmare scenarios and Daemon-Wolves. He awoke to warm lips pressing on his and looked into Tamara's face, startled. "What're you doing here?" asked Jonrah. "We said our goodbyes yesterday."

"I had to say goodbye one more time," she whispered. "What if I never see you again? What if you find someone prettier than me in the past?" Long blond hair framed the soft white skin of her face. A tear traced its way down her cheek. She pulled Jonrah close, her hair tickling his cheek. "Promise me you'll come back."

"Of course, I will. Don't worry so much." Jonrah gave her a quick kiss and sat up in his bed.

"What if she's prettier than me?" Tamara looked at him, seriously.

Here we go again, thought Jonrah. "Don't be ridiculous. She's my sister!"

"I don't care. Majik changes everything. Elemental kings and queens in the past were married brothers and sisters you know!" Her eyes held him.

"That was the past! Nobody does that anymore!"

"But you don't understand. She *is* from the past! The past, Jonrah!" she implored, tears welling up.

"Really? You're jealous of my big sister whom I can barely remember?" Jonrah shook his head.

Tamara dropped her chin, sulking.

"She's not just my sister, you know. My parents say she'll help us end this war! And besides, she's over a hundred years old."

Tamara glared at him and pouted.

He lifted her chin and kissed her gently. "Don't worry, my heart'll always belong to you."

Tamara met his eyes and reluctantly smiled. Then she brightened. Wisps of smoke rose from her fingertips as she stood up and walked slowly and seductively towards the door. She wanted him to miss her. Smoke rings spun above his bed — her signature goodbye.

Tamara's so beautiful, but so possessive, he groaned inwardly. *The other young women of the White Keep are careful to avoid me, understandably afraid of Tamara's jealousy.*

He earnestly hoped his big sister didn't have the same temperament as Tamara. If she did, he wouldn't want to be around if the two of them got into an argument. They would burn the kingdom down. Besides, if Selara was capable of doing the things his father thought, Tamara would lose that argument and possibly her life. Fortunately, Tamara had Seanna to talk some sense into her when she got heated. Seanna was the only one who could calm her down since she came to live with his family after her parents died. Tamara should have been a step-sister to him, but natural attraction had other plans for the both of them. Jonrah smiled to himself.

Part of him wished Tamara hadn't come back to say goodbye again. It was hard enough the first time. Now he was lying awake, thinking about her. Missing her. Her beautiful eyes, her sly smile, and even her wicked temper. He wished she slept in his arms tonight, but his mother, even with her limited majik, would speak to the stones in the castle walls to make sure her charge was safely in her own room. He remembered finding out his mother's so-called limited talents the hard way.

It was still dark when Jonrah slipped out of the castle. The hearths were stone cold, and the animals were quiet. His mission needed to remain a secret to everyone but his close family. Spies were everywhere, even within the castle walls. He had to be careful. Part of the reason he was chosen to retrieve his sister was his unique ability to speak and think in the old languages. This made his true intentions invisible to a Thought Listener. Jonrah grew up under Saffron's tutelage, and he was very adept at languages and basic majik.

Jonrah travelled on foot because he never learned to ride a horse. He spent so much time with his books and study, that learning to ride was never a priority. His castle friends liked to tease him about his lack of horse sense. He rationalised that for this mission, being on foot was better because he could easily slip by soldiers and Marauders, rather than travelling the open roads on an expensive horse, attracting unwanted attention. At least that's what he told himself. He wondered if his big sister learned to ride a horse in the past.

Jonrah travelled as quickly as he could for three days, concealing himself carefully from Marauders and Manoliths. He camped without a fire. He wished he could fly like the Wind Elementals of old, but no one in his generation inherited that talent. Besides, if he were seen flying, it would attract attention.

He knew where he had to look for the time talisman. Talon had shown him on an old map. It was in a small cave in the Valley of the Skulls. Talon hid the stone in the very place his family had taken shelter from Daemon's forces. The stone acted as a kind of anchor in time so that one could depart and return to the same point, keeping them from becoming lost in time, or worse. One of the last Earth Elementals helped create it so that when Selara was of age, she could return to fulfil her destiny. If she had remained in this time, Daemon would have stopped at nothing to have her put to death, and he would have certainly succeeded.

The sun melted slowly into orange twilight when Jonrah descended into the Valley of the Skulls. He traced his way down a dry creek bed and found the small weathered cave. A few ruined buildings were not far from the cave with headstones standing stoically beside the old house. As he turned towards the cave, his curiosity nagged at him. He had to see what was inscribed on the gravestones. He waded through the tall grass and approached the first stone. He held his breath. *If my sister's name's on any one of those headstones, I've already failed.* He reached down and brushed away the moss. It read, "Fayna, loving wife and mother." The rest of the inscription was worn away, but he made out her burial date. He had never heard of the name Fayna and wondered who she was. He did recognize the names on the next two markers. The first was inscribed "Petra, loving grandfather" and the second "Olga, loving grandmother." His grandmother had passed away first and his grandfather had died not long after. But Fayna had died before the both of them. *But who had buried them and fashioned their gravestones? Was it Selara? Who was Fayna?* He shook the dirt from his gloves and headed back to the cave.

His father told him that the stone was small and would glow to reveal itself when he spoke the first incantation. Talon spent hours making him memorise the two incantations until he could say them both perfectly from memory. He was only allowed to speak them in the protective presence of his father, who could keep the spells from working so that he wouldn't accidentally activate the dangerous time spell without an anchor or a pre-planned pathway. He recited the first incantation and waited. Seconds went by, and nothing happened. A faint whisper of panic rose in his chest. He circled the cave anxiously as the daylight faded. He said it again, only louder this time. The sun was setting, and he couldn't make out the walls of the cave.

He heard a faint humming and followed it to an outcropping covered with earth and moss. Jonrah scraped away the debris. The sound became louder until he saw a faint glow. He picked up the stone and brushed it off. He stopped. He heard howling in the distance. Somehow Daemon knew Selara was coming. He tried to focus. A spiral etched into the quartz glowed brighter than the rest of the stone. Placing it back carefully, he said the second incantation. Instantly, the world spun around him, and he felt dizzy and sick. He felt like he was dying. Colours flashed around him, and he floated. Then he was face down on the ground. He spat out dirt and leaves and sat up, getting his bearings.

The moon shone brightly. He saw the outline of a cottage and a few buildings in the distance. He marvelled at seeing the ruins completely re-built. He heard and smelled farm animals. The gravestones were gone. *That's a good sign,* he thought. Everything around him had changed. The trees were smaller, and there was smoke rising from the newly resurrected chimney. Welcoming light shone through the windows of the cottage. *I've done it! I'm alive and just pulled off one of the most dangerous spells ever written.*

His heart beat faster. He desperately hoped his sister and grandparents were well and living in this house. He forced himself to stand up. He covered his face to keep his identity a secret. He didn't have much time. For all he knew, his grandparents may have changed alliances over the years and would not release Selara to an Elemental — his identity had to remain hidden.

They were just finishing supper when a faint knock sounded at the door. Selara jumped. They never had visitors. Her grandparents merely glanced at each other as if they were expecting this interruption. The truth was they had been, every night since Selara came of age. A light of anticipation glowed in their eyes. They had kept Selara safe for the next stage of her life.

Grandmother rose slowly to open the heavy wooden door. The old hinges squealed loudly, heralding a tall dark figure covered entirely in black robes, standing like a defiant shadow in the lamplight. "Come in," said Grandmother, looking the figure up and down. The tall figure glided as it entered the room, a black storm cloud floating into the warmth of their cottage. His face was covered by a thick black cloth, exposing only two piercing green eyes.

Selara assumed it was a 'he' by the way he carried himself. The figure scanned the room suspiciously. When his eyes focussed on Selara, they went wider, showing surprise, and held her gaze a little longer than comfortable. The figure seemed shaken. *Emotional?* wondered Selara.

He spoke to her grandparents in a language that Selara didn't understand. They conversed in hushed tones briefly as if the very walls were straining to hear. Grandmother suddenly threw her arms around the figure without warning and held him tightly. When she finally turned to Selara, her face was wet with tears, but she was excited. Something important was happening. Selara's heart beat faster. Grandmother told her to pack her things quickly and get ready to leave.

"I'm not going with him! Where're we going? What's happening? I'm not leaving you alone," she sobbed, her voice breaking.

Grandfather hugged her. "You must go and fulfil your destiny. Don't be frightened. I have something for you." Grandfather went up to his bedroom and returned with the talking book. "Take this with you. You're going to need it."

She took the book and let her fingers trace over the familiar leather markings. Then Grandfather walked over to the figure and embraced him warmly. *Who's that?* she asked herself. *Is the figure crying?*

Selara climbed the stairs to pack her belongings. She was overwhelmed but excited. Maybe this was the answer to her prayers. Something important was happening, and she knew she was entering the next chapter of her life. She had never left her home for any length of time since she had run away so long ago. As she packed up her bag, she held her little doll and paused. *Selara's rule: Big girls don't play with dolls.* She chuckled to herself. She set it gently on her pillow. She was leaving her childhood behind for good.

When she came downstairs, the figure was pacing back and forth impatiently. Grandfather and Grandmother were crying. Selara gave them both a long goodbye hug, slung her bag over her shoulder, and followed the figure out the door.

From the peak of the cottage roof, Bird watched Selara leave with a strange man. They entered the small cave not far from the cottage. Bird was concerned. When the man suddenly grabbed Selara's arm, Bird dove down to intervene. The figure recited an incantation. Selara heard the fluttering of wings before her whole world spun out of control. Glancing back, she saw the only home she had ever known spin, shimmer and fade away. Selara and the figure hit the stone floor of the cave hard.

It was cold, silent, and dark when they woke up. The figure recovered first, roughly pulling Selara to her feet. Jonrah didn't want to speak. A Thought Listener could determine their exact location with one word. After Selara stood up, she glanced back at the cottage. It was reduced to ruins, only one wall standing. It was covered with moss, and trees grew through it. In the moonlight, she saw the silhouette of three gravestones standing in the garden. She stared in confusion and disbelief. She wanted to stop, but the silent figure didn't let her. He acted as if they were being chased by someone or something.

Selara kept up with him easily, having spent her whole life navigating the maze of gnarled roots and slippery mud washes of these moors. But everything was different—these weren't the same moors where she grew up. The trees were larger, and her landmarks had altered. Regardless, her feet danced smoothly over the vines and slippery twists in the swampy shadows. Sometimes the moon peeked out from behind the inky, black clouds and cut strange silhouettes from the dark curtain of stars surrounding them. *What happened to our cottage? What happened to my grandparents? Why're there three gravestones in our garden?*

The shadow figure stopped periodically, making sure Selara was close before stopping completely. He listened intently.

Out of the blackness came a guttural scream and an explosion of fangs. A hellish beast leaped from the dark shadows at Selara. The black figure drew a glowing blue sword. Selara had to shield her eyes. He slashed a wide arc with the sword, and the snarling ball of fury went silent, its head parted from its twisting body, its eyes scanning wildly as its jaws still snapped. The sword was swallowed into darkness, and the figure motioned for Selara to hurry. They moved quickly while the creature still convulsed. A chorus of howls and snarls echoed in the distance. They were closing in on all sides. The tales that Grandfather used to tell her as a little girl resurfaced in Selara's mind with a chilling word: Werewolves.

As Selara and her companion approached a clearing, he stopped and quickly removed a small leather bag from his cloak. Pouring a white substance out of the bag, he traced a broad circle around them.

This is what Grandfather and I did on the farm.

The figure spoke an incantation in the same strange language that she heard earlier that night. A tunnel of wind rose, sending her scarlet hair blowing in all directions. The wind increased in intensity, surrounding both of them until a black gloved hand pulled Selara from the circle.

As she looked over her shoulder, she stared in disbelief. The tall, dark figure and another Selara were still standing inside the stormy circle. It was like they had stepped out of their bodies. They moved swiftly over the rocks and branches, leaving only their empty spectres behind them. Menacing, snarling beasts appeared one by one out of the darkness, surrounding the two figures in the swirling circle, snapping violently with their deadly jaws. The misshapen creatures howled in frustration as they struggled in vain to reach the figures.

Selara sprinted in shock with her silent partner, still failing to comprehend what she just saw. After what seemed an eternity, blood-curdling howls rose up louder in the distance as the creatures realised they were deceived. The howls faded into the morning as day slowly marched across the mountain peaks. The journey was long and hard as swamps and moors gave way to rocky dry pathways cutting into the mountains like jagged scars.

The figure led Selara to a dry cave under two massive boulders and motioned for her to lay down. He opened a black leather bag and unfolded a thick wool blanket with golden spirals woven in the seams. He folded it once and spread it out on the hard ground for her. Selara had a multitude of questions racing through her mind, but they were no match for the complete and utter exhaustion that overtook her like a sleepy fog. Even though it was chilly and there was no fire to warm her, she fell fast asleep, dreaming of howling creatures, glowing swords, and piercing green eyes.

chapter iv

Rule 4: Never enter a village or a city

The next day, Selara woke to a deadwood fire. The familiar sounds and smells of crackling wood greeted her like an old friend as she struggled to open her eyes. Small birds darted in and out of a small copse of trees below them. She looked down. She was covered from head to toe by a black cloak. In the ribbons of the faint morning light, she saw a tall young man with red hair staring into the valley. His features were carved from white marble; his gaze was singular. He was lost in thought. His dark crumpled hood rested on his back, revealing a slender neck. The mysterious shadow figure had changed into a rather ordinary looking young man roughly her own age.

Hearing her stir, he turned to face her. "Good morning," he said. "How're you feeling?" The young man's voice was friendly enough. He was no longer the strange, silent, menacing creature. She felt safer.

"I feel like a Valerian ditch pig trampled me, ate me, and then shat me out," Selara replied. She suddenly worried she was being inappropriate. She fussed with her hair. What did she know about boys?

Jonrah laughed. *My sister's awesome!* He wanted to tell her who he was, but he was under strict instructions not to share more with her than absolutely necessary. She was not to be told what really happened to her or that their parents were waiting for her at the White Keep.

"You've found your voice!" Selara said.

"Yes. It's safer here, Jonrah continued, safer to talk far away from things that hear your thoughts. My name is Jonrah."

"What's happening?" she asked. "What happened to my cottage, my grandparents — my life? Why were there firkin' Were-Wolves near my cottage? I grew up there, and I've never seen even one firkin' Were-Wolf. Who are you, and where are you taking me?" Jonrah pondered what kind of a story he could tell her. There were too many questions, and he didn't know how to lie fast enough. "It's a long story."

"You've got to be kidding me!" she said, her cheeks reddening. "It's a long story? You're going to have to do better than that!"

"All will be revealed in good time!" He was trying to be nonchalant like Saffron, but he knew he was in trouble. Selara was standing up now with her hands on her hips. She glared at him dangerously. The façade Jonrah tried so desperately to maintain crumpled, and he dropped his act and whined like a toddler. "Please, Selara, I'm not supposed to talk to you about these things! I was told …."

"You were told by whom?" asked Selara, "and how do you know my name?"

"My parents, your parents, I mean …." Jonrah felt the blood rushing to his cheeks.

"What?"

"I mean I can't answer your questions right now. It's important!"

Was he starting to cry? thought Selara.

"Please, Selara," he pleaded.

She nodded and relaxed, feeling guilty and awkward about bringing the first teenage boy she ever met to tears.

Jonrah went on, "The creatures we saw last night were not Werewolves. They were Daemon-Wolves sent to kill you. I can't explain why you've never seen one before, but I'm really glad you haven't — didn't, I mean. They're nasty creatures. I have to say, I was quite proud of the glamour spell I used to get those monsters off our trail. It was the first time I ever got it completely right. Did you like the sword? Saffron taught me."

This person's a moron! thought Selara. *It's a wonder we're both not dead!* She walked over to the fire and sat down. *Okay, a cute moron,* she admitted to herself.

Selara poked a stick into the fire. Jonrah sat down across from her. "So you can do majik tricks?" asked Selara, more like a statement than a question.

"They aren't tricks! They're important tools. Not everyone can use majik, you know! Some people are born with it, and some people learn it from books."

Selara remembered the book in her bag. She reached in and pulled it out.

"I think this is a majik book, right?" she asked.

Jonrah reached over and took it from her. He opened it to the first page and closed it quickly. He gave it back. "This book is dangerous, Selara. Where'd you get it?"

"It's ... was ... my grandfather's book."

"Whatever you do, don't read it unless you have someone like Saffron or my dad with you."

"I can't read it. It's written in some kind of crazy language. I did try to read it once when I was a little girl."

"What happened?"

"I don't really want to talk about it."

"Okay," said Jonrah, wondering what happened to her. "I guess telling you a few things wouldn't hurt." Selara sat up. "I was sent by my father and mother to keep you safe and to bring you to the Keep for training."

"Training? I'm not a dog or a horse!" replied Selara, indignantly.

Jonrah ignored her and continued, "They told me you wouldn't know how to use your powers yet, and you would be as defenceless as any Nomaji. Daemon knows this and wants to kill you before your powers emerge."

"That sounds great! But there's only one problem."

"What's that?"

"I don't have any powers. The most I can do is conjure up a little fire worm if I have to. I'm nothing special. Tell this Daemon character that he doesn't have to worry about me. Problem solved." She pretended to wipe the problem from her hands. "Look, I'm a peasant girl who has nothing, is nothing, and will probably be nothing. I'm not majik, I can't do majik, and I'm nobody's problem." She tucked her knees in tight and rested her chin on them, rocking gently.

Jonrah laughed. "If you're a simple Nomaji peasant girl, then I'm a Valerian ditch pig! You are the most powerful Elemental of us all."

It was Selara's turn to laugh. "I don't even know what an Elemental is." She rolled her eyes. "I'm not powerful, and I think everyone's made a huge mistake. I'm going back to find my grandparents!"

"You're an Elemental just like me," insisted Jonrah.

"Okay, prove it!" she said.

Jonrah realised things were not going as well as he'd hoped, but then he had an idea. Without warning, Jonrah reached into the fire with his gloved hand, scooped up a coal, and playfully tossed it to Selara. He shook off his smoking glove, shaking his hand to cool it down. She caught the coal instinctively. "Good reflexes," said Jonrah, matter-of-factly.

Selara opened the palm of her hand in wonder at the glowing orange coal lying there harmlessly. "Is this one of your majik tricks?" Her eyes narrowed. She turned the burning ember over in her hand. "What did you do to this?" Selara casually bounced it in her hand. The glistening object felt as cool as any ordinary stone. Then an icy panic crept into her. She realised that there was a hot coal in her hand. As the thought of the hot coal grew, she smelled her skin burning and blistering. She tossed it away.

Then it happened. *Oh no,* thought Selara. *Rule number two, rule number two,* she repeated over and over. But it was too late. She was losing control. She screamed in pain and rage, her flaming red hair swirling and glowing.

Oh no, thought Jonrah, *this is not going well at all.*

The glow around Selara grew, and her hand held a flaming green ball. She launched it at Jonrah's not-soon-to-be-smiling face. He dodged the flaming projectile just in time to feel it sizzle past his ear. Three more fireballs flew at him, this time bouncing harmlessly off the shimmering blue shield in Jonrah's hand. Jonrah switched shield hands, trying to shake the pain away.

"That hurt," he complained. Glowing, Selara eyed him menacingly. *Not a fire serpent, please not a fire serpent, please not a fire serpent,* Jonrah repeated.

Just breathe, thought Selara, *just breathe.* "Clear blue pond…Clear blue pond," she repeated to herself, breathing in and out slowly. The rage storm subsided. She clutched her right hand in pain. Her eyes glazed over again, and she started muttering in another language, "You vermin bog sloth, carnivorous worm, twisted mud serpent! Why on earth did you do that to me?"

Jonrah was surprised and perplexed. He understood her. He stood smirking, looking like a deflated bat wearing what was left of his cloak. Sweat glistened on his face and the edge of his hair smouldered. The sound of a small fire crackled in the trees, just beyond the cave entrance.

"Why did you do that to me?" she screamed.

"I was just proving a point!" said Jonrah. "It didn't quite go as planned. But I did give you proof that you've got powers."

"Oh right! You did that. It was just a majik trick! You tricked me with your majik into thinking I have powers," she said, her eyes narrowing suspiciously.

Tamara and Selara're going to be great friends, he thought wryly.

"Why would I give you the power to throw fireballs at my head and burn my own hair?" he asked. "Just to prove a point?"

Selara sat down, shivering. Her hand throbbed.

"Please give me your hand."

"No! I don't trust you!" She pulled her hand away defensively and turned her back to him.

Jonrah moved in closer and carefully and gently took her reluctant hand. He was concerned that it might explode into flames at any moment. He whispered something under his breath, and a cool breeze blew over the angry blisters.

She stared at her hand. The blisters were gone. *This moron might be useful,* she reflected. "Okay, I lied," she admitted. "It wasn't your majik trick. I didn't want you to think that I was a freak. I can't believe I let that happen. The most important rule Grandmother taught me was never get mad and lose control."

"Our grandmother knows that you have powers?" *Firk,* he thought, hoping she hadn't noticed his mistake.

"Oh, these aren't powers. This is just me losing my temper. It's normal for me."

"Do you know any normal people your age that can throw fireballs?"

"Actually, you're the only other person my age I've met, so ... no."

"Okay, then let me be the first to tell you that normal girls your age can't make fire balls when they get mad. The only women who can do that are called Fire Elementals. Which makes you a Fire Elemental, not a normal peasant girl."

"But I don't want to be a freak! I had this thing under control for so many years, and now you've come along and made me mad. This was *your* fault. I haven't seen my fire serpents since I was a little girl."

Please no fire serpents, thought Jonrah. "You're not a freak," he assured her. "You're an Elemental, but you have no idea how to use your powers. Do you?" *And what's with the green fireballs? Elemental fire is orange. Did I imagine them?*

"Maybe everyone would be a lot safer if I just went back to my old life. Take me back. You can fight off the were-things with your majik sword, and ... I ... can ... find Grandfather ... and ...." She burst into tears. Jonrah wrapped his arms around her tentatively as she sobbed. She felt safe and then suddenly a bit uncomfortable. She stood up quickly and brushed herself off.

Jonrah stood up and looked at her. "I'm sorry, Selara. I can't explain everything to you right now. You have to trust that I'm telling you the truth. Your old life's gone, your cottage's gone, and your grandparents're gone. But your new life is going to be amazing. I promise. Now we have to keep moving. We have a long way to go."

Selara nodded and kicked the sand. "Not until I've something to eat. And don't you have any horses at your castle? Why are we walking?"

Jonrah winced. "We needed to be stealthy and not attract any attention."

"So you don't know how to ride a horse?" she asked.

"No. That's not what ...."

"Do you even own a horse? I used to ride the plough horse all the time with my grandfather!"

Jonrah rolled his eyes. "Of course, you did. Okay, there's a village on our way, and we can buy something to eat. But we can't attract any attention."

"Like if we were riding horses," said Selara.

Jonrah shook his head. *His big sister was acting like, well, a big sister.* He smiled to himself, then looked at her seriously. "We're being hunted, Selara! We're not going to be safe until we're deep inside the walls of the Keep."

Selara shrugged and began picking up her belongings.

Jonrah picked up Selara's blanket roll. With a flourish, he turned it inside out and put it on like a cloak. He gave his best impression of a statuesque warrior. "That was pretty cool, wasn't it?" He glanced at Selara. "Right?" he added.

Moron, she thought, walking.

They followed the winding trail that descended down the mountains. The silence was uncomfortable, so Jonrah asked "So what are your grandmother's other rules?"

Selara decided to humour him. "Rule number one: never curse. Or say things like firk, firk, firk, firk! Rule number two: never get mad and burn the house down."

"How many rules are there?" Jonrah interrupted.

"Rule number three," she continued, "never hold, possess, or look into a mirror and actually see if you look halfway decent."

"Actually…"

"I'm not finished. I have one more rule."

"What is it?"

"Rule number four, and we're going to break it!" she said, beaming. "Never visit a village, town, or a city where there are lots of people and interesting things to do and see."

Jonrah smiled. They were definitely going to smash rule number four.

The mountain trail levelled out as it meandered past blossoming fruit trees, babbling creeks, and a decrepit old mill. They crossed a mossy stone bridge where a motley group of peasants were redirecting water from the river. They eyed the two travellers suspiciously. One young man became distracted by the stunning young redhead, and slipped, falling head first into the water to the cheers and laughter of the other men.

She waved at them, shyly. *Did I cause that?* she asked herself, smiling. *Maybe I do have powers.* She chuckled and blushed.

"We're not supposed to attract attention," Jonrah whispered to her through clenched teeth. "Keep walking."

The cobblestone path was soon filled with people and lined with houses, shops, and even an inn. The sounds, colours, and smells of the village intoxicated Selara. She didn't know where to look first.

Jonrah had to keep stopping and pulling her along while she fixated on anything and everything that took her fancy.

Colourful flags danced in the wind while musicians and singers sang stories. For Selara, this place was pure majik. A little girl ran to Selara with a handful of bright daisy crowns. Selara bent down to let her place one in her hair. "Why, thank you, princess," she said, bowing to her. After Jonrah placed a coin in the little girl's hand, she curtsied and scampered into the crowd. *She reminds me so much of me when I was little*, she thought. "I can't believe I've missed out on all of this!" She jokingly shook her fist at an imaginary grandmother.

The inner streets were a maze of alleyways, and ancient houses with paned windows pressed in like curious onlookers. The fragrant smell of cooking meat made Selara and Jonrah's mouths water as they realised just how hungry they were. They followed the source of the heavenly fragrance to a makeshift fire grill at the corner of an alleyway. Jonrah reached into his bag to pay, but the cook made a grand gesture for him to stop. "All I require is a smile from the lovely maiden!"

Selara blushed and beamed. Jonrah looked at Selara and feigned vomiting. Selara was not used to having so much male attention, and she revelled in it.

Jonrah held onto the skewers of meat with one hand and dragged Selara away with the other. They turned and sauntered down the alleyway, finishing their skewers. Jonrah pretended to stab Selara who parried with her skewer for an impromptu sword fight. *This is the best day of my life*, thought Selara. She spun around and was immediately distracted by a wooden table with several woven baskets. Baked bread was neatly placed in rows. "This is just like Grandmother used to make," she said, smiling. The baker had left a bowl with broken crusts on a special shelf above her table. Just as Selara was about to ask about the bowl, a Night Bird flew down and snatched up a piece of bread, answering her question. The woman dropped to one knee and made the Holy Sign of the Night Bird. Jonrah did the same out of respect to the baker. Selara reluctantly followed thinking of the scolding her grandmother had given her grandfather about this ritual.

The portly woman gave them a warm smile while Jonrah pulled out a few coins to pay her. Her smile quickly vanished, replaced by a worried frown. She looked around her and then back at the spiral insignia on the golden coins. "This is too much," she said in a hushed tone, looking around her. She gathered up the coins quickly and pressed the warm loaves into Selara's hands. "This money has the stamp of the old king. Don't be showing them to anyone else. You seem like a nice couple. I wouldn't want anything to happen to you. The runes on these coins will only bring you misfortune here." She looked worriedly at Selara and then retreated into her hut taking the remaining baskets of bread with her. She shut the door quickly.

"What's all that about?" asked Selara.

"I think I've made a mistake. We should probably leave."

In the Valley of the Skulls, Fletcher woke up under a blanket of stars. "Every feather hurts," he groaned. Selara and the figure were gone. He was worried about Selara. He could hear the howling of wolves in the distance. She had been taken by a strange Hu-man. Bird flew up, circling to find his bearings, but everything was so strange. Selara's cottage was an empty ruin swallowed up by moss and trees. The valley was crawling with foul-smelling creatures. He felt dizzy. Exhausted. He decided to look for Selara at first light.

They can't have gone very far on foot. Bird flew in the direction of the Clan forest to rest. He blamed himself for Selara's kidnapping. *If I'd only flown faster, maybe I could've stopped that Hu-man. I'll tear him to pieces when I find them.*

Fletcher's wings felt heavy by the time he reached the trees. He knew something was horribly wrong. The trees had grown taller and hundreds of new baskets were woven into the branches. *When did this happen?* he wondered. He flew from basket to basket, trying to find his family's weavings. When he found his home, he was met by a stranger.

"Who are you, and what business do you have here?" barked an old bird.

"My name is Fletcher, and I live here."

"My wife and I have lived here for twenty moons! Are you mocking me?"

"I don't understand. Where are Flank and Terra?"

"I don't know anyone by those names."

"What's happening, Father?" asked Winn, poking her head over his shoulder.

"Some crazy bird can't remember where he lives," said Flint.

Winn looked curiously at Fletcher. He was handsome and carried himself well. He spoke with a strange accent, which made him even more intriguing.

"Maybe he can perch in the guest chamber until tomorrow," she said. "We must follow the Code of Hospitality, Father. We can talk to the Elders tomorrow, and maybe they can help find out where he lives." Winn knew how to manipulate her father. Ever since her mother had died, her father would do anything for her. And the code was the code. Flint had no choice but to relent.

"All right," he said. He turned away and headed back to his sleeping area. "And no funny business, Winn!" *She always does this to me,* he thought. "The Code of Hospitality indeed." *She knows Clan Law better than the Elders do.* "But just until sunrise," he added.

Winn shyly led a confused Fletcher to the basket chambers that had been his childhood home. *Where are my parents?* he wondered.

"Stay here, and we can go together in the morning," said Winn. She casually brushed her wing along his. Fletcher nodded obediently and surrendered to exhaustion. He wondered if he had truly lost his mind. As he drifted off, he thought, *Winn's a beautiful bird.*

Winn couldn't sleep. She was much too excited to have this stranger arrive in the middle of the night. She was smitten. *And sleeping in the next basket!* she thought. *My friends'll be insanely jealous.* She couldn't wait to tell them. Winn curled up in her roost, her mind racing.

The sun rose tracing golden threads over the weavings of the Night Bird dwellings, ranging from simple utility to wooden palaces beyond imagination, a woven canvas of intricate colours and spiral shapes.

The early morning was filled with the cries of birds feeding in the crisp air. Hundreds of homes dotted the branches like open mouths yawning. No humans had ever seen the Clan hives. Even Selara respected the privacy of the Night Birds and never ventured into the Clan forest.

Fletcher woke up, wishing to wake from this horrible nightmare. Nobody knew him or his parents. Strangers lived in his home. Selara was kidnapped. Something terrible had happened to her house and her elders.

Winn poked her head through the looking hole, interrupting his thoughts. "It's time to fly to the Circle, and then we can go fly for food." Her eye caught his. She looked away shyly. "Follow me," she said.

Winn swooped into the clear morning, followed closely by Fletcher. Winn's father barked out something, but Winn ignored him. She, energetic and spontaneous, was roughly Fletcher's age. Winn wove her way in and around the other Night Birds going about their morning routine.

The trees have grown twice as tall overnight, thought Fletcher.

They approached a large woven circle surrounded by the homes of the Elder Birds. Winn and Fletcher landed at the edge of the Circle and waited as was the custom. An old bird, seeing them land, waddled slowly into the Circle. Winn bowed her head respectfully, and Fletcher did the same.

"I see you have come to be mated!" croaked the elder.

"No," gasped Winn. She was visibly embarrassed, but secretly wished that it were true.

"A shame, you make a fine couple," said the old bird.

"We've come to ask you some questions, respected elder. My friend here is confused and lost," said Winn.

"Ask your questions then. I'm not getting any younger."

Fletcher summoned up his courage and asked if the Elder Bird had heard of two birds named Flank and Terra.

"Why are you speaking like that?" *He speaks like those of the old Clan,* he thought.

"What do you mean?" asked Fletcher.

"No one speaks like that anymore."

"I don't understand."

"No matter. I haven't heard anyone speak those names in many moons. They're two of our founding citizens. Long dead, of course. Shame about their only son. Tragic. Are you trying to play a joke on me?" he asked, his feathers ruffled.

"No, of course not! How could they be dead? I only saw them yesterday," said Fletcher. "I'm their son!"

Winn looked at Fletcher with concern.

The Elder eyed him seriously. "I must speak with you alone." He turned to Winn. "Come back later, dear."

Winn was annoyed but did as she was told. She flew off, grumbling to herself.

The Elder Bird took Fletcher into his home. "If you are, in fact, speaking the truth, there's only one way that this could be happening to you. Majik! Only Hu-man majik is responsible for the story you're telling me. Did you do something to offend a majik Hu-man?"

"No but…" Fletcher remembered the dark figure from the night before. "There was a strange Hu-man who took my friend away. I tried to stop him, but everything went dark."

The Elder Bird nodded sagely. "The majik Hu-man must have taken his revenge on you by bringing you here, far away from the old Clan and the parents who love you. Most likely to punish you. You must find the majik Hu-man, so he can return you to your parents." With that, the Elder waddled back into his sleeping chamber as if everything were resolved.

How can I ever persuade a majik Hu-man to return me back to my parents? I can't even speak his language, he thought. Just when everything seemed hopeless, Winn swooped in and playfully knocked him over.

"Let's go find some food," she chirped. "I'm starving." With nowhere else to go, Fletcher followed Winn, and before long, he left his problems behind. The two flew side by side past the forest to glide on the warm updrafts from the neighbouring mountains. She glanced at Fletcher. "So what did the Elder Bird tell you?"

"He told me a majik Hu-man brought me here. The only way to return to my parents is for him to send me back."

"Hu-mans," she spat. "They're nothing but trouble." Winn was secretly glad that Fletcher was stranded here with her. She wanted him all to herself.

Fletcher didn't agree but kept his thoughts to himself.

They flew silently until they spotted a Hu-man settlement far below. An elderly Hu-man was walking by herself. She was carrying food, and Winn was hungry.

chapter v

Rule 5: Never try to control Dark Majik

Alan climbed over the rocks, through thickets and under fallen trees. He couldn't afford to be seen. He was determined and focussed. Many people were depending on him. The path sloped abruptly and followed a rushing river. He needed to move quickly. He ripped off his shirt, folded it, and stuffed it into his waterproof bag. He had treated the leather bag with oils especially for this purpose. Soon he was completely naked and his pack, bulging. Sunlight glimmered around him and passed through his body, bending like a prism, casting rainbows in all directions. He became more and more transparent before he poured himself into the water until nothing was left of him. His leather bag floated, guided by an unseen hand.

The river tumbled and foamed over polished rocks and flowed over mossy green stones. *This always feels like flying,* he thought, enraptured by the experience. Unencumbered by a solid body, he was pure thought, guiding his bag through the swift current. Trout flew by like silvery birds in the translucent sky. Water bugs skittered and twisted on the rushing water. He tried to calculate just how far he needed to travel but struggled because time seemed very different when he was part of a rushing river.

The water opened up to a large pool where the current slowed. The bag floated and drifted, caught momentarily on the edge of a branch before being snatched by a translucent hand. The hand became solid, attached to a shivering arm, chest, and then complete body. In his water form, he had no concerns about temperature or pain. In his human form, Alan was always reminded of just how fragile the body was.

Alan dressed quickly, letting his dry clothes absorb the leftover river water. He made his way along the path by the river's edge. He was close to his target. He heard the voices of people walking on the road. The river path passed under a bridge. Here he climbed up and followed the road to the castle. He blended in as a peasant worker and planned to sneak his way inside the gates.

He knew the plan was foolhardy. Too many things could go wrong. He clung to the faint hope that the element of surprise would work to his favour. He knew that only an insane person would ever try to steal from Daemon, especially something as precious as the circlet. Everyone in the kingdom knew that the circlet must be resisting Daemon's efforts to use it. Otherwise every single Elemental would be dead by now. Alan steeled himself. *Fortune favours the bold!* he thought. And his mission was indeed bold!

Alan arrived at the gates in the late afternoon. He carefully hid a bag of extra clothing and sandals inside the hollow of a burnt-out tree. From the blackened tree, he could see a tower window a hundred feet above. The window would be his exit point. Being careful not to draw attention, he made his way back to the main road. A few peasants chatted as they walked, not paying much attention to him. Alan trudged along, blending.

Before him lay the Dark Castle. It was a foreboding monstrosity with towers stabbing defiantly into the azure sky. Two massive, misshapen creatures stood on either side of its gaping archway. *It hadn't always been this way,* thought Alan. His father told him of a time when this was a Nomaji castle ruled by a generous and compassionate king. Unfortunately, he and his soldiers were no match for the ambitions of the Dark Queen. During the attack, even the king's mightiest wizards were defeated. The rest of them retreated to the forests until they re-appeared to fight alongside the Elementals at the Battle of Albright.

During the battle, a miracle happened: The Miracle at Albright. Many people still whispered of the vision. A young prophet appeared in the centre of the battlefield, wearing a cloak of a Dark Majik serpent and an Elemental serpent. A young Night Bird perched upon her shoulder. It was said that the bird's eyes burned like fire. The young girl held out the book of the prophets and stood bravely and defiantly before the Elemental and Dark Majik armies. She single-handedly stopped the war before disappearing, leaving only a blackened circle upon the ground. The black circle was considered a warning of what would happen if the people didn't stop their warring and didn't honour their Gods.

The soldiers who bore witness to the vision believed the prophet was telling them to live in peace. The Holy Night Bird became a symbol of the judgement of the Gods. People now lived in fear of Night Birds, believing they carried the dark spirits of judgement. These portends reminded the people always to seek peace. Dark Majik practitioners called her the Dark Princess of Peace while the Elementals called her the True Queen of Peace. Dark Majik practitioners began a peaceful co-existence with the Elementals, and many Elementals began to trust and befriended Dark Majik practitioners. For many years there was a fragile peace until Daemon took up the Dark Queen's old campaign. He dragged the kingdom back into war and claimed the castle for himself.

The eyes on the two beasts shifted menacingly as they sniffed and eyed the steady stream of travellers, watching for anything out of the ordinary. Alan did his best to keep his fear in check, worried that even one errant thought would bring these unholy creatures down upon him. Alan composed himself and walked as confidently as he could. Suddenly a Night Bird flew low over them, causing many travellers to drop to one knee and make the Holy Sign of the Night Bird lest judgement fall upon them. Alan used the distraction to slip by the beasts and through the gates. Inside the castle walls he breathed easier, but the hard part was yet to come.

Alan missed the hustle and bustle of the castle: the children's laughter, people arguing, dogs' barking, and the general chaos of life. Ever since he manifested his powers and Daemon inhabited the castle, he was kept hidden from the people. If he were identified as an Elemental, he would be a target and mysteriously disappear like so many before him — like his father. Even with so many fascinating powers, Elementals had limitations. Sometimes using their power for long periods of time weakened them like any muscle overused. While Elementals remained in human form, they were vulnerable to injury or death like any other Nomaji.

Jonrah's father Talon, predicted that the True Queen would be the strongest Elemental. Alan felt pride that he was able to help Selara escape, carefully hidden from Daemon until her true powers emerged fully and she could protect herself. Alan helped to conceal them all by using his ability to call upon millions of droplets of water from the marsh air to create a fog so thick that both her parents and the Elemental resistance could escape. Alan's depleted powers had so exhausted him that he had to be carried away as the group escaped their attackers.

Talon sent a message that Selara was returning soon. It was more important than ever that he complete his mission. Today, he needed to retrieve the most important Elemental relic in existence. It was stolen from the White Keep by Daemon's network of spies. The relic, a majik circlet allowing the wearer to communicate with all creatures, was created long before the Dark Majik-Elemental wars. It was intended to be a tool for unification and harmony created by Wraiths from another realm. They were careful to ensure that the wearer must possess the qualities of truth, justice, and compassion. Anyone unworthy would burn or far worse. Alan steeled himself and waded through the chaos of the courtyard towards the Black Keep.

He did his best to clear his mind as his father taught him. There were creatures here that read thoughts and discerned motives. It took a disciplined mind to thwart them, confuse them or divert them. As he zigzagged his way towards the ominous building, he constructed a misleading scenario in his mind. He was Argot on his way to seek work as a labourer at the castle. He'd fought with his father and fled their home to seek refuge in the castle.

When he entered the circular archway of the Black Keep, he saw Marauders milling about. Some were guarding the entrance. He knew he had no legitimate reason to enter and no convincing lie to get him through the door. Then he remembered barrels of water were brought to the kitchen every day for cooking and washing. He saw some outside the kitchen door. A plan hatched. He walked to them casually and rolled an empty one to join its fellows. He pretended to be fixing it. He took the lid off the barrel, climbed inside, and pulled it shut using the bung hole. He pushed the bung back in from the inside. Now he waited. If he was lucky, he'd be rolled in with the others. When everyone went to sleep, he would kick off the lid, and roam the castle to find the circlet. He knew that anyone could carry the circlet safely, but woe to the unchosen who tried to wear it.

Inside the palace kitchen, Lucy busied herself stirring a huge pot of stew. Dishes clattered, and her daughter and the army of helpers neatly stacked the copper dishes and mugs. Lucy kept an organised kitchen, an oasis in a sea of disorganisation and horror. She hated Daemon for taking over the castle, but at least he kept his horrific creatures out of her domain. They ate the cooking scraps. *Like animals*, she thought. *And those poor women, taken from their families to become his slaves.* If they ended up in her kitchen, she found a way to sneak them back to their families. *Some of them couldn't even remember their names!*

Outside the kitchen, Salvan helped Bartoff load the water barrels. "I thought she asked for ten barrels!"

"There are ten barrels," replied Bartoff with annoyance.

"No, there are eleven barrels!" *Where does Lucy find these people?*

"I've ten fingers — not eleven!" Bartoff held up both hands. "You said ten and that's what I filled up. Ten." He scratched his head, wondering if he had actually filled up one more barrel by mistake.

"Lucy needs ten water barrels, not eleven. Did you fill up an extra barrel?"

Bartoff looked at his fingers, confused. *Why does it matter anyways? Who cares? Ten barrels, eleven barrels, or even twelve barrels. They're going to use them all anyway,* he thought. *Salvan always worried about numbers* "But you see these barrels go to eleven! Maybe I should just dump one out. Would that make you happy?" He was about to kick over one when Salvan glared at him.

"You've also got extra toes. You'd better start counting those too! Just shut up and load them into the kitchen. And quick sticks, or Lucy'll have our heads."

Bartoff rolled the barrels up the wooden ramp and stacked them in the corner of the large kitchen. When he rolled in the last barrel and stood it up, it didn't slosh.

"I think there's something wrong with this barrel," said Bartoff, stopping to catch his breath.

"Then open it up," said Salvan. "We can't have you poisoning everyone in the castle, can we?"

"Oi! What're you two doing over there?" shouted Lucy.

"Something's wrong with this barrel," replied Bartoff.

"Let me see," said Lucy wearily, putting down her stirring spoon and waddling over. She snatched the small tool out of Bartoff's hand and pried off the lid. She peered into the barrel. There was silence. Lucy cuffed them on the back of their heads and threw the tool on the floor "It's just water!" she shouted, hurrying back to her stove.

Salvan cuffed Bartoff, mimicking Lucy. "See, it's just water," he repeated as he stomped off.

Bartoff paused. "Shouldn't we put the lid back on?"

"No! Let her do it herself!" scolded Salvan.

Lucy cursed. Those two dough heads had distracted her long enough for the stew to start thickening. It was burning. She stirred it quickly. "Val! Run over and fetch me more water. Quickly," she directed, tossing her a small copper bucket.

"Mum, there's no water in this barrel. Somebody's left their washing in it." Val dropped the pail and covered her eyes. "There's a naked man in our kitchen!"

"No, please, let me explain," pleaded Alan. He completely lost track of time. In his water form, time passed quickly. He tried to think of an explanation.

Lucy approached him, brandishing her largest kitchen knife. She gave him a quick look up and down. "Who're you, and how on earth did you get in here?"

Alan did not answer but ran through the stone archway, leaving Lucy, and all modesty behind him. He appeared to vanish into steam that drifted through the castle.

"An Elemental!" she spat. She turned to her daughter who was still covering her eyes. "Alert the guards. Don't just stand there, move! And there goes dinner!" she complained, throwing the knife in disgust. "The monsters'll be feasting tonight!"

The fog crept from room to room, hanging like an impenetrable curtain. The translucent being moved stealthily through the maze of halls and corridors. Alan knew the general layout of the castle from his father who had worked on castle repairs in the early years. The fog caused enough confusion for Alan to move past the miserable hordes of castle creatures. As he rounded a corner and headed up a winding stairway, he heard shouting.

At Old Mill Village, Fib hauled in the water bucket and heaved it onto the table. There was a muted thunk, and the water splashed back and forth. "I'm starving!" he said, lifting the pot lid to check supper. "When's father gettin' home?" he asked, reaching for a piece of bread.

"He'll be 'ere soon. Leave the bread alone!"

Fib chewed the piece of bread quickly and sat down on a chair near the stove. His mother was busy folding clothes.

"Tam told me he saw the Marauders at White Owl Village," he said matter-of-factly.

His mother stopped what she was doing and stared at him. "When?" she asked, concerned.

"Not long ago," he said.

"We need to find your father," she said, tossing the rest of the clothes onto the shelf.

"What's wrong?"

Without a word, she rushed out of the house, dragging Fib along.

Behn was standing in the street, talking with a group of men when the two interrupted him mid-sentence. The look on his wife's face told him everything he needed to know — Marauders, and they were collecting taxes.

Daemon was demanding more taxes which shop owners couldn't afford to pay. Many refused, vainly hoping with group solidarity that Daemon would relent. Instead, Daemon sent his Marauders to make an example of the dissidents.

Behn, his wife, and Fib hurried down the crowded streets to collect what little they could from the family business, but it was too late. Hoof beats sounded in the distance, echoing in the alleyways. The family took shelter in Behn's wood shop, huddled together. Behn tried the door. Someone barred it from the outside. Behn slumped down, defeated. He kissed his wife and son goodbye.

Not far away, Selara stopped to listen. "Is that thunder?" she asked. She picked up her pace to catch up to Jonrah.

The hoof beats echoed in the narrow street. A group of Marauders rode into the village, headed for Behn's shop. Commander Dane already knew the family was trapped inside. His spies made sure there was no escape. He was ready to teach a lesson to the shop owners of Old Mill Village.

Selara and Jonrah hid themselves behind a hay wagon while men and women rushed from the trampling hooves. A large man scooped up the little flower girl and brought her to safety. The heavily armed men stopped at a little building with a front shop attached to it. The building was strategically chosen because it was far enough away from the other buildings to prevent the entire village burning. *Obviously,* thought Commander Dane.

Polished metal flashed as a huge armoured man with a long-braided beard and a curly waxed moustache motioned for his second-in-command to give him a flaming torch. The commander loved theatre and always blackened his eyelids and eye sockets to make him look foreboding. Holding up a torch as a mighty symbol of authority, he warned, "Let this be a lesson to you maggots who refuse to pay their taxes to the great King Daemon!" The torch unceremoniously went out.

A few anonymous snickers escaped the assembly. Selara felt a tingling sensation in her fingers. The Commander's fire appeared burning in her hand and then disappeared.

"Stop that!" hissed Jonrah.

"I can't help it," whispered Selara. "It's happening all by itself."

The bewildered commander had his assistant bring him another torch, and before he could utter another word, it too went out.

An errant guffaw erupted from someone in the middle of the crowd, and there were more snickers. Even some of the Marauders smiled.

The fire appeared again in Selara's hand. She shook her hand to put out the flame. "Firk, firk, firk," she cursed softly.

"You have to stop this. They're going to find us!"

"I'm not doing it on purpose!"

Commander Dane was angry. Losing his audience, his theatrical moment was ruined. *But the show must go on!* he thought. His black eyes scanned the surrounding faces for even the slightest smirk.

This is such a waste of good majik, thought Dane as he reluctantly reached into his saddlebag. Pulling out a glass bottle filled with flowing green liquid, he held it up to the crowd, pausing for dramatic effect. The liquid glittered menacingly in the bright sunlight. With a flourish, he flung the jar in a high arc. It smashed on the wood shop roof.

"No!" shouted an old man. He was the only one who knew the contents of the jar. "You don't know what you're doing!" The old man tried in vain to warn the crowd of the danger. There was an explosion of sparks, and angry green flames burned ferociously.

"C'mon, Pip!" Dane said. "We've got more villagers to frighten, and more people to burn!" He laughed and spat at the old man, dismissively. He dug in his heels. His horse charged forward. Satisfied with his performance, he led his men to the next spectacle.

As the green flames burned, an angry green fire serpent stretched out its emerald neck. It eyed the crowd with malice and split into new heads which wrapped themselves around the thatched roof, completely encasing the house in its fiery grip. Faint screams and cries for help were heard through the thick cushion of acrid smoke. A crowd of onlookers and would-be rescuers watched helplessly behind the growing wall of heat. The old man shook his head in despair.

"We have to go now!" commanded Jonrah.

Selara gave him a look of disbelief. "Those people'll die in there. We have to help them!" She punched his shoulder. "Use your majik, dummy!"

"I can't," Jonrah cried. "My majik'll just make that thing stronger."

"What do you mean?" screamed Selara, not caring if she was over-heard. "We have to help them! Use your majik!" Her green eyes blazed at him. "Why can't you help them?"

Jonrah looked at her helplessly before looking down to avoid her gaze.

She felt panic and rage rising up inside her. The thatched roof was a tangle of green tentacles and belching black smoke. "Why won't you help them?" Selara screamed again. The heat was rising inside her. "Rule number two, rule number two! Firk rule number one and number two!"

Before Jonrah could stop her, she leapt up, glowing brightly. What happened next became a legend told and sung in every county for a thousand years. The storytellers said that a beautiful red-haired stranger walked slowly through the helpless crowd as if enchanted. Her eyes blazed as she stared straight ahead into the growing flames.

The crowd parted as she strode forward, advancing on the green hydra. Everyone screamed as two fiery serpents exploded from the ground and wove around her, towering over them. Some onlookers fell to their knees, made holy gestures, and muttered prayers. The old man watched her, smiling.

"It's the prophet reborn," he shouted, nodding. Most of the crowd stood frozen with their mouths gaping. The old man watched her, smiling in anticipation, his dark eyes sparkling.

An unnatural glow surrounded her as her majestic serpents dwarfed the green hydra. Selara walked as if in a dream. Everything moved in slow motion. It felt good to have her serpents back. She smiled at Greenwald and in this strange and fiery space in time, she named her second serpent Nova.

The green hydra before her was a living, breathing thing: a primi-tive creature that stared at her through many eyes in awe and more strangely, fear. It abruptly stopped eating the building. All seven heads transfixed on the girl. All seven necks bowed to Selara like obedient subjects before their queen.

It recoiled from her as she stepped forward. Her sandals vaporised, her feet melting the sand into glass at each step. The rippling curtains of heat caressed her gently. Fiery robes engulfed her as she sang an ancient song for the flames in an alien language.

The barred door burst open, and green fire drew back as Selara approached the family. The family exited, coughing. They drew close to her and the little group moved as one, Selara still singing her fire song until the flames were replaced by astonished faces. Greenwald and Nova faded into thin air. Relief and amazement quickly turned to fear when Selara stood before the crowd, unburned and still glowing brightly. Her green eyes glistened like burning coals.

"Leave, witch!" shouted a terrified, old woman from the crowd.

The old man fell to his knees and spoke in a language only Selara understood. "Hail, Dark Princess of Peace, I'm your faithful servant!"

Some fell to their knees, praying and reverently bringing thumbs together and fingers spread apart.

Others continued to shout "Witch" and "Demon!" But they were out-numbered by the sea of grateful well-wishers.

Covered in soot and ashes, Fib ran to embrace the radiant being. Oblivious to him, Selara continued chanting in the strange language until the green flames extinguished themselves.

The old man stood up in the middle of the crowd, rejoicing and shout-ing, "The prophet has returned!"

"Shut up, you crazy, old man," said a burly villager.

But the old man continued to shout.

Selara fell to her knees, exhausted, the little boy catching her as best as he could. Jonrah rushed to the little boy to heal his burns. Miraculously, the boy was unhurt.

Fib said, "Thank you," and ran back to the arms of his parents.

Jonrah stood in shock. All whisperings and rumours were true. He saw it with his own eyes. He swelled with pride. She defeated Dark Majik. She really was the prophet described in the legends. *But how?*

Jonrah was secretly ashamed. He was too embarrassed to tell Selara that even with all of his talents and training combined, he was no match for this type of Dark Majik. His sword and his shield were like toys against the Dark Majik hydra. He would have died, and Selara wouldn't be reunited with her parents.

Selara felt exhilarated. She embraced her powers, realising that she was no freak. She was a hero. She could use her powers to help others.

Jonrah stood among the well-wishers and reflected, *If she used these powers the night before, she'd have incinerated those Daemon-Wolves in the blink of an eye.* The appearance of the green serpent was strange. How did she conjure it? He knew there was bigger problem. They had definitely attracted unwanted attention. They would have to move quickly.

chapter vi

Rule 6: Never make friends with Ogres

Shouts echoed down the corridors of the Dark Castle. "Impossible! Fifty Daemon-Wolves against two children in the open country, and they escaped? How can this be? And now the most powerful Elemental of them all is loose in my kingdom! She must be found and put to death as quickly as possible!"

"The people love them," croaked Oag, absently. His one large eye blinked. He basked in their thoughts. "They have allies."

"Where are they now?" screamed Daemon.

"They hid their thoughts by speaking the language of the ancients," he lied. The gnarled Thought Listener saw Daemon's anger growing like clouds before a storm. Having experienced the flood of emotions of the villagers, Oag saw the pieces of his ethereal game falling into place. Something more powerful than all of Daemon's ambitions was emerging: Hope.

"Then what good are you? What good are you to me?" Daemon turned and stormed out.

Oag barely avoided the random kick intended for his eye.

Daemon descended the stairs and down dark, dank passageways where unnatural creatures passed without notice. He had battled the Elementals and taken over much of the kingdom. Only splintered factions remained. He was slowly rooting out and eliminating them. Soon he would be the ruler of all of these lands, and his children's children would be kings and queens.

Daemon walked stiffly and purposefully up the spiral stairs to the Crown Room. He was consumed by the puzzle of the circlet. It sat in its crystal case, mocking him. No matter how hard he tried, or what incantations he used, the crown would not rest upon his head. When he tried to wear it by force, a fiery ring scorched his hands and hair. Daemon reasoned that when all the Elementals were killed and he controlled every river, rock, and tree, the circlet would relent, bestowing him an incredible power. Then M would have no choice but to become his queen. He would lift her curse, and she would do his bidding, for it was said that the wearer of the crown could master the minds of all creatures.

M was his greatest addiction, an obsession beginning in his teenage years. She was much older than him, but he didn't care. She toyed with his heart, teased him, and strung him along. The night she finally promised to meet him and give him his heart's desire, she never showed up. He stormed back to his grandfather's library and found a diabolical curse, a death curse that killed anyone who spoke her name. Her entire family died before she understood his cruelty. She lived in isolation until her curse was lifted or he was able to bend her to his will with the circlet.

His need for power grew from childhood. At that time, his grandmother controlled everything: the household, the finances, his life. His grandfather stood by and let her. He was more preoccupied with his own pursuits although he encouraged Daemon to develop his majik abilities, praising him for each small breakthrough. For Daemon, majik was his refuge and his way of feeling strong. He hid most of his skills from his grandmother — especially his Daemon-Wolf. By the time she passed on, he was a master of his craft. When his grandfather died a short time later, he inherited all of the property and investments. He was rich, but his lust for power continued, an insatiable hunger.

"The castle's under attack!" came shouts from down below. A dense fog was filling up the stairwell. Daemon spun around and slammed the door behind him. *Who dares defy me?* he thought, almost tumbling down the now invisible stairway. He was so distracted that he failed to realise that he was not alone. A faint glint of light sparkled off a polished translucent face, slipping into the Crown Room as the door slammed behind Daemon.

Grog drank deeply from his wooden cup. With no war to occupy his time, he was lethargic. In his prime, he lusted for the blood and the heat of battle. But now the war was reduced to talk, talk, talk, talk; plan, plan, plan; and hide, hide, hide. His brother and sister Ogres left the castle years ago, but Grog remained. With his family gone, he had nothing left.

This is no life for a warrior, he thought. He was living the life of a common castle guard, walking aimlessly up and down empty halls, preparing for threats that never came … until today.

The day started like any other. He strapped on his weapons belt and tested the edge of his sword. He walked up and down the halls, his massive muscular body sometimes touching both walls at once. He looked out the stone windows. It looked like the day would end like any other: boring, dull, and inactive. Another day of pacing these halls and serving a master he despised.

He noticed a strange mist creeping into the hallway towards him. Grog was easily confused, and confounded. *What was the fog doing inside the castle instead of in the marsh?* After a few moments, he found it impossible to see anything. Grog walked forward, tentatively touching the walls of the passageway to keep himself oriented. He heard Daemon barking orders to the rest of his hoard army downstairs. They were all just as helpless and confused as Grog.

It was pure dumb luck when Grog caught sight of a small glowing disc carried by a man of glass. At least it looked to Grog that the man was glass because, even in the fog, he saw right through him. He knew the glass man didn't belong in the castle, but the disc did. Grog let his broadsword speak for him. With one mighty blow, he cut the man in half. His sword passed through him harmlessly.

Grog stared in wonder. He stepped in front of the glass man and wrapped his powerful arms around him. *Crush!* thought Grog. The glass man turned into water and reappeared behind Grog, still carrying the shiny thing. Grog, annoyed and confused, snatched at the glowing thing, but the man ran away.

Grog spun around in pursuit. *Finally, something to fight*, thought Grog. At the end of the passageway, a large open window overlooked the fields below. A defiant stream of daylight drew angular lines in the stubborn fog. The glass man followed the lines and leapt into the open air. He splashed onto the jagged rocks below. A faint metal clink rang out as the shiny thing bounced once before the glass man snatched it. But he wasn't a glass man any more, he was a small normal man without any clothes. The man looked up at the window, smiled, and waved at Grog. Grog waved back, slowly.

Alan shivered, stepping gingerly onto the rocky ground to retrieve his bag of clothes from the hiding tree. He dressed quickly, knowing that the dark hoards would soon be looking for him. Alan exhausted his powers, producing so much fog. He wouldn't be able to transform again until morning. He was incredibly vulnerable. He slipped the circlet into his bag and forced his tired legs to move. Deep in Daemon territory, he was about to be hunted by Marauders, Daemon-Wolves, and Thought Listeners.

Keeping off the main roads, Alan favoured the crooked overgrown pathways through the dark woods, knowing the Marauders couldn't ride their horses through the thorny underbrush. It was growing late, and Alan needed to put more distance between him and the castle. But his heavy legs refused to move. He climbed into the arms of a burned-out tree and hid in its hollow trunk.

Back in Daemon's meeting room, Grog thought about the glass man as a short leather whip stung his leathery face.

"You, idiot!" ranted Daemon. "The Thought Listener said you had the thief trapped and you let him go!"

Grog didn't register any pain or allow his expression to flinch. Grog knew better than to speak when Daemon was mad.

"How could you let this happen? You, stupid oaf! Your whole family's dead, so I can't even have the satisfaction of killing them again! Go! Join the others, and don't come back until the thief's captured and the circlet returned!"

Grog listened to the insults without emotion. He was used to being punished and insulted. It had been his life here at the castle after Daemon took over. This memory stung. It was true that his whole family was dead and Daemon was responsible, but Grog had no place to go, and for years he stayed, suffering in silence.

Grog hated Daemon-Wolves. They were unnecessarily vicious, remorseless creatures that fought without honour, killing everything in their path. He hated being near them: they smelled worse than him. He joined the Daemon-Wolf search party that was attacking and killing men, women, and children in the hunt for the thief. Grog thought about the Glass Man. He was a bold thief. Grog respected him for that.

Deep in the woods, Alan slept fitfully as his dreams turned into nightmares with the terrifying howls of the Daemon-Wolves nearby. He was still too weak to use his powers or his legs.

The full moon, like a searchlight, lit up the forest. The sound of the howling Daemon-Wolves indicated they'd picked up his scent and would soon be upon him. He stumbled out of his hiding place and walked on stiff legs. Three sets of glowing eyes appeared in the shadows. They found him. Eyes multiplied, too many to count.

Alan knew he was going to die. He was foolish to have stolen the circlet on his own with no clear plan of escape. Now he would pay, and the circlet would be back in the hands of Daemon. He couldn't think of a more horrible way to die, being ripped apart by Daemon-Wolves and eaten alive.

Massive hairy figures, deadly shadows in the silvery light, stepped out from the darkness one by one. Their stench made him queasy. He was surrounded, but strangely the beasts were showing restraint. The air filled with unsettling snarls and howls. He felt the hot, foetid breath as the alpha male advanced.

Alan squeezed his eyes shut and steeled himself for the worst possible pain. If only he could transform for even a moment, he might escape. *Why is the brute waiting? This was torture!* Lightening suddenly lit up the forest, and thunder exploded afterwards. As rain pelted down, Alan heard a choking sound.

Alan cautiously opened his eyes. The massive creature was being strangled — the life squeezed out of it while the pack backed away, momentarily subdued. Howls in the distance warned of a larger pack advancing. Alan recognized the Ogre guard. *He's gone rogue!*

"Go!" blurted Grog, thickly as the alpha male collapsed into the mud. Grog was taking revenge on Daemon.

In the ensuing confusion, pure adrenaline propelled Alan and his useless legs into the bushes and down towards the river. The nearest monster turned to pursue, then slumped to the ground.

Grog swung his broadsword in graceful sweeping arcs. There were too many attackers for Grog to kill, but he didn't care. Grog was back in the heat of battle, and he revelled in it. The sword was a blur in the moonlight, blood spattering, fur flying, legs and heads disembodied. Bloody trophies piled around him. When the Daemon-Wolves overtook him, a crooked smile curled on his torn and bloodied face. In the purple fog, Grog saw his wife and his daughter waving to him from the Second Realm.

Alan half-ran, half-rolled down the hill to the river. He slid down the bank and splashed into the rushing water. He hoped the Daemon-Wolves would have trouble tracking him there. He waded desperately into the centre of the freezing torrent. The rain fell in sheets. A dislodged tree moved in the current with crooked boughs — a giant's arms reaching out. Alan desperately clutched onto a branch, holding on with all his strength. The tree gained speed, carrying him safely down the river. He thought of how ironic it would be for him to drown in this river while water was his greatest gift.

Jonrah and Selara tried to leave the village quietly, but the people showered them with more food and gifts than they could carry. One villager asked Selara what was her heart's desire. She replied, jokingly, "A horse." Selara was just teasing Jonrah. As they struggled to pack up their presents, a very grateful Behn walked through the crowd with a beautiful white mare. She whinnied at a beaming Selara.

Before she could protest, he said, "She's all yours. You saved our lives, and we owe you everything. Ride safely. Her name's Storm, and I hope she can make your journey more comfortable."

Selara wiped tears of joy off her face as the villagers strapped bags and parcels onto Storm. She was always told to keep her power hidden, but using it to help these people filled her with happiness. She felt loved and accepted. The little flower girl ran to Selara and gave her a new daisy crown. Selara bent down and allowed her place it on her head. The old man handed her a pair of beautiful sandals. She bent down to put them on. They fit her perfectly. When she looked up to thank him, he was already deep in the crowd.

Fib locked his fingers together and offered them as a boost onto the horse. Selara mounted, and a nervous Jonrah followed up behind her. He wrapped his arms around her waist, afraid of falling off. Selara stroked Storm's neck and took the reins. She squeezed her legs, and the horse trotted slowly out of the village to the shouts and cheers of the villagers. Jonrah leaned in close to Selara and whispered, "So much for not attracting attention."

In the next valley, Winn and Fletcher circled an old crone as she hobbled down the stony path towards the village. Large white rocks poked their polished heads through the sand like skulls raising empty sockets to the dying sun. Winn caught sight of a loaf of bread poking out from the worn leather bag. Fletcher dived playfully at the woman, trying to make her lose her balance and drop her bag.

Winn held back. She waited for the elder Hu-man to give them an offering as was the incomprehensible Hu-man custom. This Hu-man ignored the ritual. Winn found this annoying and disrespectful. She looked for an opportunity to swoop down and snatch the bread herself. Fletcher made a wide circle and gained speed. The old woman struck out with the speed of an angry serpent, striking him hard on the wing with her gnarled cane. Blinding white pain flashed through Fletcher as his wing snapped and he spun. A second blow hit him in the head, and he smashed onto the rocks of the path. Winn made a hasty retreat and landed by her fallen comrade. *Later I'll kill the old Hu-man and feast on her entrails!* Winn promised herself.

Night Birds can't cry, but her heart broke, seeing the wreckage of her dear, new friend. She wasn't strong enough to carry him, but their Clan wasn't too far off. She needed to fly back quickly. It was a sacrilege to let lesser animals defile the body of a Night Bird. Winn beat her powerful wings and rose into the wind. Fletcher was a black mark on the path below. The sun was a golden ball, dropping into the late afternoon.

Jonrah shielded his eyes from the sun. "We're going to have to pick up the pace if we're going to make it to the Keep by nightfall." The two rode steadily into the afternoon, alternating from paths to open roads until the sun bathed the trees in gold and long shadows stretched their weary arms across the pathway. A tar black heap lay in front of them.

"What's that?" asked Selara, climbing off Storm. She tied the reins to a nearby tree. Storm was happy to stop and chew on the tender grass.

"It looks like a dead Night Bird," replied Jonrah, tumbling off Storm.

Selara stepped cautiously towards the pile of twisted feathers, a look of concern on her face.

"Careful!" cautioned Jonrah. "Night Birds are dangerous, especially if they're wounded."

Selara was not afraid. Her best friend was a Night Bird. She didn't believe that they'd ever hurt her. She bent down, gently picking up the bird. Jonrah shrank back. The size of the bird was enormous. She looked hopefully at Jonrah.

"What?" he asked.

"You healed me from my burns. Maybe you can heal this Night Bird."

"The bird's badly hurt and probably dead. I've never tried to heal a dead bird before — let alone a Night Bird! I don't know what'll happen. What if it doesn't work?"

"Then we'll bury him."

"We don't have time for this, Selara!" He knew reasoning with her wouldn't do him any good. Jonrah took a deep breath. "Okay, bird," he said, "don't hurt me if I bring you back to life." Jonrah dropped to one knee and performed the Sign of the Holy Night Bird.

Selara rolled her eyes.

"It can't hurt," he argued. Jonrah passed his hands over the lifeless body and began his incantation. He blew gently onto the bird. Its dying lungs slowly filled with air. *If you're going to bring a creature of the wind back to life, who better than a Wind Elemental,* he thought.

In the Second Realm, Fletcher lay on a mountain under dark purple skies. He was at peace. His mother, father, and his long dead family and friends silently watched and waited for him. Ceeka was there too. He was not afraid to enter the Second Realm.

All at once, a blinding blue explosion lit up the mountaintop. Jagged streaks of lightning pierced the dark clouds and surrounded his body. It snatched him up violently and spun him around. The circle of relatives scattered, and his very soul seemed to tear apart while his entire being shuddered. The pain was overwhelming, sending him into deep darkness.

There was a cracking and snapping sound like twigs breaking as bones returned obediently to their proper places. His feathers unruffled, and his heart began to beat, drumming against his breast. He felt part of the sky. His body and his spirit were completely restored. His eyes opened slowly. They met two beautiful green eyes, the same eyes he saw every day. He was filled with joy. The full weight of his body was held by the one creature he loved the most in the world.

Jonrah stepped back, smiling. *I've done it!* He felt a flush of pride and relief after being such a failure at Old Mill Village.

Without warning, Fletcher stretched out his powerful wings and lifted out of Selara's hands. She watched him as he rose up, twisting gloriously into the golden sky. Selara and Jonrah shielded their eyes as they watched the bird rise, soar, and swoop into the clouds. But he didn't fly far. He circled above them, waiting.

"What's he waiting for?" asked Jonrah.

"I'm not sure," said Selara, untying the reins and remounting Storm. She reached down, locked arms with Jonrah, and helped swing him up behind her. He almost slid over the other side, but held onto Selara.

The Night bird swooped down to rest gently on Selara's right shoulder.

Jonrah stiffened. "I don't like this," he whispered. Jonrah leaned over towards her left shoulder and asked, "What's wrong with this bird? Night Birds don't do this, Selara."

"I grew up with one who did. He spent most of his time riding right here." She touched the shoulder. "It feels kind of nice actually. I've missed this."

Jonrah marvelled at how such a vicious and dangerous bird was so gentle with Selara. *Maybe this power over Night Birds is part of her majik,* he pondered. Its claws were as sharp as razors and its beak could snap a broomstick, yet it perched as softly on Selara's shoulder as a black butterfly.

"It looks like you've found a new friend," said Jonrah, eyeing the bird nervously. "And after I did all the work!"

Selara reached into one of the bags and broke off a piece of bread. She lifted it up to the bird, who bit into it hungrily. He pushed his feathered head into her hand to say thank you.

"There's something very familiar about this bird," remarked Selara. "What shall I call you?"

As if in response, the bird let out a strange croak.

"He seems friendly enough, but I'd be careful! You know what they say: 'Never trust a Night Bird!'"

"That's ridiculous. I've spent my whole life with Night Birds. They mostly left me alone, but they certainly didn't like my grandparents very much."

"That's because they don't like people in general. Unless they're hungry," said Jonrah.

High in the trees, the Night Birds watched in horror. Winn, Thrush, and Arrow kept their distance, perching on the outreaching branches of a tall tree while they watched the two Elementals looming over Fletcher's body. The three were too afraid to intervene, respecting the incredible power that each Elemental wielded. They watched helplessly as the Fire Witch picked up Fletcher's body and offered it to the Wind Elemental. Winn panicked at the thought of Fletcher being eaten by these two Hu-mans. *Maybe the Fire Witch will roast him before they eat him!* Instead, the Wind Elemental brought Fletcher back to life, and Fletcher was obviously enchanted and not in his right mind.

Has he bonded with the Witch? Winn wondered. *Why else would he travel with them and most disturbingly, touch a Hu-man?*

They flew back to the Clan to tell the Elder Bird.

From Selara's shoulder, Fletcher regarded the young Wind Elemental sitting behind him. He was the mysterious stranger who had kidnapped Selara. He didn't seem so mysterious now. He reconsidered tearing him apart as he planned earlier. He seemed a friend of Selara's, and he did bring him back to life, after all. His heart beat faster. Would this majik Hu-man send him back where he belonged? But what about Selara? He didn't want to leave her here. He loved her, so deeply that he would die for her.

Selara glanced up and spoke to the bird, "I grew up with a Night Bird like you, you know?" Turning to Jonrah, she said, "This bird reminds me so much of him. Do you think that he could be the same bird?"

The bird eyed her carefully. *Girl … Selara, I am the same bird.*

"I don't think so, Selara," replied Jonrah. "Night Birds stay pretty close to their Clan and their territory. Besides, your grandparents closed the time portal after we left the cottage, so he would have remained in that time realm." Jonrah almost choked on his words, realising the gravity of them.

"What do you mean, time portal?" asked Selara, stopping Storm. Her voice rose slightly, the blood rushing to her cheeks.

But before Jonrah could reply, Selara jumped at the strange voice in her head. *Girl … Selara, I am the same bird.*

Overhead they heard a rush of wings and a battle cry as three Night Birds dove out of the trees and targeted Fletcher in tight formation.

Fletcher flew up in alarm. He recognized two of the birds from the Clan. He knew why they were here: bonding majik was felt by Elder Birds from hundreds of miles away, and these birds were sent to be his executioners.

They dismounted Storm quickly, and Jonrah spoke an incantation. A bright blue shield rose up in front of them, its translucent edges humming with power. The same blue sword that had dispatched the Daemon-Wolf now vibrated in Jonrah's right hand, ready for battle, razor-edged and glistening like glass. The attacking birds gained speed and broke formation, trying to work themselves around the shield. The flanking bird was cut in half by the arcing blue sword, but its partner managed to dodge the subsequent sword stroke, somersaulting behind the shield, intending to squeeze its razor-sharp talons around Fletcher's throat.

"Enough!" screamed Selara, now glowing a menacing green and orange. Greenwald appeared, vaporising the bird in a shower of sparks. The lead attacker was not discouraged, however. He somersaulted like his partner, but this time an angry orange Nova waited and swallowed up the bird completely in a shower of sparks and feathers.

Selara was breathing heavily. As her glow faded, tears fell. She felt betrayed. Growing up with her grandparents, the Night Birds always kept their distance. She was never afraid of them. *What's changed?*

It's my fault. It's forbidden to bond with Hu-mans, and I've bonded with you. I couldn't help it. I've loved you ever since we were very young, but I've never been able to tell you. Please don't be mad.

Selara stared at the bird in shock, her eyes glistening. *You are Bird, no, … Fletcher,* she thought, burying her fingers deep into Fletcher's soft black feathers. "In my heart, I knew it was you. You didn't need to use words to tell me that you loved me, I knew it every day of my life."

If Night Birds could cry, Fletcher would have matched Selara tear for tear. He was finally able to communicate on a deeper level with his childhood friend. It was worth the pain of being snatched back from the Second Realm to have this second chance.

"How'd you get here? How is this possible?" asked Selara.

I tried to protect you from the majik Hu-man, but I came here. My parents are gone and your elders are gone too!

"I think I'm beginning to understand what's happened," she said, glaring at Jonrah.

"It's not my fault!" Jonrah insisted, looking at her, trying to piece together the one-sided conversation Selara was having with the Night Bird.

Jonrah watched the two of them bewildered. *How could this possibly be the same bird?* he asked himself. "He should've been dead for over a hundred years! The only way this could have happened would be if he had…"

"You majik'd him here, you moron!" said Selara, finishing his thought.

"Did the bird tell you that?" asked Jonrah.

"He was trying to protect me from you, and you brought him here with us!" she said. Her eyes blazed.

"Listen, I didn't know…"

"What was I doing in the past?" she asked.

"I'm not supposed to talk…"

Selara leaned forward, her eyes narrowing. "Oh, you're going to talk, Mister, or Fletcher here is going to start breaking fingers!"

"Okay!" he relented. "Okay! You were sent into the past to keep that maniac Daemon from killing you! He sent a firkin army, Selara! He had spies and assassins everywhere. You were not safe. No one could protect you. Your grandparents volunteered to go back to the past to take care of you. They knew it was a one-way trip. They made up their minds and knew exactly what they were getting into. Now please, I can't tell you anymore. I've told you too much already." Jonrah shook his head. He wasn't supposed to be telling her all this.

Selara sat down, trying to process everything she heard. "So why did you bring me back now? Why not earlier?"

"Because we had to wait until you came of age, and you could claim your powers," said Jonrah.

Selara nodded her head.

I think you need to trust your friend, said Fletcher.

She agreed. She stood up, and Fletcher perched on her shoulder as she untied Storm's reins.

Jonrah watched her, standing there with Fletcher. *Wow!* he thought to himself. *With that Night Bird on her shoulder, along with her two fire serpents and her grandfather's book, she really could be the Peace Prophet! Two serpents!* His father probably suspected that Selara was a Dark Elemental. This answered so many questions for him, but he didn't like the answers. He was worried for his big sister.

They resumed their journey without talking. Storm filled the silence with her steady clopping rhythm on the muddy pathway. Selara laughed, giggled and smiled as she was having an animated conversation with herself. Jonrah assumed she was speaking to the Night Bird. He himself had no experience with human-Night-Bird bonding practices. Almost nobody had. It had been years. Long before Jonrah's time. He decided to remain silent and let the two of them catch up.

He felt a pang of jealousy. He got his sister back, and now he childishly wanted her all to himself. He knew that in the days to come, she would have much more important things to do than spend time with her little brother. However, it was good to see her so happy. The days ahead were going to be challenging enough and happiness would be in short supply.

She glanced back at him, smiling, the golden light of the sun, turning her red hair to copper.

chapter vii

Rule 7: Never bond with a Night Bird

The wizard Saffron walked slowly up the path over the stone bridge towards Old Mill Village. Sparrows darted from tree to tree, and the sun painted red and gold ribbons across the sky. The smell of cooking fires wafted on the evening breeze. He was lost in thought. He had been communing with the forest wizards from Albright. They were the descendants of the very wizards that were rumoured to have dispatched the Dark Queen in retaliation for her attack on the Nomaji King over a hundred years ago. Once, every ten years, the wizards of the kingdom gathered in the evergreen forest at Albright to share ideas, old majik, and this year, to celebrate the hundred and tenth anniversary of the fall of the Dark Queen. Saffron's head was still groggy after celebrating the night before, so he wanted to spend a night at the inn in the village.

As he approached the village, he heard a party going on. Music and people filled the streets. Jugglers, fire-eaters, and sword swallowers delighted the bystanders. They couldn't be celebrating the downfall of the Dark Queen. The only ones who knew about the hundred and tenth anniversary were the wizarding families.

Saffron looked around, curiously. A little girl approached him, carrying daisy crowns. Saffron couldn't help but smile at her. "Young lady, could you please tell me why everyone's so festive?"

"The Princess of Peace returned. I saw her with my own eyes," she said excitedly. "She has two serpents just like in the window at the chapel. We didn't see her Night Bird though—he was probably out flying somewhere. The soldiers tried to roast Fib and his family in their shop with a Dark Majik hydra. The soldiers didn't even stick around. They had business elsewhere. After they left, the lady appeared out of nowhere."

Saffron's eyes went wide. "Who appeared?" asked Saffron. "What did she look like?"

"The Princess of Peace, of course. She's beautiful with long red hair. She has grown up! She told the Dark Majik hydra to get lost, and then she went and got the family out. I think the hydra was scared of her fire serpents. My grandma thinks she's just a witch trying to trick us, but I know better. She's the Princess of Peace."

"Did you say there were two serpents?" asked Saffron.

"Yes, one green one and one orange one."

"You know you shouldn't lie to an old man!" warned Saffron. His eyes narrowed.

"May the Gods strike me down, sir, if one word of what I told you is a lie." The little girl went down on one knee, bringing her thumbs together and fingers outstretched, and handed Saffron a daisy crown. She scampered away.

Saffron held up the daisy crown, not quite knowing what to do with it. He shrugged his shoulders and placed it on top of his hat. He continued on to the inn, making his way through crowds of revellers. He considered what the daisy girl had told him. *How ironic*, he thought. *That this woman would appear on the hundred and tenth anniversary of the Miracle at Albright. Could this be a coincidence?*

Near Daemon's castle, Whig, the ancient Earth Elemental, witnessed the magnificent battle between the Ogre and the Daemon-Wolves from his hiding place. He watched the brave Ogre fight valiantly until he was overwhelmed and killed. After he died, the remaining Daemon-Wolves abandoned the body. Whig approached the bleeding corpse, cautiously. He leaned over the broken hulk. He was conflicted. He stood up and paced back and forth. He stopped. He made his decision. He decided to do something he vowed he would never do again. He could still see the pale little face of the Fire Girl, who died so very long ago.

Animals and birds were different from human beings. They didn't drain his power. But every time he restored a humanoid life, a part of his life force was given up in return. He calculated he could bring only two more humans back in his lifetime and die on the third attempt. He wondered if an Ogre counted as two. If so, the next human life he restored would be his last, a life for a life. *But these are desperate times*, he rationalised, and he needed a powerful ally. Whig tentatively placed both palms on the ground in front of the Ogre and hummed softly. The sand and the soil came to life. The ground around the Ogre softened and melted. The bubbling earth rose up and consumed the Ogre's body. Tiny tendrils of roots extended and multiplied over his skin.

Three days passed by. The air filled with rot. The Night Birds feasted on the remains of the Daemon-Wolves. Left over limbs, heads, and bodies were clean to the bone. They ignored Whig, focusing on the bloody carnage that surrounded him. He was glad he acted quickly before the Night Birds showed up. *I can't bring a skeleton back to life*, he chuckled mirthlessly. *The Night Birds are efficient scavengers. That man they were looking for made good on his escape. Good for him!*

The sun was a faint glow on the horizon when Whig spotted small cracks forming around Grog's tomb. In the Second Realm, Grog felt strange — he was fading. The faces of his loved ones blurred as he was drawn away. The aches and pains of his embattled body flooded back to him as he struggled through the black sand, desperately seeking air like a drowning man. His large head burst through the sand into the darkness. Tiny pinpricks of light danced above him decorating the twilight sky. Grog was back in the world again. He felt his lungs fill with the cool night air. It was both exhilarating and sad. His resurrection was a steep fall from the bliss of heaven to the aches and pains of mortality. Grog looked around bewildered.

A short distance away, he saw a small old man with wild white hair, sitting in front of a small campfire, watching him intently. Grog sniffed. The rabbit stew drew him to the fire beside the man.

Whig was not afraid. Very little could harm him when he was well rested and his powers were at full strength.

Grog pointed to his chest and uttered, "Grog," eyeing the steaming pot of stew.

"Whig," replied the man, pointing to himself. Whig ladled out a large portion of stew into a wooden bowl and passed it to Grog.

Grog took the bowl gratefully and drank it down in one gulp. He stuck out the bowl for another scoop. Whig gave him another bowl, and Grog took more time with this one. Grog had many questions churning in his brain, but he couldn't seem to hold onto any of them.

Whig covered himself with a thick blanket and said, "Sleep."

Grog was exhausted, and the mere mention of sleep sent him tumbling into unconsciousness. Both rested soundly, Grog having been reborn and Whig having formed a new alliance with a formidable companion. The dark forest wasn't as menacing. In the morning, they would travel in the direction of the White Castle.

Grog awoke to the smell of fish cooking in clay over a charcoal fire. Grog liked this Mouse Man. He was clever and gave Grog food. Grog sat up and tried to snatch one of the fish from out of the fire.

"Not yet," scolded Whig, knocking away Grog's gigantic hand.

Grog instinctively gave his new friend a smack on the head (as was Ogre custom), but his hand bounced off stone. "Ouch!" Grog blurted, looking at his bruised fingers.

Stone Whig changed back into person Whig, laughing heartily. Grog realised Mouse Man was like the Glass Man, only he could turn into stone instead of water. Grog shifted his body impatiently until the little old man pushed the clay fish towards him and tapped the clay to crack it open. He ate happily and noisily. "Good." Grog nodded at Whig.

Whig knew this was going to be a mutually beneficial partnership.

When the two finished eating, Whig repeated the word 'friend' as he pointed to himself and then to the Ogre.

Grog patted the Mouse Man on the head carefully and followed after him after retrieving his weapons. He wiped off some of the dirt and blood. *Clean later,* he thought to himself.

There was a bounce in Grog's step. The birds sang, the sun sparkled through the leaves, and he was no longer a slave of the cruel Daemon. He missed his family, but they knew he had unfinished business and he would see them again.

Whig walked quickly to keep up with the gigantic strides of Grog. He focused on the far peak of a withered mountain where it cut into the blue horizon. They needed to cross the summit and travel to the Valley of the White Castle.

Whig, one of the last of his kind, sought sanctuary in the last Elemental stronghold. He would pledge allegiance to the queen and protect her with his life. Grog was his bodyguard, but he didn't know it yet. There were very few humans, or even majik creatures, that would take on a fully-grown, battle-seasoned Ogre. It took fifty Daemon Wolves to bring down Grog, and only a few survived to claim victory. This is why Whig felt a wave of confidence with Grog by his side. By himself, Whig was constantly hiding and camouflaging himself to keep from being discovered by Daemon. With Grog as a companion and with Whig's powers, they would be unstoppable.

Far, far away from the Keep, growing clouds clustered on the darkening horizon. The telltale smell of damp earth foretold the coming of a storm. The trees were black with birds as they roosted, waiting for the elder to speak.

With the loss of his three assassins, Gavel pondered a new plan. When he broke the silence, he chose his words carefully.

"Daemon is at war with the Elementals and their allies. The Night Birds have been careful never to choose sides. Now one of our own has bonded with an Elemental."

There was an explosion of angry croaks and screeching.

"This bonding may bring this war to us. We have no choice. This Fletcher Bird must die!" The Elder Bird Gavel turned and paced away from the gathering.

That cursed bird. Why couldn't he have died? Doesn't he know how much danger he's putting us in? he thought. *How many have we cast out for even discussing bonding with Hu-mans? Fifty. Maybe a hundred. There can be no bonding while that evil Hu-man Daemon is alive. This strange Fletcher bird's given us no choice. Daemon must know we're not conspiring with the Hu-mans or the Elementals. If he believes we are, we're all in grave danger.*

Winn flew into the evening sky, conflicted and heartbroken. Gavel chose her to be the lone assassin.

The Elder Bird was happy with his plan. He knew that Fletcher befriended Winn and that she could get close enough to deliver a killing blow. He told her to make sure he stayed dead this time. The Elder also knew a single Night Bird would draw less attention than a large killing crew. The fewer birds who knew, the less likely Daemon would think Hu-mans and Night Birds were collaborating.

What the Elder didn't know was that Winn was falling in love with Fletcher. When the first Elder Bird had mistakenly thought the two had come to be mated, she now secretly wished it were true. Her heart was divided between her loyalty to the Clan and her love for her new friend.

Winn could see angry clouds conspiring in the distance. The temperature dropped rapidly. Winn needed to find shelter before the storm hit. Fat raindrops fell. She was still a long way from where she saw Fletcher die, but she had no choice but to wait out the storm and resume her search after it passed. In the growing darkness, Winn could see a faint square of flickering light coming from an abandoned, old building by a rushing river.

The farm looked deserted, but someone or something had a fire burning in the old hearth. Smoke valiantly rose from the crumbling chimney, only to be beaten down by the strong wind. Gliding through the open window, she saw a Hu-man shivering by the fire, pulling off his sopping wet clothes, and wringing them out onto the dusty floor. Winn was well able to handle herself if this Hu-man proved to be dangerous. She moved tentatively towards the fire, trying not to startle him.

When he saw her, he jumped back in surprise. "A Night Bird!" he muttered, through chattering teeth. He stared at her for a full minute, trying to decide what to do. He shook his head. "I'm too tired and too cold to care." Turning away from her, he stooped close to the fire and fed it more dry twigs. Winn flew to the other side of the room. She couldn't understand what he was saying, but she understood what he was trying to do.

Within moments, she returned with a beak full of twigs and dry leaves and dropped them in front of him. The man chuckled, gathered up the offering, and fed it to the flames. With the addition of a few broken chairs, the fire was soon roaring, its welcome heat filling the room.

The wind screamed and howled outside the ramshackle building, causing the old shutters to swing and bang. The naked, shivering Hu-man walked to the windows and forced the wooden shutters closed, securing them with more pieces of broken chair. The man carefully draped his clothes over an old mantelpiece rod, leaving them to dry in the heat of the fire. He opened his leather bag and unfolded a thick woollen blanket. Wrapping the damp blanket around himself, he inched closer to the fire. As sleep took hold of him, he imagined the Night Bird tossing more twigs into the fire.

Alan dreamed about flying. He was soaring over fields and houses. It was exhilarating. He awoke to find the Night Bird burrowed into his blanket and pressed up against his back. She was warm and soft. *How do I know it's a she?* Alan decided that all the stories he heard as a child about Night Birds were wrong. He rose quietly, trying not to wake her, unsure of what she might do if startled. He threw more twigs onto the coals and blew over them. Soon tiny new flames joined the wisps of smoke. He put on his clothes and placed his hand into his leather bag to reassure himself. The circlet was still there — he breathed a quiet sigh of relief.

Winn spent a warm restful night dreaming. She dreamed of sunny days and blue skies. The Hu-man was also in her dream, and the two of them talked in a garden. *Night Birds are very resourceful,* thought Winn. Sharing a fire and a blanket with a Hu-man made perfect sense under the circumstances, and everything she had been told about what happens when you touch a Hu-man was wrong. Of course, she could have killed the Water Hu-man at any time, but she decided that the two of them could help each other if she let him live. *How do I know he's a Water Hu-man?* she wondered. She stretched out her wings lazily in the growing fire.

"You're awake!" said the Hu-man, now fully clothed. "Thank you for keeping me warm last night."

Winn was groggy and confused. *Why can I understand what the Human's saying?* She didn't speak the language of Hu-mans or understand it. Then a slow and icy realisation rose up in her. It wasn't a dream! She had accidentally bonded with this human while she slept. Her heart started beating quickly. She flapped her wings in panic.

"It's okay, Winn, calm down. What did I just say? How do I know your name? Do Night Birds have a language?"

This is bad, whispered Winn. *This is really bad! First Fletcher, now me. Gavel'll be beyond furious!*

Alan was in shock. He didn't know what was happening. The Night Bird was speaking to him in his mind, and he was speaking to her.

"How's this happening?" he asked.

We've bonded, said Winn, exasperated.

"What does that mean?" asked Alan.

It means we can speak to each other and see through each other's eyes.

"But I didn't ask for this," said Alan.

Neither did I, replied Winn, helplessly.

"Well then un-bond us," said a confused Alan.

The bonding cannot be undone, groaned Winn.

Alan paced back and forth in the small room while Winn watched helplessly. "What are we supposed to do now?" asked Alan.

I don't know, replied Winn, realising the gravity of the situation and not experienced in the rules of bonding.

"I have to deliver this circlet to the Queen. I almost died stealing it from Daemon's castle last night!" Images of the Daemon-Wolves and the sword-wielding Ogre filled his mind. Winn saw them too, and drew back in horror. She could see and feel his memories.

And I'm sent to kill my friend, Winn said, sadly.

"Not just a friend," replied Alan, looking directly into her eyes. Images of Fletcher and her feelings for him surfaced as well as the Elder Bird and the details of her mission. The two of them sat facing each other in the grey light of the morning, thinking. The only sound in the room was the random crackling and popping of dry wood in the fire and the whispering of the wind. Even though Winn was still struggling to deal with this accidental bonding, she found their communication oddly comforting. Because of their bond, this Hu-man sympathised with her, and strangely enough, cared about how she was feeling. She now felt that she didn't have to face these problems alone and had an ally named Alan.

As Alan readied himself to leave, Winn made the decision that she would remain close to him. She still needed to find Fletcher, but her mission changed. She was now a criminal just like him. She was both relieved and conflicted. Maybe the two of them could help each other get what they both wanted, what they both needed.

A day earlier, the spires of the three marble towers of the Keep glowed white and gold, reflecting the setting sun. The castle rested like an elegant swan on a silent lake. A patchwork quilt of tiny farms, buildings, and villages surrounded White Castle Island. It was a haven for the non-Majik, or Nomaji, as well as the Elementals and Dark Majik practitioners sympathetic to their cause. The smells of dung, wood smoke, cooking, and industry filled the air.

"We're almost there," said Jonrah, excitedly, looking forward to being home.

The lands were olive green and alive with every manner of flower, bird, and insect. The Elementals had enriched this valley, creating harmony and balance.

Fletcher eyed the circling insects hungrily. As the landscape stretched out before them, Selara had to catch her breath. She'd never seen anything so beautiful in her entire life. She wanted to drink in every moment and lock it away in the pages of her memory. She wished her grandparents were here to see it.

The lake surrounding the castle was crystal clear and deep. There were several large supply barges lined up along the dock by the end of the road

Selara turned Storm towards the boats.

"Not that way," said Jonrah. "We have a family entrance." Jonrah took Selara around a cluster of trees to a blank wall of stone. The same runes on the gold coins were carved into the wall. There was a finely woven design split into four sections. Each one represented a different Element. Jonrah placed his hand on a swirling symbol and asked Selara to touch the adjacent symbol. The two stone pieces slid to the sides and a door-sized opening appeared before them. The air blew pleasantly through the tunnel and the torch-lit hallway.

The two dismounted and took their bulging bags from Storm. Selara unbridled the horse and let her loose to graze in the meadow.

"Will she be okay here?" asked Selara.

"We can send a boy out to bring her into the castle stables when we're safe inside," replied Jonrah.

Selara patted her horse and thanked her for being so patient with them. Storm whinnied as she walked over to drink in the lake.

As they entered the tunnel leading to the White Castle, the torches flamed on. Selara watched in wonder as the majik torches lit themselves as they advanced and then went out after they passed. She took a few steps forward then shuffled back to see if they came back on. She laughed as they obediently relit. She tried to confuse them by going back and forth.

"What are you doing?" asked Jonrah.

"Just having a little fun," she replied, smiling. The majik fascinated her.

They walked slowly down a hallway made of smooth marble, hearing only the soft shuffling of their feet. Fletcher flew into the darkness somewhere ahead, too far away to be seen or heard. *The torches ignored Fletcher, possibly because the majik only responded to humans,* thought Selara.

Far ahead of them, Jonrah's little sister Sara hummed happily to herself. She enjoyed this silent hall that was seldom used by her family. She stopped and concentrated hard. She felt her feet lift off the floor, if only for a moment. It had been an accident the first time, and neither her parents nor her big brother believed her. Since there was no record of any Wind Elemental having the ability to fly for years, her claims were easily dismissed. Sara didn't know of any other girl Wind Elementals either. Only the boys had those powers, so no one ever took her very seriously.

A bat whistled by her head, and she giggled. An invisible hand grabbed hold of the bat and sent it spiralling. Sara was practising controlling tiny wind patterns. The unfortunate creature flew directly into the wall. *Oops,* thought Sara. She continued to play her own version of hopscotch with the polished stones when she heard a rushing sound in the chamber directly in front of her. She stopped in mid-skip as a huge bat-like creature swooped down and landed on the floor in front of her. The bird was large enough so that the two of them were almost eye-to-eye. The silence was filled with the soft crackling of majik torchlights while shadows danced softly on the walls.

"Hello," she said tentatively. The bird tilted its head. "You're such a pretty bird!"

In the tunnel far behind them, Selara turned to Jonrah and asked, "Who's the little girl?"

"What little girl?" he asked, staring into the blackness of the long tunnel. New torches lit up beside them.

"The little girl with the white dress that Fletcher's talking to."

"That bird's too far ahead. What are you talking about?"

"Fletcher has found a little girl in the passageway!" said Selara.

"That must be my little sister! How can you possibly know that Fletcher's talking to her? And what's she doing down in the tunnel anyways? What if he attacks her?"

"She's so cute," purred Selara. "He said he'll keep her safe until we get there."

"So now you can talk to the bird when you can't even see him?" said Jonrah. *Just like a Thought Listener,* he surmised.

"Yes, and I can see what he sees," said Selara.

It wasn't long before the torchlight lit up Sara, who squealed at the sight of them. She ran to her brother and hugged him.

Selara bent down. "Can I get a hug too?"

Sara wrapped her arms around Selara. Sara was star struck. The news of Selara's battle with the Dark Majik hydra had spread to the castle. Sara looked at Selara wide-eyed and speechless. Selara was a celebrity.

Jonrah smiled, seeing his two sisters reunited.

When Sara finally found her voice, she babbled about the news of the castle: her friends, her enemies, and all of the excitement around Selara. She walked along with Selara, holding her hand and feeling that just being near Selara would raise her to celebrity status. "Wait until my friends hear about this!" Sara was too excited and too impatient to be walking along at this snail's pace. "I'm going to run ahead and tell everyone you're coming!" she said, skipping down the corridor.

Silently, Selara sent Fletcher along with her to keep her safe. Fletcher leaped from her shoulder and followed Sara. Selara smiled at their ability to communicate. She wished she had bonded with him years before.

"She really doesn't need watching, you know. She wanders around these tunnels by herself all the time," said Jonrah. "And that Night Bird following her is going to raise a few eyebrows!"

"I know," said Selara. "But she has a big sister now looking out for her."

If she only knew, thought Jonrah. *If she only knew. Soon ….*

As Sara entered the Keep, she trotted and skipped past guards, cooks, and servants. They were shocked to see one of the notorious Night Birds inside the building. Many went down on one knee, making the Sign of the Holy Night Bird. Little did they know that this was the very bird responsible for the origins of the Sign of the Holy Night Bird. Because Sara was Talon's daughter, no one interfered with her or even asked her why she had a Night Bird flying beside her. The castle staff were more concerned with their own safety, growing up with the strange tales and superstitions surrounding the birds.

Sara skipped towards the main hall. Fletcher landed, perching gently on her shoulder as she pushed open the heavy door. Sara rushed in, her unruly mop of red hair bouncing with enthusiasm.

Talon, Seanna, and Tamara sat open-mouthed as Sara cut their conversation short, standing in the doorway like a little white doll with a large Night Bird on her shoulder. Several of the servants went down on one knee, performing the ritual. The news bubbled out of her before her stunned parents could speak.

"Jonrah brought Selara here. She's so pretty. She has this Night Bird for a pet. Isn't he awesome? His name's Fletcher, and he's so soft. Is she going to marry Jonny? Can I have a new dress for the wedding?"

Seanna and Talon smiled at her and exchanged glances.

Back in the tunnel, Selara giggled.

"What's so funny?" asked Jonrah.

"It seems that your little sister is looking forward to our wedding!" she said, laughing and blushing in the half-light.

"Keep walking, the sooner we get there, the sooner I can stop her from talking!" Jonrah muttered, not amused.

Selara smiled to herself and did her best to stifle her laughter. Through Fletcher's eyes, she could see three people in the room. One was a pretty blond woman around Selara's age who looked very upset.

As Selara and Jonrah opened the doors to the Keep, they were met with thunderous applause. Servants, noblemen, people of Dark Majik, and Elementals overwhelmed them with goodwill, praise, and encouragement. Several people took their heavy bags and followed them as they slowly made their way through the welcoming crowd. Everyone wanted to touch them or shake their hands. The crowd dispersed as Selara and Jonrah opened the doors to the dining room where the family waited for them. Sara sat cross-legged on the floor, tossing pieces of bread to Fletcher. Talon, Seanna, and Tamara rose from their chairs quickly.

Tamara raced over to Jonrah and threw her arms around him theatrically, passionately kissing him.

Selara stepped back, feeling a faint misplaced twinge of jealousy. *Who the firk is this?* she thought.

Tamara released Jonrah just long enough to give Selara a quick, cold obligatory hug. She added pretend kisses to her cheeks. She returned quickly to Jonrah, locking her arm firmly with his.

Seanna glared at her.

Talon rushed up to Jonrah, embracing him. "You did it, son! I'm so proud of you!"

"Thanks, Dad."

Selara smiled at the ridiculous behaviour of this blond girl firmly latched onto Jonrah. She wouldn't even let go of him to let his father give him a hug.

What a freak! thought Selara. She was not comfortable with this girl having her hands all over Jonrah.

Be nice, said Fletcher in her mind. He groaned inwardly.

Seanna stood frozen, staring at Selara as if in a trance. She was so proud of the young woman she saw standing before her. It had been ten years. *But what's become of my tiny red-haired moppet?* she asked herself sadly. *I've missed all her growing-up years.* She silently cursed Daemon for his obsession with killing her. He stole ten years from her relationship with her daughter, and she would never get that back. The last time she saw her there were no gentle goodbyes. She had been screaming and crying, her heart breaking to let her go. She knew that Selara wouldn't recognize them now. Majik had been used in the final moments of the time shift so that Selara wouldn't remember who they were, helping to ease her pain and loss. *What a beautiful young woman she has become. Thank you, Petra and Olga, and thank the Gods!*

Seanna wished with all her heart that she could tell Selara who she was right now, but she knew this wasn't the time. Selara had much to do, and she couldn't be distracted by an emotional family reunion. She might never forgive them for sending her away. She might even decide to leave them, dashing all hopes of ever defeating Daemon and restoring peace to their kingdom. And then there was the matter of the Dark Majik that dwelt inside her. If left unaddressed, it would tear her apart.

Seanna knew how hard this mission had been for Jonrah as well, seeing his sister and grandparents for the first time and not being able to reveal to her who he really was. It must have been hard to leave Petra and Olga there to die by themselves with no family and no grandchildren. Seanna felt tears welling up in her eyes as she approached Selara. "I'm so glad you're both safe — I was so worried. Everyone in all ten burrows hasn't stopped talking about you defeating the hydra and saving that family! We're so proud of you!" Selara bravely fought to keep her tears in check.

Tamara stared at Selara then back at Seanna. *She looks so much like Seanna,* she thought. *And she's so beautiful. Well she can't have him. He's mine.* She clung possessively to Jonrah, pulling his arm around her waist.

Selara looked at everyone there. Talon and Seanna were so familiar, and they were speaking as if they knew her. She hadn't thought of her mother in a very long time, but Seanna reminded her of her. Everything felt so strange.

Seanna sensed what Selara was thinking and rushed to her, embracing her tightly. It was a mother's embrace. Talon tried to catch Seanna's eye, but she was overwhelmed at seeing her long-lost daughter and didn't care about the need for secrecy.

Selara lost the battle with her tears. She sobbed uncontrollably, releasing a pain that was buried deep inside her for so many years.

Seanna sobbed as well. Amid the tears, Selara could have sworn she heard Seanna whisper, "Please forgive me."

Jonrah and Talon stood by watching the two of them. The tears were infectious. All of the young table servants struggled to control their emotions as well.

Even Tamara cried in spite of herself.

Selara felt strangely safe and accepted in Seanna's arms. It was as if she was home now. Her grandparents had loved her as best as they could, but they were no replacement for what now felt like a real mother and father.

Talon joined Seanna, along with Jonrah and a reluctant Tamara, in a group hug.

As her sobbing subsided, Selara felt the addition of two small arms wrapping gently around her legs. She sighed deeply and smiled, feeling she had finally found the family she always longed for.

As they released their embrace, Seanna looked seriously at Selara and Jonrah. "Now as much as I love you both, you stink," she said. "Baths will be prepared for you upstairs and some clean clothes laid out. We'll have your bags brought up to your rooms. Come downstairs for dinner when you're ready."

"Can I go up with Selara?" asked Sara.

"No, we need to give her some privacy," said Seanna.

"Can Fletcher stay?" pleaded Sara.

Seanna looked at Selara, and Selara nodded her head.

Tamara was about to follow Jonrah upstairs, but Seanna stopped her.

"I need to speak with you alone," she said firmly.

Tamara relented, but she wasn't happy.

Jonrah and Selara went their separate ways, looking forward to a wash and some fresh clothes.

In Old Mill Village, Barnard carefully stacked a collection of priceless glass artefacts near the altar in the Temple of the Peace Princess. He divided them into orange and green piles. Barnard treated each delicate piece with reverence.

"The time's at hand, Sheer," he said to the large Night Bird perched by the window. "Daemon's reign's coming to an end."

Sheer nodded. *We must do all that we can to help her.* Sheer spread his wings and lifted himself up and out through the open window.

"Yes, you must call on the Brethren." Barnard's eyes sparkled. *This has been the most wonderful day of my life*, he thought. He had met the Peace Princess, the prophet who'd been the centre of his existence. Everything he did supported the ideals of her first appearance: peace, cooperation, generosity, and justice. As he watched her with her two majestic serpents battling with the Dark Hydra, he was in ecstasy. He wished that all the Brethren had witnessed the miracle of the Peace Princess' return with him. He hoped to see her Night Bird as well, but he didn't attend the miracle. He may have other responsibilities that were far beyond Barnard's comprehension.

He ritually lit the green candles on the altar below the painting of the Peace Prophet. The prophet stood proudly, clothed in fiery serpents and holding the holy book with a young Night Bird on her shoulder, Both Elemental and Dark Majik soldiers surrounded her, their faces in exaggerated awe.

Barnard sat on one of the polished wooden benches and muttered several ancient prayers. He devoted himself completely to the preservation of the ideals of the Dark Princess of Peace. He studied writings about her appearance at Albright. He knew all the legends about her from memory.

When he was very young, a flock of outcast Night Birds weaved homes in the trees near his farm. One by one, people bonded with the birds, forming a strange new community, devoted to the Dark Princess of Peace. In their village, Night Birds and humans used their abilities to enrich each other's lives. Night Birds shared their woven baskets with the humans, and the humans shared their food with the birds. They would hunt together, work together, and play together. They called themselves the Brethren.

The Night Bird Clan shunned the outcast birds and were horrified at the number of Night Bird-Hu-man bondings. The Brethren community was located far to the East in the kingdom, isolated and self-sufficient, away from prying eyes. Their Night Birds kept a vast communication network with Brethren members throughout the kingdom, awaiting the return of the Peace Princess. The heroic act of defiance and power witnessed at Old Mill Village inspired the Brethren. The Dark Princess of Peace had returned, and they made plans to fight with her.

Barnard finished his prayers, making the Holy Sign of the Night Bird, and shuffled to his precious relics. He held one of the green glass arte-facts up to the candlelight. He marvelled at each finely formed crease and crevice. It was a perfect impression of Selara's right foot.

chapter viii

Rule 8: Never try to reason with a Daemon-Wolf

Laughter echoed in the elegant dining room as the group shared news of the kingdom and the travellers' adventures. Sara sat close beside her newly adopted big sister.

Tamara eyed Selara, suspiciously, pinning Jonrah's arm close to her possessively. Selara was even more beautiful than she had ever imagined, and Selara made her feel threatened and uncomfortable. Seanna scolded her for her earlier behaviour, so she was doing her best to be more understanding and less overtly jealous of Selara. She winced, however, when Jonrah told the story of the distracted young man falling into the water at Old Mill Village, completely taken with Selara's beauty. And then again when Jonrah talked about the grilled meat seller who wouldn't accept Jonrah's coins, but only a smile from Selara. Even little Sara, Tamara's confidant, was completely taken with Selara. Tamara felt as if she was being replaced.

Selara shared the story of how Jonrah brought Fletcher back to life. She beamed at him, making Jonrah feel uncomfortable. He changed the topic quickly and shared how Selara unknowingly stole the torch fire from the commander. They all laughed at how annoyed the commander had been — but the laughing stopped when they talked about how he used Dark Majik to create the hydra.

"That family would've been burned to death if it weren't for Selara. She was furious with me!" said Jonrah. "She didn't understand that I didn't have the power to fight that thing."

Tamara pulled him closer and kissed him on the cheek.

Selara placed a comforting hand on his hand, causing Tamara to bite her lip to keep her composure.

Jonrah pulled his hand away, pretending to scratch his hair. He sat stiffly between the two young women at the table. He didn't know if it was his imagination, but he could literally feel the temperature of the room rising.

One of the pretty servant girls smiled at Jonrah as she re-filled his cup. Tamara glared at her, and she moved quickly to the other side of the table. Seanna shot her a quick glance of disapproval, and she relented.

Jonrah wished he could tell Selara that she was his sister now, but his parents told him that this wasn't the right time. He hoped the right time would come soon.

Fletcher watched the gathering and listened intently from the home-made perch Sara made him at the end of the table. Through his bond, he understood the Hu-man conversation, and he found it fascinating. There was a separate, more private conversation going on between himself and Selara.

I know Jonrah didn't tell you about Tamara, but it's nothing to be upset about, Fletcher spoke soothingly. *She's not giving you dirty looks.*

Even though she really is, thought Fletcher to himself. *And it's not nice for you to keep calling her a freak.* He wasn't used to the surging feelings he was now feeling from Selara. He almost wished he were the same ignorant bird of the past, simply nodding his head when Selara was upset, not having to negotiate the complexities of her thinking.

It was strange for Selara to have the ability to see herself sitting at the table through Fletcher's eyes. She was like a stranger enjoying a meal with her friends. Having become used to the sensations of the bond, she was now able to control the connection between them. She could manipulate the nature of the bond in such a way to give both her and Fletcher the privacy of their own thoughts. Fletcher knew this instinctively. Each of them were now the eyes and ears for the other when they wished.

Selara was grateful for the warm reception at the Keep. She couldn't help but wonder why Seanna and Talon would risk having their only son hurt or killed for a person who was virtually a stranger. There were many unanswered questions that bothered her. She particularly wondered why she felt so comfortable with Talon and Seanna.

Talon and Seanna were a mature, attractive couple. They shared the same flowing red hair that Jonrah and his sister had, but Talon had a tiny grey-green streak like a lightning bolt rising from his temple, giving him a distinguished air. The two of them wore no crowns nor robes of office, nothing to indicate their importance.

After dinner, Seanna took Selara by the hand and led her through empty passageways and up a set of winding stairs. Moonlight beamed, and torchlight wallpapered the stairway with warm shadows. Seanna opened the heavy door and a comfortable, cheery room greeted her. Fresh flowers adorned the tables. A large ornately carved wooden bed stretched across the middle of the room with dressers and a table on either side. Moonlight played on the lake through the window and painted the dark green hills stretched out like velvet curtains. The noises of Keep City echoed through the alleys and pathways far below them.

Selara started to cry.

Seanna put her arm around her. "What's wrong—should I find another room for you?"

"No," she said through her tears. "I've just never been in a room so beautiful." She felt like a princess.

Deep in the forest, on the edge of Daemon lands, Dane stretched and stared into the dim light. He was cold. Rain was dripping onto his face, causing his black eyeliner to meander down his cheeks with a disturbing effect. He wanted to go back to sleep for a few more hours, but the thought of returning to the Dark Castle without the thief was worse than the discomfort he felt. He forced his aching body off his bedroll. The smell of smoke from the early morning fires and mutton sizzling over the open flames tantalised his nostrils. Then a vile odour crept into the morning air, the smell of death and decay. The Daemon-Wolves camped not far from them. If sleeping in the woods could be considered a camp — not far enough, Dane thought.

He remembered when he and his men first joined Daemon. At the time, Daemon was just a boy with a hungry look in his eyes who made many promises. Dane was tired of petty robbery and decided to trade his sporadic raiding life for the security the boy could provide. No one imagined how things changed so quickly for that boy. A bastard son whose father was barely young enough to shave when he met his mother. And that so-called father wanted nothing to do with him. *Guess he was just a kid himself really,* he pondered. But that boy's grandparents left him a lifetime of riches. *And I have no problem helping him spend it,* he laughed. *But those monsters! The kid couldn't just leave those wolves alone.* Once he made one, he had to have more. *Now we're up to our eyeballs in them,* he spat.

Dane emerged from his tent to the nods of his men. There was no word on the thief, only that stupid Ogre's help in his escape. At least the oaf had the decency to die and take out a few Daemon-Wolves in the process. *I'll raise a glass to him for that.* The horses whinnied as he passed, anticipating the hunt. They were bred to endure miles of travel, and their speed was unrivalled in the kingdom. He patted the head of his steed, affectionately.

"We'll get him today, won't we, Pip?" The horse nickered enthusiastically. Dane walked over to the fire, tearing a leg off the blackening beast and chewed it hungrily. "Let's get moving. He couldn't have gone far on foot!" At this, the underlings scrambled to break camp. Dane squinted his eyes. Downriver he saw the outline of three buildings. *Maybe he took shelter there,* he thought.

Gliding high above the forest trails, Winn saw the tiny form of Alan moving slowly away from the abandoned farmhouse. It felt good to tilt and rise on the northern wind, letting her fears and worries disappear into the hazy clouds that drifted over the land below. The morning sun warmed her face, and she felt peaceful until she saw the dark creatures emerging from the forest like an oily stain. A squadron of Marauders on horseback led by a pack of Daemon-Wolves. They were winding their way towards the farmhouse and would soon overcome Alan.

All at once, Alan felt his stomach lurch as the path ahead of him tilted. He saw Daemon's army closing in on him as if he was flying high above them. Smaller groups broke off from the main group, creating a three-pronged attack to trap him against the mountain. Hiding in the trees or rocks was not an option: he wouldn't be able to evade the keen smell of the Daemon-Wolves. He heard the sounds of horses and the grunts and howls of the Wolves closing in fast. Without more rain, he couldn't cover his scent. His powers were at full strength, but if he used them now, he couldn't hide the circlet. He was too late; he saw a flash of grey just beyond the trees.

We've got him cornered, thought Dane, his swirling black beard buffeted by the northern wind. "Those cursed creatures can track a mouse through a corn field, but the smell," he remarked, his nose wrinkling in disgust.

"You never get used to it, do you?" said Bard, watching his commander's face. "But they do all the work, and we just clean up afterwards — not a bad life, yeah?"

"There's no place for him to run — unless he's a mountain goat," Dane chortled. That's when he noticed something glistening at the bottom of a deep puddle. "The Gods are smiling upon us!" he exclaimed, jumping off his horse.

Dane went down on his hands and knees and reached down to the bottom of the pool. His hands grasped the glistening circle of metal, and he raised it into the air triumphantly. His celebration was cut short as a black meteor swooped down from nowhere and snatched the prize from his hand. Several of the more superstitious men knelt down and made the holy sign, helping Winn escape. The archers had serious misgivings about the judgement they and their families would face if they put an arrow through a Night Bird. The flying thief was already in the clouds when the confused and superstitious soldiers got themselves organised. The golden circlet now glistened like a misplaced star in the morning sun.

"Firk!" screamed Dane in frustration. "Superstitious idiots!" The group of pursuers turned and followed in the direction of the flying Night Bird. Winn made a wide circle and flanked the group as they marched in the opposite direction.

Down on the forest floor, bubbles rose from the bottom of the pool. They soon coalesced roughly into the shape of a human, then a perfect glass-like version that solidified into a shivering Alan. The Daemon-Wolves were momentarily distracted by Dane finding the circlet and didn't find his bag. *They would've ripped my clothes to shreds, and I'd surely have frozen to death,* he thought. Winn landed softly behind him as he pulled up his pants. She dropped the circlet on the ground, glad to have her beak free. "Thank you," said Alan. An exhausted Winn nodded her head.

Alan laced his sandals and looked at Winn. "Thank you for doing that, I know that this isn't how you thought things were going to work out."

Everything's wrong. I was sent here to kill my friend because of his bonding with an Elemental, and I have done the very same thing. I'm just as guilty as he is, and now I don't know which way to turn.

Alan came close and gently ran his fingers along the feathers of her head. She instinctively tensed, then relaxed. She knew Alan cared about her and her problems. Her fear and aversion to Hu-mans had evaporated when she was able to share their thoughts. Both of them were running from something or to something, the only difference was they were now in this together.

Why's this circlet so important? she asked.

Without a word, he showed her the power of the circlet. He showed her how desperately he needed to get it to the True Queen so that she could keep their world from tearing itself apart.

Winn nodded, understanding Alan's commitment to his quest. Her quest seemed to have mercifully ended because she was also an outcast and most likely marked for death. She decided she needed to find Fletcher — this was her quest, and fortunately, their destinations were the same. There was nothing left for her to do but press on.

Winn flew up and circled, watching for enemies. Alan was far below, moving further into the mountains. She could see the path through the mountains to the valley. If only Alan could fly like her, they would be through these mountains in minutes instead of hours! But he was only a Hu-man, and she had wings.

"Maybe you can fly, but I can swim," he said excitedly as he reached the summit, his voice in her head.

Stop listening to me thinking without my permission, thought Winn.

Alan stripped off his clothes, carefully folded them, and stuffed them into his bag. "Can you pick up my bag for me and meet me at the bottom of that valley?"

"Maybe I should just let you go naked, Hu-man!" She teased. She swooped down and snatched up the bag as Alan dissolved into the mountain stream. She was a strong Night Bird, and carrying Alan's bag was easy. She found that she enjoyed having a companion to share her thoughts. She felt more than a magical bond with Alan: she was starting to care for him. If her father could see her now, he would be scandalised. She flew hard on the east wind, trying to beat Alan into the valley. She flew fast, a blur of feathers streaking down to the small clearing at the base of the mountain. As she rounded the trees, Alan was already there, warming himself in the sun. She dropped his bag, exhausted. She had to admit, she couldn't out-fly a mountain stream.

Alan smiled at Winn. He had been alone for so long. It was comforting to have a companion to share his days. Maybe this bonding was more of a blessing than a curse. Winn felt his thoughts and, a little uncomfortable, turned away.

Why don't your clothes turn into water as well? asked Winn.

"I don't know how the majik works," replied Alan, "I change completely, but my clothing doesn't."

That's too bad. I guess you're lucky you've got me to be your maid servant! she quipped.

"The first time I transformed, I was just a child, and I ended up miles from home. It took me hours to get back, shivering the whole time."

Winn felt a strange emotion. It felt light and bubbled up inside of her. She was laughing. Laughter was uncommon among Night Birds. They couldn't cry or laugh, but through the bonding with this Hu-man, a new world of thought and emotion was available to her. It was sad that her kind were forbidden to experience this world of deep feeling — except Fletcher. She immediately felt the pang of missing him. She steeled herself. She was becoming too soft and needed to focus.

Talon was awake and pacing. The nightmare replayed itself like a spectral dagger driven into his heart over and over again. The nightmare continued to torment him even in his waking hours. But it was more than a nightmare—it was a painful memory, polished by years of guilt and regret. It always began with thick acrid smoke billowing around them. Sounds of clanging swords and innocent screams filling the air. Some monsters exploded in flames while others sank into the earth. It was Talon who had to make the final decision. They were losing the battle. Wave upon wave of Daemon-Monsters kept coming with no sign of relenting. They surrounded the small band of Elementals. The family huddled together momentarily safe in a small cave in the Valley of the Skulls. Whig turned the ground around the cave to quicksand, making it impossible for the advancing army to get to Selara, but they were surrounded.

Selara drew close to her mother, tears tracing down the sides of her frightened cheeks. Talon and Seanna looked helplessly at each other. There was no other way. To leave Selara here would result in her gruesome death. To send her to the past was a last resort. It was dangerous. If his father's incantation failed, then at least her death would come swiftly and painlessly. She needed to go now. There was no guarantee it would work. This kind of incantation had not been used in decades and was unpredictable. If it failed, both of his parents and his little daughter would simply cease to exist. When Selara disappeared into the past, Daemon's forces would be called back, believing she was dead and their campaign a success. They would have to retrieve her when she was old enough to take care of herself. *And all of us*, he thought.

Selara screamed and frantically tried to run back to her mother. Her grandmother wrenched her from Seanna's arms. Seanna turned away as the incantation began. Grandmother's face showed no emotion as she held her struggling granddaughter tightly. Selara's grandparents chanted in unison, their very words bent the air and smoke around them.

"Make her forget!" screamed Seanna. Then the world wavered and the frightened little face of Selara vanished with her grandparents. There was no way of knowing if the incantation was successful. It would be years before Talon and Seanna would know if their desperate gamble paid off. Talon held his wife close as they both wept, knowing what this decision would mean. Daemon's forces suddenly stopped as if an unseen command reached them all. Their target abruptly vanished. Daemon could feel it too, and in the confusion, the small band of Elementals escaped in the dense fog that appeared out of nowhere on a safe path provided by Whig through the quicksand. Deep in his castle walls, Daemon celebrated.

Seanna entered the chamber to see Talon agitated. She sat down by the dim light of a candle.

"What are we supposed to say to her?" Talon wiped the perspiration from his forehead.

"She looks so beautiful!" Seanna said wistfully, staring into the darkness oblivious to her husband's words. "It's so good to have her back here with us, safe and sound."

From the arched window, there was a faint glow of moonlight. The candle fluttered and danced as if it were trying to escape the conversation.

"We had no other choice," whispered Talon.

"It was wrong! We should have fought harder — we should have found another way. There must have been another way!" said Seanna, her eyes unfocussed tears streaming down.

"She would have been killed, torn to pieces by those brutes. Is that what you would have wanted for our little girl? To die like that? The only reason we're all still alive is because of that sacrifice!"

"Yes, I know," she replied, sighing. "But she had no choice. She was just a little girl."

Talon put his arm around her slim waist. "You don't regret it, do you?"

"Of course not," she said as she pulled him close.

"I know there was no other way. It's just she was so young, and all of those precious years were lost to us."

"But she's here now," said Talon, looking hopeful.

"In many ways, she is in more danger now than she ever was when we sent her away," said Seanna.

"Her power's so strong now. Can you feel it?" insisted Talon.

"I can't feel what you feel. I can only feel her Elemental fire, and yes, she is strong, and soon she has to make peace with that demon inside her, or we're all lost."

"What about Jonrah?" asked Talon.

"He's a good son, loyal to the cause — he can keep a secret! He must! We can't let her become distracted from what she must do. If she discovers what we did, she may abandon her destiny and leave us. With the power that she wields left untrained — it would be better if she never returned at all."

"Don't say that! Everything will work out! Everyone needs to play their part until the time is right," said Seanna.

"I only hope this secret doesn't crush us all. Have you talked with Tamara?"

"Yes, but you know Tamara. Once she gets something in her head, you can't get it out."

"She needs to hold it together. We can't have her letting things slip or start openly fighting with Selara," said Talon.

"She'll be okay. We just have to keep things under control until Selara has time to work with Saffron. He should be back any day now."

"You haven't told him about Selara's condition, have you?"

"Of course not. Everyone's sworn to secrecy. If the Nomaji find out she's a Dark Elemental, they'll panic. Everyone remembers the last time a Dark Elemental was born in this kingdom. Saffron will determine what needs to be done when he meets her."

Hiding in the shadows by the door, Sara was listening intently. Now she knew that Selara really was her sister, and for some reason, her parents hadn't told her. She smiled to herself, and crept back to her room, quietly.

After losing sight of *that damn Night Bird,* Dane was furious. He sent the Daemon-Wolves out in another direction to search for the thief who somehow disappeared into thin air. Elementals, he thought, always playing tricks on honest common folk like him. The thief was no longer important now that the Night Bird stole the circlet. The focus of his quest changed. What would the Night Birds even do with the circlet? Why would they pick a fight with Daemon? Are they in league with the Elementals? he wondered.

The men rounded a copse of trees when they spotted a tiny old man with a massive Ogre, blocking their way. He recognized the Ogre immediately and silently cursed the Elementals. They somehow brought that firkin' Ogre back to life.

Dane realised his day was about to get worse. Before he could utter a single command, the ground beneath him became unstable. It turned to sludge in seconds. The panicked horses and riders sank into it waist deep, leaving the group trapped and completely helpless. The Ogre casually went from soldier to soldier, knocking each unconscious.

Grog was amused. The battle ended in seconds as Commander Dane himself slipped into unconsciousness.

After Grog and Whig relieved the unconscious soldiers of anything of value, Grog stomped happily through the woods, carrying a huge bag on his shoulders, grinning from ear to ear next to Mouse Man. Grog was happy to do what he did best. He looked at his skewed reflection in his shiny new shield.

Whig giggled to himself, thinking of the surprised looks on the faces of the unsuspecting soldiers.

The road twisted and soon dissolved into broken rocks, forming a crude stairway ascending up to the withered peaks. Sweat dripped down Grog's face by the time the sun dipped below the horizon.

Whig found a deep cave, and the two made camp for the night. Whig decided to risk another fire, knowing that the cave and the wind would disperse the smoke.

It was Grog's turn to provide the evening meal. He pulled out the provisions of the defeated soldiers. They feasted and drank until late into the night and then slept well into the next afternoon.

It was morning, and Sara bubbled with excitement. She had a real sister! Tamara had been her adopted sister, but Selara was the real thing. The secret wanted to explode out of her, but she knew she had to keep it. There must be a good reason her parents were keeping it secret.

Sara rushed downstairs and ate a hasty breakfast. She navigated the twisted paths of the courtyard quickly. There were the familiar morning sounds of chickens and little children playing. She sauntered down the cobblestones to the far edge of the castle. Around a collapsed section of wall was a small unused courtyard — her secret hiding place. It was here that she first lifted from the ground. Today she was determined to do it again. She felt different. The news of her new sister made her feel lighter, and she approached the problem of flying differently. She heard the soft cooing of a mourning dove nestled in the north wall of the Keep. She looked up and smiled. She closed her eyes and imagined that she was the dove, gently drifting like the clouds. It felt wonderful.

When she opened her eyes, the Keep was far below her. She panicked and started to fall. She quickly composed herself and brought the dove back into her thoughts. Her heart pounded in her chest. She stopped falling and stayed suspended in the breeze with her white dress flapping in the wind. The feeling of panic subsided, but now she had a new problem. She was drifting over the lake like a kite towards the forest. She couldn't control her direction, and she was afraid to change her thinking, lest she fall. She drifted at the mercy of the north wind.

She only wanted to fly a few feet above the ground, she thought helplessly. No one could teach her at the Keep. *No one believes me anyway,* she thought. Her mind raced, not knowing what to do as she got further and further from the safety of the Keep.

Tiny animals, houses, and trees spread out below her. She constantly fought off panic. Despite her desperation, she was overwhelmed by how beautiful it all was. She thought about how lucky she was to see this. No human in over two hundred years had seen the world in this way. She saw Night Birds drifting far below her and herds of cattle grazing in the open fields. She saw men on horseback riding in groups and horrid creatures walking in front of them. She was glad she was in the clouds.

By late afternoon, she was miles away. She experimented in changing her direction. When looking at the clouds below her, she saw one shaped like a bat. She remembered accidentally causing a bat to spin into the tunnel wall. Sara tilted her hand and pushed. She could feel her direction change slightly. After practising all afternoon, she had some control over her movements. *It's like swimming*, she thought. But by now she was far past the forest and over a range of mountains.

chapter ix

Rule 9: Never speak a cursed name

During the mid-day meal, Tamara was the first to ask the question, "Where's Sara?"

"I don't know," replied Seanna. "She's probably out playing with her friends. She'll be back by dinner."

The day passed, and everyone became more and more concerned. Selara and Jonrah joined the search, asking her friends if they had seen her. They checked all of the various tunnels and hiding places, but Sara couldn't be found.

By evening, Seanna was panicking. "Where could she be?" She turned to Talon. "You know what you have to do."

Talon looked haggard. "It's too dangerous. We need to do everything we possibly can before—"

"What if she's injured? Or dying or kidnapped?"

"There will be consequences. Daemon'll sense what we're doing, and he'll know we're looking for her. And then there's M."

Seanna stiffened. She knew all too well how M could be. She remembered a much younger M, a seductive sorcerer, doing everything in her power to tempt Talon and seduce him. M even tried to stop their wedding, claiming Talon should never marry an Elemental, but rather a person like herself who descended from pure Dark Majik. She was extremely unpredictable. Daemon knew that too and put a curse on her name after she had toyed with him mercilessly and spurned his advances. Being much younger, Daemon was ill-equipped to manage a viper like her. Seanna took a deep breath; her eyes met her husband's. "Do this for me."

Talon gave her a gentle kiss and left the room.

Talon climbed the winding stairs of the east tower until he came to a room with a heavy door adorned with a golden spiral. A large iron lock kept the door secure. He pulled a circle of keys from his cloak, and finding the oldest one, pushed it into the keyhole. Its hinges squealed. A round table with an ornate mirror sat in the centre of the room. At the back, an assortment of books, scrolls, and curiosities littered the shelves. Talon stood before the mirror and cleared his mind. He wiped the thick dust from the glass. His face distorted in the dark reflection. He chanted in an ancient language, and a light green mist formed around the mirror. He could feel his chest tighten as his power gradually grew.

In a tiny cottage, a few miles from the Keep, a tall cat-like woman sat up in her bed, sensing majik reaching out to her. A wicked smile slowly curled her lips. She brushed her long green hair away from her eyes in the darkness. "What brings the great Talon to my bedchamber at this hour? Have you come to play? Does your little wifey know you're here?" she asked mockingly.

"I need your help."

M sighed. "I can see you're going to be no fun at all."

"My daughter Sara's missing, and we can't find her. We fear something's happened to her."

"Sara? Is she the one whose life you ruined by sending her into the past with those boring parents of yours? No, that was Selara! She was a little spitfire, that one — I liked her. Now she's all grown up! Have you told her yet? You haven't, have you? Daddy's such a coward!

"I will help you find Sara. But only because I choose to. She has a little secret I've heard, but I'm not telling. I may ask a favour of you in return.

You don't mind, do you? Let's get started. I hope you realise our mutual friend'll want to join the party!"

Talon ignored her taunts and concentrated. He felt his heart beating in his chest. A second heart began to beat slightly out of sync with his, then the two beat in rhythm together.

"Cosy, isn't this?" purred M. "Just like old times."

A third smaller heart throbbed in the centre of the mirror.

"At least she's alive!" remarked M.

"But where is she now?" asked Talon.

"Reach out!"

Their hearts beat faster, and Talon and M moved as one astral body in the direction of the smaller beating heart.

"There, in the Dark Mountains!" M rejoiced.

But just as Sara was coming into focus, another presence entered their consciousness like a dark cloud.

"What are you doing?" thundered the astral Daemon.

"There you are, you scum worm! Go back to sleep, we're busy!" screamed astral M.

Talon didn't want to confront Daemon and desperately tried to break the link, but M clung on.

"You're so pathetic. Such a coward, up there in your big castle playing with your little monsters!" M chided. "And those poor women you bewitch don't really love you, do they? Such a lonely, lonely man! You poor, poor, thing."

Daemon was beyond furious, but there was nothing he could do in this state of consciousness. "I'll tear you to pieces and feed you to the Valerian ditch pigs, you wench!"

"No, you won't. You need me and you know it! Say my name!" she teased. At that moment, M released the link, and Talon felt a light unwelcome kiss from astral M on his lips. "Good night," she said. "You're welcome." Their link disappeared.

M lounged in her bed, smiling. *That was fun,* she thought. *Things are about to get interesting.* She yawned and drifted back to sleep.

Far away in his Castle, Daemon was livid. He shouted at the guards. "Send word to the Marauders! Have them search the mountain territories at first light! There's an Elemental girl out there, and I want her brought back alive!"

A woman with long brown hair in his bed remained sleeping, not remembering who she was, or why she was there.

When Talon awoke, the room was dark. He didn't relish telling his wife the news. He rushed towards the bedchamber, locking the door behind him. His wife was waiting for him.

"She's alive. But she's far away in Daemon's mountains," said Talon.

"How's that possible? Did someone take her there? My poor Sara!" Seanna started to cry.

Talon held her in his arms. "Daemon knows she's there, too. M started arguing with him just as we found her."

"Of course, she did," spat Seanna.

"She'll be alright. You know Sara, she's a survivor," he soothed.

"But she is so young, and so defenceless. How could this have happened?"

"We'll send a search party out tomorrow. It's too dark to go looking for her now!"

News of Sara's disappearance spread quickly throughout the Keep. Immediately after Selara heard, she reached out to Fletcher. *Sara's missing in Daemon's mountains. Please, you have to find her!*

He bolted through the window, his powerful wings propelling him into the early morning skies. Fletcher was growing very fond of Sara. He worried for her safety. Selara sat quietly in her room, scanning the countryside through Fletcher's eyes.

Dane rode all day after he and his men dug their horses out of the mud. At least the two thieves left them his saddle rope. As he approached the castle, a messenger told him they were to scour the mountains for an Elemental girl.

Dane slunk wearily back to the barracks and began retrieving new supplies and weapons. It wasn't a very good week. It started with the family who should have been justly punished for not paying their taxes. He heard later that his work was undone by a young girl. A Fire Elemental — even after he used Dark Majik! Then, after cornering the Elemental circlet thief, he somehow disappeared, even though he was surrounded by hungry Daemon-Wolves. Dane shook his head wearily. He came so close to claiming an enormous reward from Daemon for finding the circlet when *that damn Night Bird* stole it. Now he and his men had to re-supply because an Ogre who should have been dead, came back to life, teamed up with an Earth Elemental, and stole all of their weapons and supplies. Upon thinking, he brightened. *How much trouble could one little girl be?*

Far away in the Dark Mountains, Grog watched the clouds go by. "Flying Girl," Grog said matter-of-factly.

"What are you talking about?" asked Whig.

"Flying Girl."

"How much of that mead did you drink last night?" He knew his companion drank the small keg of mead they took from the Marauders.

Grog pointed to a small white shape drifting over them, waving its arms frantically.

Whig squinted his eyes. *What!* He couldn't believe what he was seeing. He heard stories of Wind Elementals flying, but he never believed them. He stood up and shielded his eyes. She didn't seem to know what she was doing. *A child*, thought Whig.

"Help," screamed the flying girl in the distance.

Grog picked up a bow.

"No, Grog! Shooting an arrow into her isn't going to save her." Whig scrambled to his feet. He shuffled up the path, following her.

She was drifting slowly above them. She managed to lower herself just enough so she could be heard. "I'm scared. I don't know how to land."

Grog and Whig jogged below her, Whig struggling to keep up.

"Can you make yourself fall?" huffed Whig.

"I think so," shouted the girl.

"Then think of falling, and Grog will catch you."

"Grog catch flying girl." he shouted thickly, keeping pace with her through the grass.

"I'm too scared. Isn't that an Ogre?"

"Think of falling," assured Whig.

Sara closed her eyes and held her breath. Suddenly, the floating white feather became a rock and Grog lunged forward, placing himself under the screaming girl. Grog's muscular arms broke her fall. She stopped screaming and then looked squarely into the face of her rescuer and started screaming again.

"It's okay," Whig said. "He's a friend."

Grog put the flying girl down on the ground and gently patted her head. "Grog catch," he repeated with a crooked smile.

Sara slumped down, exhausted, and hugged the ground. "Thank you, thank you," she moaned. She flew for an entire day and through the night. *It felt so good to be back on solid earth,* she thought.

"I'll never fly again," she breathed.

"Sure you will," replied Whig. "What's your name?"

"Sara," she said tentatively, unsure of her rescuers. *Why's a full-grown Ogre travelling with this old man? What are they doing this close to the Dark Castle? Can I even trust them?*

"Where did you come from?" asked Whig.

"From the Keep. My parents are going to be so worried about me," explained Sara, wondering how much she should tell them.

"You're in luck. Grog and I are headed to the Keep ourselves. We can take you there."

"Is he safe?" asked Sara, pointing at Grog with her eyes. "He won't eat me, will he?" She had heard too many scary stories involving Ogres.

"Of course, he's safe. He saved your life, didn't he? And besides, he's already eaten," Whig joked. "We have to keep moving. Can you walk?"

"Yes," said Sara, afraid that the Ogre would have to carry her.

Sara did her best to keep up with the Ogre and the old man. *He looks like he's a hundred years old, but he sure walks fast,* thought Sara. The Ogre was moving quickly even though he was carrying all of the supplies on his back. Sara had never seen an Ogre in person before. He was big and scary, but surprisingly not smelly.

"It's been a long time since I've set foot in the Keep!" said Whig.

"Why are you going there?" asked Sara as she puffed from the exertion.

"I want to spend my final days in the service of the True Queen."

"I think she's my big sister," contemplated Sara. "She saved a family in Old Mill Village from a Dark Majik hydra. She's awesome!"

"Well, well, Grog!" he said, turning to the Ogre. "We're escorting a Wind Elemental Princess back to her sister who'll help us overthrow Daemon! Our mission is now critical!" said Whig. "You know, when I was very young, I met a little girl just like you."

"Really? What did she look like?"

"She had red hair and looked exactly like you! She could have been your sister. She had a little Night Bird as a pet. But that would have been over eighty years ago."

Sara furrowed her brow. "That's weird!" she said. "My big sister has a Night Bird. His name is Fletcher." Sara started to wonder about Selara. She pieced together everything she overheard and assumed that her parents sent her to live far away with her grandparents in another kingdom.

Sara scrunched up all of her courage and decided to talk to the Ogre. "My name's Sara," she said looking up warily at Grog.

"Grog," replied Grog.

"Where do you come from? Do you have a family?" she asked, trying her best to start a conversation as her mother taught her.

"Family dead. Daemon kill them. Grog have no home."

Sara looked at her feet and began to feel sad for him. "I'm sorry, Grog," she said. She reached up instinctively and wrapped her tiny hand around one of Grog's pinky fingers.

"Flying Girl," he mumbled, looking down at Sara, as he continued to tramp forward — Sara in tow.

By the end of the day, Whig and Sara were exhausted and needed to set up camp. Grog could have kept walking, but he stopped for them. Whig asked Sara to gather some firewood while he went fishing for their evening meal. Grog followed Sara, crunching large branches into tiny pieces.

"Do you like being an Ogre?" she asked.

"Yes," replied Grog.

"Why?" she asked, gathering some small branches in her arms.

"Fighting, smashing, crunching, breaking, eating, drinking." It was three too many words, and Grog's head was starting to ache. *The Hu-mans like words more than eating*, thought Grog. *Always talk, talk, talk.*

"I think if I was an Ogre, I would like all of those things too!" she said, trying to be polite.

The sun dipped under the mountain range, and the clouds drifted in the pink and orange sunset. Sara built a firehouse, starting with the smallest pieces and gradually building up the circle. Sara admired her firehouse for a moment and looked up at Grog. "Do you have a fire maker?"

"No. Mouse Man has."

"If only Tamara or Selara were here," she said, disappointed.

"Flying Girl make fire," Grog said earnestly.

"I'm not a Fire Elemental," replied Sara.

"Make storm. Make lightening," urged Grog.

Sara sat thinking. Why would Grog think she could make a storm? She was barely able to control her flying, and she never saw Jonrah make a storm or use lightning. She assumed that somewhere in Grog's life he had seen a Wind Elemental make lightning.

Sara was cold and didn't want to wait for Whig to make fire. She closed her eyes and remembered what it was like to watch a lightning storm. She could feel her fingers tingling. Suddenly she heard a crackle and a sizzling bang. When she opened her eyes, she was floating above the firehouse. It exploded, smoke rising from its centre.

Grog was holding onto her ankle like the string on a balloon. "Lightning Girl," Grog said happily.

Sara was shocked and pleased. She willed herself to fall and plunked down beside the Ogre. She sat, smiling.

When Whig returned with his prepared fish, he saw Grog and Sara warming themselves by a roaring bonfire. He reached down absently to feel the fire starter in his pocket then shrugged his shoulders. He pushed the fish into the coals to let it bake and sat down.

An owl hooted in the distance. The first stars dotted the evening sky.

The three of them sat gazing into the flames. "Your parents are probably out looking for you," said Whig.

"I know. I wish there was a way I could tell them I'm safe," replied Sara, worried.

"When you learn to control your flying, I'll send you on your way and you'll be back in no time."

"I know, but I'm scared." She made a gentle breeze to fan the coals.

"Maybe we can help teach you tomorrow. I have an idea!" Whig said, tapping a branch on one of the clay fish.

The three of them slept soundly after supper. Sara never imagined in her wildest dreams that she would be sleeping next to an Ogre.

In the morning, they ate the leftover fish and some of the remaining provisions courtesy of Commander Dane. Grog busied himself collecting the supplies and tying bags together.

"Come here," he said to Sara. Whig was untying a long coil of rope.

"What are you going to do with that rope?"

"You're going to learn how to control your flying. And the rope is going to keep you safe."

At the thought of flying, Sara's feet lifted from the ground, involuntarily.

Whig quickly tied the rope around her waist, and she tentatively rose up above them.

"Please don't let go of the rope," cried Sara, looking down on Whig and the Ogre who looked like shrinking dolls on the ground.

"Don't worry, I've got you. You're going to practise rising and lowering yourself and controlling your direction."

This must look ridiculous, thought Sara. She was glad her friends weren't here to see this.

"Flying Girl," sighed Grog, the supplies clattering and shifting on his back as he walked.

As the day went on, Sara got better and better at controlling her rising and falling. She also spent time pushing herself in different directions with Whig securely holding onto the rope.

Two passing Night Birds narrowly avoided a mid-air collision, seeing a Hu-man flying without wings. They circled curiously before resuming their journey.

By late afternoon, Sara controlled most of her movements. Much of the time the rope fell slack as she needed it less and less. Despite her growing confidence, she was still too scared to fly without it.

They set up camp under a large group of trees. It was a clear night, and a blanket of stars stretched across the sky above the treetops. The fire crackled softly. Grog was already snoring while Sara sat quietly, looking at the stars. Whig poked at the fire with a stick and stared into the flames.

"There'll come a time, Sara, when the wars will end, and none of us will have to look over our shoulders. I believe it will come in your life-time."

"I've never seen war. I've lived my life in the lands of the Keep. I don't think I would be much of a soldier. I don't want to have to hurt anyone."

"None of us are soldiers until we have to be. We defend our families. We defend our right to live. I've seen many days, Sara, and I'm tired of wars and conflicts. I know in my heart that peace is coming, and I believe that your sister, the Queen of Peace, will heal this broken world.

"I've visions about your sister. She is the bridge between the Majik of the Elements and the Majik of the Darkness. She'll bring balance between the two. Peace isn't the absence of conflict, it is the balance of conflict. Majik is a tool, Sara. Both people of Elemental and Dark Majik can abuse their powers. Evil lies in the heart of the individual, not the majik. Power can be seductive, Sara. When it is used for the health and prosperity of all creatures, it is a force for good. When it is used to corrupt, manipulate, or enslave, it is a force for evil."

Sara listened as long as she could before her eyelids grew heavy. She pulled her blanket around her and fell fast asleep.

Daemon's blanket lay on the floor. He tossed and turned. In his night-mare, he saw a woman, tall, dark, and threatening. She told him his days were numbered as ruler of this kingdom and soon she'd come to claim what was rightfully hers. She looked at him with disdain and disgust, calling him a spoiled child. In his nightmare, he struggled to recognize her, but her face was a blur. He woke up in a cold sweat. *The Elementals are even haunting my dreams,* he thought. *But this woman isn't like any Elemental I've ever seen. Maybe the Thought Listener would discover her identity in the morning.*

He left his latest companion in bed, dressed, and found food. Some of the Nomaji women he wanted came willingly, believing they would be pampered and treated like royalty. Others were attracted to his power, not caring about the price of being with a rich and powerful man. Daemon knew this and took advantage. He trusted no one, so no one came close to knowing him or understanding him. He could easily bewitch any Nomaji woman to serve him, but the only woman he ever truly wanted was M. He sought out tall, attractive women that reminded him of M. These women were his proxy M's until he grew tired of them. Then he would send them to work in the kitchens or worse, as concubines for his Marauders.

But being in love with M was like falling in love with a candle. She could keep him warm or just as easily burn him. M was unpredictable, uncontrollable, and intoxicating. She was a drug, and he was an addict. As a younger man, he tried everything to make her want and need him. He gave her lavish gifts that she kept but spurned all his advances. He made himself vulnerable, and she embarrassed him, cutting him to the core. With the loss of the circlet, his one chance of possessing and controlling her was gone.

He wound his way down the halls until he came to a secret exit. He stepped into the sunlight, dressed entirely in black — a dark shadow on a new day. The people of the castle gave him a wide berth as he passed them. He followed the descending path to the forest. It held a special attraction for him. He remembered when he was just a boy walking in the forest. Life seemed easier then. He often sat, wondering what his father was like. His grandparents told him that his father left him and his mother alone because he was selfish and not interested in a family. After a while, he grew to hate his father — a faceless man who robbed him of all the things a father meant to a growing boy. He fought back tears, making sure there was no one near him to see his weakness.

Growing up, he was talented in the ways of Dark Majik. His grandfather said he was a genius and encouraged him to delve further and further into Dark Majik lore. It became an obsession for him, wanting to please his grandfather, who was the only real father he ever knew. He couldn't remember his mother ever being healthy. She was always weak and sick. He loved her dearly. When she died, he was only nine years old. He was heartbroken. He used majik as a way to forget the pain. As time went by, his pain found a voice as the Dark Majik bent and twisted him until he was unrecognisable even to himself.

He took more and more chances with his majik, pouring over ancient texts in his grandfather's library. One day, while he was out walking in the forest, he encountered a wolf. Using a combination of majik and training, Daemon made him his house pet. The wolf became his constant companion. It followed him everywhere.

He remembered one horrible day when two older boys, who always tormented him, found him walking with his wolf in the fields. The boys were talented archers and decided to have some sport with him. Daemon panicked as one arrow after another narrowly missed him. Daemon's wolf, sensing the danger, ran to attack the brothers. Terrified of the wolf, they put an arrow through his heart and ran away. The arrow might as well have pierced Daemon's heart. He felt closer to the wolf than his own family.

Daemon carried the body of his wolf home. He was devastated. He never cried as hard as he did that day. His icy grandmother ordered him to stop whimpering like a baby, and bury the thing immediately. He didn't answer her. The truth was he cared very little what his grandmother said to him. It was as if her very heart was removed when she was very young.

He remembered an Earth Elemental who could bring creatures back from the dead. But no one knew where he was, and he was expressly forbidden to talk to Elementals. He wondered if he could do the same thing with Dark Majik. He remembered a spell from an old book he studied only weeks before. The spell was complex and involved a forbidden form of Dark Majik. After completing the spell, he needed to bury his wolf and wait until the spell took effect.

His grandmother watched him follow her advice and smiled to

herself—glad he'd come to his senses.

Every day he would go out and check on the grave, but nothing happened. After a time, he gave up.

A few weeks later, the village was in an uproar. Two brothers were found torn apart, their bodies mangled and dragged into the forest. The king's soldiers searched for the monster. The entire community was on alert, and no one was allowed to leave their homes after dark.

One night, Daemon awoke to a familiar scratching at the door. He ran downstairs, certain his spell worked. But when he opened the door, he was met by a massive wolf-like creature. It sat down in front of him, waiting for a pat. It had the same eyes as his beloved pet, but its body was a monstrosity, a demonic caricature of his pet. There were traces of dried blood on its face. Daemon was both horrified and fascinated.

He led the creature to a shed on the property and told it to stay. It understood him perfectly. He knew it was the creature that killed the two brothers. *They brought it on themselves,* he rationalised. He wondered what he was going to do with his creation. The king's soldiers were looking for it even now and he wondered if he could keep it hidden. He imagined having an army of these creatures at his disposal. He would be unstoppable. He knew the term 'Were-Wolf' and decided to call his creation 'Daemon-Wolf.' In the future, everyone would fear his name and know it was he who commanded the beast.

He snuck out at night to feed his Daemon-Wolf table scraps, or to send it hunting in the deep forest. It innately knew not to frequent the village but to remain unnoticed and unseen.

In time, his grandparents passed on, leaving the house, property, and vast fortune to him. When the Dark Queen disappeared, he made his move.

He met with the leader of a group of young outlaws that called themselves the 'Marauders.' He told them he had money and wanted to hire them to be his soldiers and his bodyguards. Two of the outlaws scoffed, saying he was just a boy. They could kill him right now and take his money.

Daemon simply pointed at the would-be assailants and said, "Kill."

Before the men could utter another word, the massive beast exploded from the trees and tore the two to pieces. The remaining Marauders stepped back as the beast chewed on sinew and bones. "So, do we have a deal?" he asked. Dane nodded, emphatically.

Daemon scanned the trees around him for threats. He worried very little about man-to-man attacks, but a well-placed arrow or dagger could mortally wound him. An Elemental assassin took many forms: a rock, a pool of water, or a breeze. He shuddered. His policy on Elementals continued to be enacted. The only good Elemental was a dead one. But they haunted him in his dreams.

Daemon prided himself on his ability to kill Elementals. If he got close enough to them or deceived them, he used spells to make them forget who or what they were. Then they were killed like any other Nomaji. He took a sadistic delight in killing them using their own Element. When he captured that despicable Fire Elemental, he would make sure she burned!

Rayne was furious. "Another three women gone — taken by that madman! He must be stopped!" he said. The men at Oman Village agreed. Rayne felt powerless. He begged the Ogre queen for help, but she refused to defy Daemon. He knew the Elementals also suffered at the hands of Daemon, but they seemed as helpless as the Nomaji. Besides, the majority of the Elementals went into hiding after the last war, and no one had any idea who they were, or how many were left. His spies indicated that many of them were under the protection of Talon at the White Keep, but why would he care about Oman Village? No Elementals lived here. In fact, Elementals were not welcome in the village. Village law banished families of children showing Elemental powers. Oman Village was fiercely non-majik, and proud of it.

The last family banished by the village leaders was some years ago. The son went missing. He was swimming with the other children when one boy watched him turn into some kind of water statue and disappear into the pond. They were terrified. They thought he was bewitched. He was found miles in the forest, naked and shivering. All of his friends were afraid of him. The village leaders knew what they had to do: banish the family. Not everyone agreed. Two families left with them in protest. Perhaps they travelled to the White Keep, but no one knew for sure.

Since that time, the Nomaji were famous for being the most talented metalworkers in the kingdom. What they lacked in majik ability, they made up in human ingenuity. Rayne imagined a future world not ruled by majik, but by the wonders springing from the creativity of the human mind. The villagers hid their most advanced creations carefully from tyrants like Daemon. The Oman Nomaji were biding their time until they were strong enough to cleanse the kingdom of both Dark and Elemental Majik.

The Makers were a covert society of mathematicians, inventors, and fabricators. They created new metals, designed complex mechanisms, and experimented with improving weapons of war in secret factories throughout the Oman Village. Their recent inventions included a crossbow that could release multiple arrows quickly and a new weapon called a Wolf-Killer, designed especially to dispatch the powerful and unpredictable Daemon-Wolves. When Rayne was sure the weapon was effective, he would mass-produce the weapons for his army with the intent to overthrow Daemon and then begin ridding the kingdom of all majik.

Night Birds knew never to raid the Oman village because they were killed or worse by the fiendishly clever traps set out for them by the Makers. As intelligent as the Night Birds were, they were not as clever as the Makers of Oman Village. Imagination and creativity were the only majik they possessed. The possibilities were endless. Rayne felt the days of majik in the kingdom were numbered.

chapter x

Rule 10: Never eat white berries

The morning fire sank into the ground, consumed by Earth Majik. Whig groaned and helped break camp, walking stiffly. Sara felt she was ready to lose the training rope. She was more and more confident concentrating and lowering herself safely to the ground. When they started out, they saw the valley far below, but by mid-afternoon, the rocky path gave way to soft grassy meadows. A fallen tree across the river provided a bridge for a wobbling Whig to balance on while Grog ploughed through the rushing current. Sara glided overhead smoothly, enjoying the advantages of her newfound abilities.

"Show off," laughed Whig as he wove his way between the dead branches.

"I could never have done this without you," she shouted back.

When they entered an open meadow, they spotted a large group of armed men.

"Marauders! Quick, take cover!" shouted Whig.

Sara landed, looked around but found none. They were trapped by a mountain stream behind them and an open field ahead of them.

Commander Dane saw the Ogre and his companion. Remembering the sinking horses, he ordered his soldiers to dismount quickly and climb onto the rocks. *Now I'll get my revenge*, he thought. "Archers!" he shouted.

Grog stepped in front of Sara, protectively.

"Do not kill the girl, he wants her alive!" Dane shouted. "Fire."

A volley of arrows flew directly at Whig and Grog. Grog roared with rage as five arrows struck his Marauder shield. The arrows hitting Whig fell harmlessly to the ground, glancing off stone. The archers cocked more arrows, aimed, and fired. Dane secretly wished he could outfit his crew with new arrow launchers from the Oman Village, but the towns-people wanted nothing to do with Daemon or anyone associated with him. When he himself asked permission to raid the village for their weapons, Daemon said he didn't care about the toy-makers from Oman Village. He believed his Majik was all that he and his men would ever need. Dane couldn't help wondering if he was making a mistake.

Sara was frightened of the Marauders and their arrows, but something far greater than fear rose inside of her.

Grog pulled the arrows out of his shield one by one while the archers readied for another volley. Grog was annoyed at the damage they caused to his new-to-him shield.

"Fire," shouted the Commander again. This time a strong gust of wind blew the arrows in all directions, completely missing their marks. Some arrows boomeranged back at the archers who fired them, forcing them to leap out of the way.

Whig looked around, wondering how that happened. Then he saw Sara floating and transforming.

Dane's jaw dropped. His men were aghast. No one had ever seen a human float before. She looked like a ghost. He had seen an illusionist levitate at a fair once, but everyone knew it was just a trick. Even with all of his advanced majik, Daemon couldn't fly. Dane could see that this was no trick. It was really happening. *How am I supposed to bring the girl back to Daemon if we can't even reach her?*

Sara glowed a faint green. Out of a bright, clear sky, dark clouds materialised over the Marauders, and the air became cold. Their breath turned to vapour. Frost formed on their weapons. The higher she rose, the more desperate and agitated Dane became.

Even from her rising elevation, Sara focussed on the menacing archers. The horses reared up in the wind, sensing danger. Dane felt an unexpected and malevolent power growing above them. He lived his whole life around Dark Majik, and what he was sensing now terrified him. Even more alarming was the faint outline of something impossibly huge emerging from the clouds. He decided to ignore Daemon's request to bring the Elemental girl in alive and grabbed a bow and arrow. Fumbling with his frostbitten fingers, he aimed quickly and shot the arrow directly at Sara's heart.

Before the arrow found its mark, a speeding Night Bird dropped from the clouds and snatched the arrow, just inches from its target. Winn flew protectively in front of Sara, clutching the arrow in her beak.

Sara screamed with fury at the offending soldiers.

Many soldiers went down on one knee and made the Sign of the Holy Night Bird. Dane rolled his eyes.

Green lightning twisted from the dark clouds and struck down the archers randomly, incinerating some and scattering others in all directions. Their horses bolted into the fields, and the remaining soldiers ran for their lives.

"It's that damn Night Bird again," cursed Dane as he sprinted into the fields.

"Flying Girl mad!" said Grog, looking up in awe. *But not Flying Girl.*

Sara calmed down slowly, and the storm subsided. The dark shape disappeared, and the clouds evaporated into brilliant sunshine. She floated down gently with the Night Bird following close behind.

Grog looked at her with concern.

Winn snapped the arrow in half and dropped the pieces on the ground in disgust.

Whig took a tentative step back from the Night Bird and turned to Sara. "You put quite a show on for us, little lady!"

A short distance away, Alan was puffing and struggling to catch up with Winn.

"Who's that?" asked Whig, wondering if he should trap him in quicksand.

Alan recognized the Ogre first.

"Glass Man!" Grog bellowed happily. He ran over and gave Alan a crushing hug, then dropped him to the ground.

"Alan," squealed Sara, jumping into his arms. Alan hugged her tightly.

"What on earth are you doing here? And when did you learn to fly?" he asked.

Sara let go quickly, too excited to answer, bent down and hugged the Night Bird. "Thank you for saving my life," breathed Sara. Winn graciously let Sara hug her, slowly becoming accustomed to the way that Hu-mans expressed gratitude.

The little group travelled together. Whig swelled with pride at the little Elemental girl's accomplishments. He felt partly responsible, having helped to train her. "You're like the Wind Elementals of old," he said. *But no one ever spoke of green lightning — that's disturbing*, he thought.

Grog secretly thought the same thing.

Whig turned to Alan, walking beside him. "So you're bonded to the Night Bird who caught that arrow? I have never heard of a Night Bird moving so fast!" he added, admiring her as she glided slowly along beside them.

Winn swelled a bit, understanding Whig through Alan's mind. She would have blushed if she could.

"Her name's Winn," commented Alan, "and she's my new best friend."

Winn was overwhelmed by the flood of compliments. The companionship and camaraderie warmed and comforted her. She felt sad that the outcast Night Birds of the past were shunned for wanting to experience this. *Where are they now?* she wondered.

"I didn't know there were any Earth Elementals left," remarked Alan to Whig.

"Many of us were killed during the war. The others went into hiding. I'm going to pledge my service to the Queen. There is a war coming, and I want to be there to help."

Alan nodded, secretly wondering how helpful this crotchety old man could be.

"You've earned your wings," said Whig, turning to Sara. "You're only a few hours away from the Keep by air. Why don't you fly ahead? We'll meet you there in the morning."

Sara beamed and hugged each of them.

"Winn says she'll fly with you and keep you safe on your journey. She has someone at the Keep she wants to catch up with," said Alan, grinning.

Winn gave him a friendly slap with her wing as she took off with Sara. Both rose quickly. Sara couldn't move as fast as Winn, but she could spin, rise and fall, mimicking the motions of the Night Bird. She followed Winn who was careful not to fly too far ahead of her. They flew in silence, both lost in their own thoughts as the first stars of the evening twinkled on the horizon.

The night before, Tamara smouldered as she lay in her bed. With Sara missing and her continuing fear of Jonrah falling in love with Selara, Tamara was on edge. Ever since Selara showed up with her long legs, her exquisite hair, and her brilliant smile, Tamara had not slept.

Oh Selara, can I braid your beautiful hair? Of course, you can have my boyfriend! No, we don't have to share him! Can I be your servant forever — can I please? she thought sarcastically.

She lay on her back, glaring at the ceiling. Tamara knew that in the ancient texts, some Elemental brothers and sisters became married rulers to promote family lines and political unity — often with disastrous results. Tamara's mind made this unlikely union into a fact. Her skin became so hot she singed her bed coverings. She got up quickly, seeing that she had ruined yet another sheet — her sooty silhouette marked where her body lay moments before.

"Not again!" she screamed, throwing a white-hot fireball through the open window, watching it explode in the night sky. Her mind was an inferno, and common sense and patience were sacrificed on the pyre of jealousy — a jealousy that was steadily growing. Tamara was going to eliminate the one threat to her happiness: Selara!

Jonrah was becoming more and more uncomfortable, and no matter what he said to Tamara, she was suspicious of every glance and every word. She fumed every time Jonrah went near Selara — or even mentioned her name.

Selara was very fond of Jonrah and having a difficult time sorting out her own emerging feelings. She thought of him as she braided her hair that morning. She wondered if he had feelings for her as well. But Tamara got him first. She made that abundantly clear. *No, Jonrah, you can't have your arm back now because it's mine. No, Jonrah, you can only look at me, you don't need to see where you're going,* Selara rolled her eyes. *Tamara's such a freak. What could Jonrah possibly see in her? She's short and so bad-tempered — Jonrah could do much better …. With me perhaps.*

Selara flipped through Seanna's clothes, deciding which outfit to wear. *Which one would Jonrah like?* she wondered. She thought about the boys in Old Mill Village who gave her so much attention. *Why couldn't Jonrah see me that way?* She settled on the green one with the gold leaf patterns thinking it showed off her figure the best. She wished she could look at herself in the mirror, but with Sara missing and the threat of a Thought Listener looking at her, she had to be satisfied with her imagination. The mirror remained covered.

It had been two days since Sara's disappearance. Jonrah and Selara were wandering the streets of the Keep together. It was one of those rare times that Selara could have some alone time with Jonrah. Seanna was having a meeting with Tamara and asked not to be disturbed. Selara looked up at Jonrah and reached out to hold his hand. She gave it a little squeeze.

He took it tentatively, feeling very uncomfortable. He could sense Selara's feelings for him were growing, and he didn't know how much longer he could keep the secret.

"Fletcher's been scanning the mountains back and forth every day, but the mountain fog's made it impossible to see anything. I wish I knew she was safe," said Selara.

"There's nothing we can do for her right now. Worrying isn't going to bring her home any faster," said Jonrah. "Listen, my favourite minstrels are in the market. Maybe they can cheer you up."

As they came closer, they heard the beat of drums and the trill of flutes. A lute player underscored the melody with syncopated rhythms. A small group of Nomaji clapped along.

Selara smiled. The music was infectious, and she was enjoying her time with Jonrah. The thoughts of worry faded into the musical strains and energetic clapping. Her grandparents never sang or played musical instruments. For her, music was pure Majik, and its novelty, sheer delight. She was immediately caught up in its rapture.

Then someone in the crowd recognized Selara. "She's here," whispered a young woman, excitedly to her friends. One of the women hurried to the lead musician and whispered in his ear, "Now's your chance."

His face turned beet red when he looked up at Selara. Several people in the crowd urged him on. He held tightly onto a large lute-like instrument with two necks and a round back like a tortoise shell. "Beg pardon, sweet lady," he said looking up at her bashfully. "I've written a ballad for you. I would be honoured to share it. It's called, " he paused for dramatic effect, "'The Ballad of the Red-Haired Maiden.'"

Selara blushed, nodding. Everyone, including Jonrah, applauded. The street fell silent with anticipation. The musician's skilled fingers traced paths along the doubled strings, and haunting arpeggios filled the silence. He began to sing from memory:

Listen good, and listen well!
You fiery creatures who burn in hell;
For good still walks this Earthly place,
A beauty bold and fair of face!
A beauty bold and fair of face!

The musicians sang the chorus together. Jonrah teased Selara, and she elbowed him in the ribs.

The black heart coward did release,
A fiery demon to make war on peace.
It breathed green fire with seven heads;
Then the black heart coward turned and fled.
Then the black heart coward turned and fled.

Some men drinking mead sang and spat, cursing Commander Dane and cheering Selara!

Of the seven heads no one could tame,
Save one brave maiden who danced with the flames!

More cheers rose up.

She sang a song that stayed the beast,
And drove it from its unholy feast!
And drove it from its unholy feast!

The people chimed in.

Of this red-haired maiden, I sing and tell,
For she sent that demon straight to hell!
For she sent the demon straight to hell!

"Selara, Selara!" they chanted.

The group cheered wildly. Selara, so moved by the singer and his song, skipped across the dance area and kissed the singer directly on the lips.

He was so stunned that he fell off his bench, embarrassed. The surrounding musicians teased and congratulated him. Everyone was talking at once. They couldn't wait to bring the story back home with them. A few men patted the lute player with powerful hands, feeling jealous of his kiss.

"I think we shall all take up the lute this very night!" they said.

The rousing music resumed, and the people resumed dancing. Jonrah playfully pulled Selara away from her admirers and onto the dance floor. She had never danced before and tried to protest, but everyone urged her on. Before long the two of them were laughing and enjoying themselves. Selara felt safe and secure with Jonrah. *My cute moron,* she thought. She liked the feeling of his strong hand on her back. Selara locked eyes with Jonrah. Overwhelmed with the music and the moment, she moved in closer to kiss him.

Wandering the streets, looking for Jonrah, Tamara was attracted to the music. Several people were dancing, but all she could see was Selara about to kiss Jonrah. What happened next came so quickly that no one could have stopped it. Tamara flew through the dancers in a rage and slapped Selara across the face.

"Firk you! You conniving little ditch pig!"

The shocked dancers backed away, and the music stopped.

Jonrah tried his best to get between the two young women, but Tamara tossed him aside like a rag doll. Then she targeted Selara like a mountain cat. She was glowing a threatening crimson.

Selara didn't have time to think about rule number two. The combination of the pain from the slap on her face and her confused feelings for Jonrah cancelled it out. *Who does this little freak think she is? Ruining my dance!* she thought. *She just slapped the wrong girl!*

A white-hot fireball erupted from Tamara's fist, aimed directly at Selara's face.

She barely dodged the burning projectile as it grazed her ear. "Leave me alone, you little freak!" screamed Selara, throwing a fireball back at her.

Jonrah had been terrified from the beginning that this would happen. His worst nightmare was about to come true, and there was nothing he or anyone else could do to stop it.

Everything happened at once. The dancers and musicians scattered, fearing for their lives. The guards of the Keep gathered quickly but stood back, not willing to intervene. None of them were brave enough to get between the two Fire Elementals or their deadly creatures. Jonrah stood frozen with the rest of the onlookers. Everything was moving too fast.

Fletcher was just returning when green and white fireballs exploded into the air, narrowly missing him. He could see from the explosions down below that his Bond-Mate and Tamara were fighting. Fletcher had expected this was going to happen. He just didn't know when.

Fletcher focussed with all his might on his bond, but Selara was unreachable, her mind a wall of fire.

Selara began cursing while Tamara matched her flame for flame. The two young women were panthers circling.

Fletcher flew helplessly above them.

Tamara struck again, sending another fireball at Selara's head. This time Selara caught the flame instinctively and sent it back exploding into Tamara's chest.

I'm getting better at this, Selara thought. The fireball burned brightly before going out.

Tamara screamed. The pain only seemed to make her stronger and more determined. A white-hot serpent circled Tamara before slithering ominously toward Selara. Greenwald appeared in response, wrapping himself around Selara protectively. Nova followed him.

The heat emanating from the two women caused some of the surrounding buildings to combust. Some onlookers ran to get buckets of water. Others watched silently, transfixed.

Tamara's serpent rose to its full height but hesitated for a split second before attacking. Nova moved in like lightning — sinking its fiery fangs into the white serpent's throat. Its scream echoed in the square as it was strangled and completely consumed in a flurry of sparks and smoke. Nova advanced on Tamara who conjured a fiery shield.

In the chaos, Selara was impressed by the fire shield and wondered if she could learn to do that too. Tamara wielded the shield bravely, but Nova attacked her mercilessly. He was able to tunnel under the shield and snap at her legs. Then he wove his body around her and burned her neck and her hair. Tamara screamed, spun around and fought back with a fiery sword. A surprised Nova drew back, retreating. The air suddenly wavered around Selara, and she was consumed by a green mist.

From out of the mist came another fire serpent, joining Greenwald and Nova, but this one split into several heads set to strike. It was the Fire Hydra. The onlookers watched in horror and disbelief as Selara used the very monster she defeated at Old Mill Village against Tamara.

They feared that they were about to watch Selara murder Seanna's step-daughter. Tamara screamed as the seven heads oriented on her, each one vying for position, making it impossible to predict which one would strike first.

Tamara eyed the lethal heads, trying to decide what to do. Her entire body was burned and disfigured, her hair was burned to her scalp, and the skin on her hands and arms were scarred with deep black fissures. In that moment, she decided it would be better to die than continue to live this way. She had no chance of defeating the Fire Hydra. She had lost her battle for Jonrah. She was humiliated in front of all these people. There was nothing left. Her anger dissipated into fear and regret. She surrendered. She lowered her fire shield and her sword, prepared to die. At least she would reunite with her parents in the Second Realm.

The Fire Hydra, seeing no resistance, moved in for the kill. But before the serpent heads struck, a cold wind blew into the square and storm clouds rushed above the combatants. Rain came down in torrents. It fell in a tight circle, extinguishing the flames and causing the serpents to hesitate, filling the air with steam as they wavered, struggling to remain solid. A winding tornado sprung up between the two women, and a tiny body floated high above them.

Jonrah gasped. "It's Sara!"

Sara's impossibly loud voice exploded like a thunderclap. "Stop! Both of you. Stop fighting! Jonrah's your brother, Selara!" Green lightning crackled and hissed, striking the ground around them.

Time froze. Tamara and Selara stood like statues in the freezing downpour. The flames hissed and spat, causing steam to rise into the twisting whirlwind.

Selara's trance ended with the implications of Jonrah being her brother and seeing Sara back safe, but flying. The serpents, who were doing their best to remain lit, vanished. Pools of water flooded the square.

The two shocked young women stared up at Sara. Onlookers splashed through the puddles, taking cover. The tiny storm expanded to extinguish the small fires licking at the buildings.

Selara felt her head spinning and crumpled down unconscious in the rushing water.

Tamara stood smoking and shivering. Jonrah ran to Selara. The onlookers gaped as Sara descended gently to the ground. Her body wavered from translucent to solid. Tiny flashes of green lightening still danced on her fingertips. She had a driven look in her eyes. The crowd of onlookers applauded.

The storm clouds disappeared, leaving only stars and a lonely crescent moon. There were cheers for Sara. The people were seeing the first Wind Elemental Princess in over one hundred years.

"Get Saffron as fast as you can!" screamed Seanna.

"He's not here. He's still travelling," shouted a guard.

"Then get Talon, he'll know what to do."

Jonrah rushed up the tower stairs. Tamara stared at the ground—her shoulders slumped. Vapour rose from the burns on her body. Seanna watched her stagger off before anyone could stop her. Seanna couldn't help but feel responsible for Tamara's pain. She was obstinate about not telling Selara the truth sooner. And now unexpectedly, little Sara claimed her Elemental powers. No one would believe her when she said she was flying.

Deep in the shadows, a hooded man watched the entire scene play out. *The Oman Seer was right! Both of these women are Dark Elementals. Something must be done quickly before they turn. How could Talon let this happen? He was irresponsible. He should have known better. All of us are in danger now!* he thought. Weaving through the streets, he rushed to the stables to retrieve his horse. He must report the news to Rayne.

High above them, Fletcher circled the square, worried. His bondmate was unconscious, and he couldn't hear her thoughts. He could see people gathering around and carrying her to safety.

Without warning, his wings were pinned and he was spinning out of control. Something grabbed him. He struggled, but powerful wings enveloped him. He was falling. Then soft feathers pressed against his face, and in the rushing wind, a voice asked him, "Did you miss me?"

Winn released Fletcher's wings just before they hit the ground, and the two of them rose up twisting into the air.

Fletcher was overjoyed. He hadn't seen or heard from Winn since he was mortally wounded by the elder Hu-man. "Something about you has changed, hasn't it?" Fletcher asked, admiring her.

"Accidentally bonded with a Hu-man," she said. "I'm learning about laughter and the deep love that Hu-mans are capable of." She looked into his eyes with affection.

"I knew that before I bonded, " said Fletcher.

"I think I love … you!" she said shyly.

"Me too," echoed Fletcher nuzzling the feathers of her soft neck. The two flew off together and nestled in the arms of an ancient oak tree growing in the Keep. It was a long and emotional day for the both of them.

Some miles from the Keep in front of a campfire, a smile crossed Alan's face. He fell asleep, chuckling to himself.

When Selara awoke, it was dark. She didn't know where she was or how she got there.

Seanna leaned closer.

"How?" asked Selara, feeling ashamed, confused, and devastated. Her face was a mask of concern. Images of the battle and the shock of Sara's words tumbled in her mind. "Are you my mother?" she whispered, tears welling up.

"Yes," said Seanna.

"I don't understand — they told me you were dead. I couldn't even remember what you looked like."

"We felt it was easier that way."

"… and Talon?"

"He's your father. He took care of you after you collapsed."

"Where is he?" she asked.

"He's recovering. The majik he used to strengthen you exhausted him."

"Will he be alright?"

"Of course, he'll come and see you when he's ready."

"Is Tamara okay? Did I hurt her? I could have killed her! Sara can fly?"

Seanna looked down. "Yes, if Sara didn't stop you, Tamara would be dead. There was nothing Jonrah or anyone here could do. The two of you are extremely powerful. Sara and Jonrah are your sister and brother. And Tamara is your step-sister."

Selara looked deeply into her mother's eyes. The old spell lost its power over her, and she recognized her mother. "Mum," Selara rasped in a whisper of tears, her eyes saying more than her words.

"I'm so sorry, Selara. We had no other choice," she said through the sobbing. Seanna embraced her daughter, hugging her as hard as she could.

"There was a war ten years ago, and your very existence was a threat to Daemon. He sent out all of his armies and all of his Dark Creatures to have you put to death. We tried so hard, but we couldn't protect you — there were even assassins in the Keep. We fled for our lives. By sending you into the past with your grandparents, Daemon and his armies could no longer sense your majik and we were able to escape.

She looked deeply into Selara's eyes. "The final war is coming, and you need to be ready. Saffron will be back tomorrow, and he'll tell you what you need to do to harness your powers. It seems that now he'll have two students."

Sara, who was listening quietly behind the door, rushed into the room and hugged Selara.

"I am so proud of you, Sara!" Selara croaked. "You saved Tamara's life! And you flew!

You were amazing!" said Selara. Sara beamed. "What better way to cool off two Fire Elementals than a rain storm?" Selara coughed. "I think there're more than a few farmers around here who would like you to be their new best friend."

Exhaustion suddenly overcame Selara, and even talking was too difficult.

"She needs to rest now, Sara. Let her sleep."

The fiery little waif, who lived most of her life without a mother, was home. She drifted off into a deep and peaceful sleep.

Jonrah knocked on Tamara's door. "Tamara, are you okay?"

"No! Go away!" rasped her muffled voice.

"I'm not leaving until you open this door." Jonrah could hear Tamara coughing and sobbing inside. No one had spoken to her since after the firefight. Jonrah's tall frame bent over, and he rested his forehead on the polished wood. "Please open the door." There was no answer. He turned around and slid down with his back to the door. "We were just having fun. Nothing was happening between us." He felt responsible for the jealous battle. If he hadn't been dancing with his sister, Tamara wouldn't have reacted. "Please, Tamara. We need to talk."

"You ran to her and ignored me!" she screamed. The sobbing continued, and Jonrah couldn't stand it anymore.

He stood up, spoke a short incantation, and the bolt on her door slid open smoothly. As he entered the room, he was struck by the smell of smoke and burnt hair. He could see Tamara face down on her bed, crying. Her clothes were torn and blackened with soot. Her back was a crisscross of deep red welds. He knelt down beside her.

"Don't look at me!" she sobbed.

He ran his fingers gently through her hair. She flinched in pain. Brittle golden strands came off in his fingers. Most of it was burnt off. "You know I love you. We were all upset about Sara. I care so much for the both of you. I told you before, she's just my sister. You're the one I want to marry."

"Marry?" she asked, the sobbing stopping suddenly.

"Why would you want to marry a crazy person like me? And besides, I'm a monster. Look at me."

Tamara turned to face him, slowly and reluctantly. The skin around her eyes was burned black. Deep dark scars were etched on either side of her jaw. Her face was a bruised, burnt skull. Only a small wisp of hair remained on her head. He lifted her hands and saw dark black streaks tracing down her arms to her fingers. Her extreme rage caused her to over-extend her powers, generating so much heat that even the majik in her body couldn't process it. "Don't look at me. I'm hideous!" she sobbed.

"What are you holding?" he asked, spotting something in her right hand.

"Nothing."

Jonrah gently pried open her fingers. He could see several small white berries in her palm. Without a word, he took them and tossed them out the window. "You don't need those," he said to her softly. Tears welled up in his eyes. "I love you for everything that you are." He carefully placed his hands on the back of her balding scalp and gently kissed her forehead. Her skin was warm to the touch. He wrapped his arms around her tenderly.

She stiffened from the pain of her ravaged skin before surrendering to his embrace.

They rocked together gently. He could feel the heat emanating from her like an oven. "Close your eyes," Jonrah said softly.

She closed them, coughing. The blisters stung and broke as tears ran down her burnt cheeks.

Jonrah spoke a gentle incantation, and a cool wind blew onto her closed eyelids. The burns and blisters faded. Her blackened eye-sockets softened and healed. Dark burns were replaced by fresh new skin.

She kept her eyes closed and breathed deeply as the pain in her lungs subsided. When he kissed her forehead again, she felt a cool sensation course through her scalp. Blisters and charred skin healed while the roots in her tufts of hair tingled. Golden hair grew and lengthened. While the brittle pieces of damaged skin repaired and hair cascaded down around her, she sighed deeply.

He brought her fingers to his lips, kissing them and then moved his hands gently along the skin of her arms. The dark scars faded slowly, and a cooling ran down to her fingertips. Her entire body felt as if a healing river was running through every cell, hair, and fibre of her being. Tears of relief streamed down her cheeks, and then warm lips pressed gently against hers. Her heart beat faster.

"Will you be my wife?"

"Of course," she said, her voice still a harsh whisper.

He pulled her close for another kiss, and the bolt on her bedroom door slid back, locking into place.

To the east of the Kingdom, over bright gold and green fields, Vector glided towards the open window of a little farm cottage. He perched on the back of a worn chair next to Agata. She stroked his feathers. *There's news from Old Mill Village that the Princess of Peace has emerged. Sheer saw the miracle himself just a few days ago. The princess transformed and brought with her, her two fire serpents. She subdued a Dark Majik hydra and saved a family marked for death by Daemon,* Vector recounted into Agata's mind.

"Good. Daemon's reign's coming to an end."

We have been tasked with gathering the Outcast Brethren and their Bond Mates.

"Then fly and spread the news. Where's the Princess now?"

She is at the White Keep, preparing herself for the coming battle.

"We'll gather at Circle Village to pledge our allegiance to her."

chapter xi

Rule 11: Never mix Elemental with Dark Majik!

It was another morning in an endless wheel of mornings for Saffron as he unpacked his bag and sat alone in the white tower, pondering the changing reflections of Crystal Lake. Normally, he felt tired after a long journey. But not today. He felt a change. He'd heard stories of the young Fire Elemental, Selara. And just yesterday, her little sister Sara flew into the Keep saving Tamara's life, he reflected. He knew Talon sent his daughter into the past to save her from Daemon. He was not privy to her unique abilities, only that Daemon used every resource at his disposal to kill her, but failed.

None of the Elementals, including himself, could understand why Daemon so desperately wanted Selara dead. He must have sensed something in her that no one else did. Perhaps his Thought Listener discovered something about her that frightened and threatened Daemon to the point that he was willing to start a war over that young girl. Recent events revealed why Daemon was so concerned. More and more powerful Elementals were emerging around the Kingdom. Soon they would threaten his plan to rule unchallenged.

But how could the stories be anything other than pure fantasy? he thought. *They were impossible tales, of course.* In a nearby hamlet, Selara commanded the green flames of a Dark Majik hydra to extinguish themselves. The people insisted that the Princess of Peace had returned. He shuddered reflexively. *Very few Elementals could influence Dark Majik in any way. What Elemental in the history of the world had this kind of power?* The story filled him with questions. The castle was still buzzing with the news that Selara was bonded with a Night Bird. *And now the first Elemental to fly for over two hundred years has emerged?* A quiet knock at the door interrupted his reverie.

A timid, young woman with flowing red hair stood before him. The fully-grown Night Bird on her shoulder eyed him cautiously. She carried an old book in her right hand.

She's the image of the Peace Prophet, the Princess of Peace, he thought. Saffron recognized the book immediately. It was Petra's book of incantations, one of the most dangerous majik books ever scribed. The hairs on the back of his neck stood on end, and shivers raced down his spine. He felt a rippling power emanating from her. One of his gifts was to sense even the subtlest trace of majik. Now he was at a loss for words. He tried to catch his breath. He taught many Elementals to control their limited powers, but she was the majik student he had waited for his entire life.

"My name's Selara, and this is Fletcher," she said in a soft voice. "I'm here for my lessons. Can he stay?"

"Certainly," stammered Saffron.

What is wrong with this man? thought Selara to Fletcher.

I think he may be a few strands short of a basket!

Was that a joke? smiled Selara, impressed at how quickly Fletcher was navigating humour. *Be nice!*

"My name's Saffron. I've heard so many won…wonderful things about you," he stuttered. He spoke as calmly as he could. Being in the same room with Selara was the majik equivalent of standing at the edge of a volcano ready to erupt. Selara had the majik potential to vaporise everything around her with a stray thought, and she had no idea how to control it. Saffron felt the crushing weight of responsibility on his shoulders. It was vital that he teach her control as soon as possible.

"That's a beautiful basket," remarked Selara, trying to be polite as she sat down, placing the book on the table.

Shoddy workmanship, Fletcher whispered.

Selara smiled, ignoring him.

"It's a very old Night Bird weaving," answered Saffron, proudly. "For a short time, long, long ago, humans and Night Birds worked together peacefully."

The wizard sat Selara in front of a table near the window. Saffron walked to the stove, bent down and piled up some kindling inside the hearth. He looked at Selara. "Do you mind?" he asked.

"Of course not." Fletcher hopped to perch on the windowsill. Selara walked over and remembered her grandfather's lessons. She cleared her mind and passed her fingers over the wood. She spoke a short incantation. A tiny fire serpent appeared, consuming the kindling and growing bigger as it ate the dry pieces of wood.

Saffron thought it was ironic that such a powerful Elemental knew so very little about her own majik potential. She was completely undisciplined, save for the tiny fire serpent she could conjure up when required.

"Who taught you how to make the fire serpent?" asked Saffron.

"My grandfather."

"I knew your grandfather, you know. He was a wonderful man; your grandmother too."

Selara brightened. "They raised me." Then she looked down, sadly. "But they never talked about my powers or taught me how to use them. My grandmother gave me her rules to keep me calm and safe. I understand now that they're both long dead."

Fletcher flew down, picked up more kindling, and tossed it into the flames.

Saffron was momentarily distracted then turned back to Selara. "If they tried to teach you too much, you would draw attention. They had to keep you hidden from enemies until your powers fully emerged."

"I brought the book my grandfather gave me," said Selara, "when I left with Jonrah, he told me that I would need it." She looked out the window wistfully, remembering what an emotional night that was. "When I was younger, I kind of had an accident with it."

"What do you mean, an accident?"

"I accidentally went back in time with Fletcher to some battle. I think it started with an A."

"Albright," said the wizard, finishing her sentence, the colour rapidly draining from his face. The implications were astounding.

"The letters in the book talked to me. I remember I wanted to fly like Fletcher, so the book took me to someplace else."

"What happened at the battle?"

"There were monsters everywhere, and I'd have been killed if it wasn't for the serpents."

"Serpents?" asked the wizard.

"Yes, the fire serpents that came and saved me from the monster that scratched my face. The monster exploded after my fire serpents tore it to pieces. I named the serpents Greenwald and Nova."

"Then what happened?" asked the wizard, trying to catch his breath.

"I picked up the book, and the words brought me back to the farm."

"And what did your grandfather do?" asked Saffron, his eyes narrowing.

"He hid the book from me until it was time for me to leave."

"Sensible," said the wizard, masking a rising panic. "I wonder if you could leave the book here with me ju… just to keep it safe."

"Certainly, I haven't opened it since that day."

"Good choice. We'll work through the book together, so there won't be any more accidents." The wizard eyed her seriously, taking the book carefully as if it would burst into flames and placing it on a high shelf.

Fletcher threw more pieces of wood into the fire and pushed the door shut with his beak and latched it. *This Hu-man asks too many questions. Talk, talk, talk.*

"Stop it," Selara said, addressing Fletcher out loud.

"Pardon me?" asked Saffron.

"Not you, sir. The bird. My friend here is getting bored, and he's becoming rather rude." She gave Fletcher a disapproving look. Selara opened the window for him. "Go, I'll see you later." With a flutter of wings, Fletcher went to find Winn and Sara.

"It must be a strange experience sharing consciousness with a Night

Bird every day. I've often wondered what that would be like."

"It has its advantages and disadvantages. Sometimes it's like having a child!" she laughed. "An awful child!"

Saffron noticed her necklace. "Where did you get that stone you wear around your neck?"

"I've had it since I was little. A little boy named Whig gave it to me. He brought me back to life after I ate poisoned berries."

Saffron was speechless. *Whig was almost one hundred years old now*, he thought. "That's a talisman from an Earth Elemental. It's very rare. Do you know how to use it?"

"No, but I keep it because it reminds me of my grandfather. He made the leather lace."

"I heard you and Tamara were fighting." Saffron took the boiling water from the wood stove and poured it into the teapot. "Someone told me they saw a green fire serpent appear, but that didn't really happen, did it?" His nervous hands trembled. He stumbled. Scalding water splashed over Selara.

The memory of Tamara's attack flooded into her mind, and Selara cried out in shock and pain. She was losing more and more control every day. *Rule number two, rule number two,* she repeated to herself, but it was no use.

Before the wizard could utter another word, Selara glowed, her green eyes transforming into white coals. She chanted a strange incantation and Greenwald appeared out of thin air, sending sparks flying in every direction, lighting up the Wizard's apartment. He eyed the wizard maliciously.

Saffron's jaw dropped as the teapot smashed to the floor.

The serpent spun around Selara, protectively. It reared its flaming head, threateningly at the old man.

Saffron's hands moved like lightning, forming a series of intricate shapes with his fingers.

When the serpent struck, it bounced harmlessly off a bright blue shield of light. It reared back and tried to attack the wizard from above, glancing off the top of the glowing shield he wielded. The shield dropped, and the serpent targeted the wizard's throat. A blue sword came down in a tight arc, decapitating the serpent and causing it to explode into a shower of green sparks. All at once, the serpent, shield, and sword disappeared, and Saffron slumped into the nearest chair, exhausted.

"I'm so sorry," she sobbed, falling to her knees in front of the wizard. "... and now Greenwald's dead." *Had she killed him?* She wondered, helplessly.

Saffron sat expressionless in the chair, staring straight ahead. He drew a deep breath and burst out laughing, shocking Selara. "It's been a long time, but I've still got it! My dear child, that was real Dark Majik!"

Selara was confused. He sounded like she'd given him his heart's desire, not threatened him with certain death. As if the green fire serpent restarted his heart rather than almost stopping it.

"And don't worry about Greenwald, he will live to fight another day! Elementals aren't supposed to be able to use Dark Majik! We have to find out why you can! Maybe it's because your father...." He stopped. "Maybe it is because of your mother, but her majik is limited. This is impossible." *She is a Dark Elemental,* he pondered. *That would explain so much.*

Selara looked at him, eyebrows furrowed.

"We must see ... I'm sorry, her name is cursed, we can't speak it ... we call her M." Saffron grabbed Selara by the hand and led her down the stairs. "Do not speak of this to anyone in the castle — promise me!" Saffron stared into Selara's eyes. "If your father found out where we're going, he would be furious with me."

Selara nodded, caught up in the whirlwind of enthusiasm generated by the old wizard. She walked quickly to keep up with him.

"But I have to show you something before we go." Saffron moved quickly, dragging Selara along. They zigzagged down narrow cobblestone streets until they came to a little stone building. "Do you know what they call this chapel?"

"No."

"The Chapel of the Peace Princess," said Saffron, opening the door for her. The chapel was dark except for a few candles and a magnificent stained glass window. Selara stared at it in awe. At the centre of the window was a perfect representation of herself as a little girl with a young Fletcher perched on her shoulder. Greenwald and Nova were wrapped around her shoulders. Soldiers and Dark Majik creatures surrounded her awestruck. Selara stood in shocked silence.

"You're responsible for almost eighty years of peace!"

"But how?"

"When you were just a little girl, you travelled back to the Battle of Albright. Your appearance there was interpreted as a sign from the Gods to stop the Dark and Elemental war. It coincided with the strange disappearance of the Dark Queen. You've heard of the Sign of the Holy Night Bird? You're Fletcher *is* the Holy Night Bird and you, my dear lady, *are* the Peace Princess!"

"Firk!" said Selara, shaking her head. She collapsed on a bench, overcome with emotion. She didn't know whether to laugh or cry. "It was an accident. I didn't try to end a firkin' battle. I was a little girl trying to fly like her pet bird!" *Firk rule number one.* "What would've happened if I'd never found that firkin' book? I couldn't even read it! I still can't," she said, pounding her fist on the bench. "Now here I'm on a firkin' picture window!"

Not here! thought a worried Saffron, glancing to see if anyone else was in the chapel.

"I almost kissed my brother and vaporised my stepsister! My life is so messed up!" She pounded her fist again. "Rule number two is not working anymore!" She screamed, frustrated. "I can't control this thing in me."

"Listen," said Saffron gently. "You've become a child of destiny. I believe the Gods have a special purpose for you."

"The old lady bird said I was a child of two rivers. What's that supposed to mean? I'm supposed to take my love and heal the world. How do I do that?"

"I have a friend who I think can help us. Her name's M." Saffron sat down beside her.

"What kind of a name is M?"

"Her name's cursed, so no one can say it and live."

Of course! thought Selara, rolling her eyes.

It was still early morning when they left the chapel and slipped out of the castle through the hidden tunnel. They quickly reached the shelter of the forest. Saffron looked back frequently, making sure they weren't followed. The dappled sunlight painted a glowing patchwork on the mossy floor of the woods and a chorus of buzzing insects and singing birds filled the air. The path was overgrown and difficult to follow.

This wizard's so paranoid, thought Selara. *Why should anyone care about them going to visit some old lady in the woods? Least of all her father.* Selara silently hoped that Saffron was right about M being able to help her.

The sunlight streamed into Tamara's bedchamber, lightly tracing the folds of her blankets. She felt like a child waking up on the Day of Giving. She uncovered the mirror and looked curiously at herself for one guilty moment. Her badly burned skin was smooth and soft. Her fingers traced over the skin of her eyelids and cheeks. She stretched out her hands and surveyed the length of her arms; they were as white as porcelain Tamara felt reborn. During the night, her hair grew long. It stretched down the full length of her back, a mass of curls. She wondered if she would keep it that long, and possibly braid it. It would be a shame to cut it. She could never grow it that long again. I've got to ask Jonrah what he was thinking. She smiled.

She quickly covered up the mirror and giggled to herself. Jonrah healed her completely — almost better than completely. She raked her fingers through the curls. And best of all, he asked her to marry him. Of course, they were too young to get married today, but she could enjoy her engagement year knowing no one could take him away from her. Her heart was light. She jumped playfully back into her bed and kissed the still sleeping Jonrah. He groaned.

She felt like a new person. *No one could be happier*, she thought. She guessed that Seanna must have been too worried about Selara to bother about the two of them. Or maybe she knew that Jonrah needed to stay with her after that terrible fight. Jonrah proposed to her even though she looked like a monster. *Did he know he could heal her?* she wondered. *What if he couldn't? Would he have changed his mind?* She didn't think so. She smiled as she looked at her hands and surveyed the length of her arms. It was as if nothing happened. As if the night before was just a horrible nightmare.

She stretched out and yawned, running her fingers through her thick curls, shaking out a few dead strands. She knew that Jonrah loved her. She would be the most loyal partner any husband would ever have. She owed him her life. But even so, she didn't think she would be able to go on living, looking the way she did yesterday. She picked the white berries years ago when her life was difficult and she'd lost everything. Seanna showed her love and gave her the strength to keep living. She was the one constant in Tamara's life, and even though Tamara struggled with her rules, she knew she loved her like her own daughter. Tamara put the berries in a jar and forgot about them until after the battle. She shivered. If Jonrah didn't insist on seeing her, she would have been in the Second Realm along with her parents and brother.

Her big worry was facing Selara. Now that Selara knew the truth about Jonrah, she must be devastated and embarrassed. Tamara felt remorse. She knew deep disappointment, and she knew loss. She understood what it was like to have her family torn away from her at a young age. When Selara recovered, she needed to speak with her and set things right.

High in the arms of an ancient oak tree, the morning traced golden paths along the branches where two Night Birds slept soundly in a happy embrace. This was exactly what Winn wished for. Ever since Fletcher came to her home unexpectedly, she was enamoured with him. *It was fate that brought us together again,* she thought. She felt warm and safe wrapped in his wings. She listened wistfully to the gentle buzzing of insects darting back and forth in the morning air, and wondered about her father. He promised her dying mother that he would always protect Winn. But she didn't need protection. She could take care of herself. And now she found the love of her life.

The morning painted sunlight onto the woven dwellings of the Clan trees. There was no word about Winn. Flank was concerned. He knew Gavel sent Winn to kill the strange bird. What was he thinking, bonding with an Elemental? he asked himself. Flank was to meet with the Elder Bird Seraphim that morning about an important matter. The messenger would not tell him what. He stretched out his wings and flew to the Council Circle. He missed his daughter. She was all that he had after his wife's passing. He was protective of Winn, but she was willful and independent. He knew deep down that she didn't need protecting.

Flank wove through the busy morning, gliding slowly until he landed on the rim of the Council Circle. A courier met him who said he'd have to meet the Elder Bird in his chambers because he was ill. Flank waddled across the council meeting circle. He entered the Elder Birds' magnificently woven home. The Elder Bird greeted Flank. He was very weak, and his voice was just a hoarse whisper.

"There is something I need to tell you, but you will need to keep an open mind."

"Of course," said Flank.

"I have had a vision, sent by the great matriarch Ceeka," he said.

Flank gasped. Ceeka was a seer and a goddess who gave her life, protecting a Hu-man. She preached about the unity for all creatures and advocated the prohibited practice of bonding.

"She told me that a great war was coming, and our Clan would be destroyed and reborn into a different world. She told me that your daughter and the strange bird Fletcher would be the leaders of a new springtime for Night Birds, a time of great prosperity and friendship with all creatures. Your daughter has bonded with an Elemental and has taken Fletcher as her mate."

Flank was shocked. Everything he believed was falling apart around him. Whatever normalcy remained was torn to shreds.

"Don't be discouraged or dismayed," croaked the old bird. "Winn will be the queen of a new Clan. Her children will do great things, and you will live to see it." His old eyes sparkled. He put his head down slowly and closed his eyes, never to open them again.

High in his tower room, Oag became more and more engrossed in the tapestry of thoughts before him. Ever since he lied to Daemon about Selara, he felt freer. He was no longer a slave to Daemon or anyone else. Oag saw the scales had tipped, and Daemon was beginning to lose his grip on the kingdom. He saw Grog die, defying Daemon, and brought back to life from the Second Realm. He saw Selara return to her family. He saw the bonding of two Night Birds with Elementals. Love and hope were a drug for Oag, and the weaving of the thoughts in front of him were sparkling with hope, burning brighter with each passing day. He studied them as an omnipresent being, watching a living and breathing chess match and revelling in the unfolding story.

Oag could not remember a time before Oag. There was nothing, and then there was Oag. He only knew he was created by one of the Ancients. There were others like him, but they had long since perished. He was not originally created to serve the likes of the Dark Queen or Daemon. He was created for the betterment of the kingdom, a kind of confessor or advisor. His purpose was perverted over the years by men and women twisted by the lure of power. He longed for a time when he could once again serve the kingdom as a trusted advisor and fount of knowledge. The girl in the pool so many years ago gave him hope once again that his dream was possible. He also knew that the girl was in constant danger, and there would be times when the tangled river of fortune might wash away his hopes and dreams. But Oag was patient. *Clever Oag,* he thought.

In her cottage bed, M stretched like a cat. Living here alone was a necessity after that maggot Daemon put a curse on her. She spat. M sat up and drained her mug of mead. She stared out the window. I guess I did give him a few good reasons, she admitted. It was fun having a little surprise visit from Talon though, she thought wistfully. She always wanted him. But Seanna got him first. The wench. That coward, she thought, settling for the prudish Seanna. She spat again.

M adored chaos. She often bewitched lost strangers who accidentally wandered into her forest domain. If they were handsome, she kept them as lovers. If they were rude, she tortured them in twisted ways. But to her credit, she let them go after she finished playing with them.

She yawned, picked up a bucket, and shuffled to the well in her furry slippers. "Why is morning so bright?" she murmured, shielding her eyes. The trees suddenly parted behind her. A massive creature came romping out. She rolled her eyes. *Why can't he just sleep in for a change?* She tried to ignore the beast, but the creature nuzzled her, almost knocking her into the well. M ran her hand gently across his fiery nose. "What a good boy you are," she cooed. Its glistening body rumbled and purred happily like an overgrown cat. Satisfied, he turned and lumbered back into the forest. She shook her head. "Every morning like clockwork," she said as she cranked up the pail and lugged it back into the cottage. When she stepped through the door, there was a polished stone pulsing green on her table. "It looks like I'm having visitors." She smiled, brushing the hair away from her face. "I hope they're interesting," she said, pouring some water into a large iron kettle.

In the forest, Selara struggled to keep up with Saffron, who moved quickly in spite of his advanced years. As they rounded the edge of a great boulder, the path abruptly ended, and a huge chasm lay before them. A slithering green fire serpent slithered around the rocks below, waiting for one of them to slip and fall. Selara stopped at the brink of the cliff and looked down.

"Which way do we go?" she asked.

"She's not going to make this easy," he said, stepping into thin air.

"No!" shouted Selara as she grabbed his shoulder.

But Saffron floated above the gorge—the serpent eyed them both with anticipation.

"It's only an illusion," whispered Saffron, turning to Selara. "But if you believe it to be true for even a second, it will become deathly real for you." Another step and Saffron was suspended in thin air on an unseen path above the gorge—the serpent became more and more agitated far below. "Just a little further," he whispered.

Selara followed him and forced herself to focus on the back of the wizard's hat. If she looked down for even a moment, she knew she would fall.

"Why's this happening?" asked Selara when the two were safely on the other side of the majik gorge. "Who would be twisted enough to do this?"

"M is doing this for our own protection," said the wizard, continuing through the overgrown path. "M was cursed by Daemon, and even speaking her name causes death and calamity. Her entire family and many of her close friends perished. She has isolated herself to protect others. And now she just wants to be left alone."

"Then why are we looking for her? Aren't we in danger too?"

"M is an old friend of mine. Because you don't know her name, you are safe from the curse. I'm careful to never speak her name. I have created a spell to make me forget it. But we must be vigilant. M has put up many barriers to prevent people from finding her. The forest and her Dark Majik provide her with everything she needs."

Selara wished the wizard hadn't explained the curse to her because now she was trying to guess M's name. *Stop thinking!* she told herself.

There was rustling in the grass. "Did you hear that?" whispered Selara. *Why am I whispering?*

"Yes, be careful and wary. I'm sure there're more dangers here than the gorge serpent." The grass around them shifted and writhed with the bodies of hundreds of tiny green fire serpents advancing from all directions. "Stand closer," Saffron said quickly as he encircled the two of them with a white powder. The tiny serpents snapped at them but couldn't cross the line.

"What do we do now?" asked Selara, panicking.

As Saffron thought of his next move, a gigantic green serpent erupted from the ground and encircled both Saffron and Selara, looking menacingly at the tiny serpents. Saffron eyed the serpent, understandably concerned. Then without warning a second serpent of orange flame encircled them both. The multitude of serpents quickly disappeared like so many tiny sparks. Selara's fire serpents evaporated as well, and Selara awoke from her trance. Saffron was speechless.

"How did you do that?" he asked, amazed.

"I don't know," replied Selara. "They just appeared. You were right! Greenwald is still alive!"

"Yes, but the two serpents together? This is most unusual." The wizard looked puzzled. He had very little experience with combined majik. The two walked on, Saffron lost in his thoughts.

The woods parted, and a tiny cottage wavered and solidified in a small clearing. An alarming crackling sound erupted from the woods as branches and leaves evaporated in the heat of something unspeakably large. It was as if the forest transformed itself into a sparkling green thing, slithering menacingly towards them. Green ribbons of flame erupted from its mouth, and shimmering scales glowed and shifted while tiny sparks sprayed a fiery mist.

Saffron's blue shield appeared, looking woefully small and inadequate in the presence of this writhing behemoth. The wizard knew there was no defence against such a beast. He could not protect them both, and he was clearly outmatched. His mind raced desperately, seeking a way for the two of them to escape to the cottage. He was so mesmerised by the fire dragon that he didn't see Selara's transformation.

Selara's skin glowed, and the grass beneath her feet wilted in the heat. She began a slow melodic chant. The dragon stopped advancing and paused, listening intently to her song.

Saffron's jaw dropped as he lowered his useless shield, enraptured by the beauty of her majik.

Selara stepped forward, and the beast bent down so she could touch its glowing face. While the scene played out, the door of the cottage opened, and a tall beautiful woman with green hair stood watching them. The dragon crouched as docile as an immense fiery cat. Selara smiled in her trance and then presumably told the dragon to leave because it rose up slowly and lumbered into the forest.

As Selara and Saffron turned to approach the cottage, the green-haired woman intercepted them and ran to Saffron, embracing him and kissing him as if he were a former lover. He was wide eyed and taken aback. *M was always finding ways to shock me,* he reflected.

Then she turned to Selara. "I am honoured that you have come to visit my humble home, my Dark little Princess. What on earth did you do to my dragon?" Not waiting for an answer, she threw her arms around Selara and kissed her on each cheek. "I've always loved this one," she said to Saffron. She let go and looked directly into Selara's eyes. "Does your father know you're here? … Of course, he doesn't," she said, laughing mischievously.

Selara didn't understand this crazy woman's reaction. She called her 'Dark Princess.' Selara had no idea what this woman was talking about. M dragged the two of them into her cottage, excited. "You command the green fire and speak the language of the ancients. We're going to have so much fun, you and I!" There was something about the woman that made Selara feel very uncomfortable. Despite this, the cottage was inviting with a crackling fire, a polished wooden table with chairs, and an overstuffed bed. There were freshly picked wildflowers and a collection of various dried herbs hanging by the window. She led them to the table with three chairs.

"So, too bad about your hunk of a brother," she said, pouring a cup of mead for herself.

"Pardon me?" Selara gasped. *This woman has no boundaries.*

"Come on, let's be honest, I'll bet you were just a little disappointed, weren't you?" chided M. "You almost burned down the Keep, fighting with his girlfriend."

Selara was stunned.

"No matter," she said dismissively. "You can have any man you desire. I'll teach you."

Selara was beginning to understand why she wasn't allowed to tell her father they were coming here. She got up and started walking towards the door.

Saffron stopped her. "M can help us," he said.

"Of course, I can!" she said, ignoring Selara's discomfort. She walked to the far side of the cottage, picked up a heavy round mirror, and set it on the table in front of them. "Maybe we will find the answers in my mirror. But the mirror never tells us the whole truth! Do you my precious?" she cooed.

This woman is crazy, thought Selara.

M removed the black cloth covering the polished glass. A green fog swirled just beneath the surface. "Place your finger tips on the edge of the mirror, honey."

Selara reluctantly did as she was told. As soon as her fingertips pressed onto the smooth wooden frame, the mirror reacted instantly and dramatically.

A sparkling green serpent suddenly appeared from out of the edge of the frame, slithering out of the thick green fog towards the centre of the mirror.

"You see. Dark Majik!" purred M, tracing her finger playfully along the serpents back. Another serpent appeared without warning, weaving its way to the centre from the opposite edge of the frame. This one was flaming orange. M pulled her hand away as if the new serpent might burn her.

"This isn't supposed to happen!" she shrieked. M glanced at Saffron, confused. The two serpents became entwined. "No, no, no, what . . .?"

M was on her feet now. The two serpents became a single serpent with flaming orange and green stripes. "Okay, this is just wrong," gasped M, turning her eyes away, afraid that the mirror might explode at any second. The entwined serpent grew and twisted around a tall black tower and disappeared into a dark window. It appeared again with a golden crown in its mouth. The green fog returned, and the mirror went black.

"Something is seriously wrong with this mirror," she breathed, turning it over and inspecting it for damage. "The Elemental serpent can't enter the mirror at the same time as the Dark Majik serpent. It can't happen, and it never happens!" M picked up the mirror again, turning it over and over in disbelief. She sat down. "Well, this is unexpected! I don't think we're going to be besties, honey."

"What do you mean?" asked Selara, somewhat relieved.

"You are a freak of nature, baby! There's no such thing as a Dark Elemental." She grabbed a bottle of wine from the nearest shelf, popped the cork, and took a long swig. "You march for both armies at the same time. No wonder Daemon wants you dead! If you find a way of using Dark and Elemental Majik together, he won't be able to touch you. There will be nothing stopping you from becoming the next queen of this kingdom."

She turned to Saffron. "You haven't given her the circlet, have you?" she asked accusingly. Saffron shook his head. "Good. Then let me be the first to toast you! All hail, Queen Selara! The Dark Elemental!" She took another long swig.

"I'll have some too, thank you." said Saffron, finally finding his voice, and not entirely surprised at what the mirror revealed. M passed the bottle to Saffron.

"How about you, honey? No, wait, you're your daddy's little girl, aren't you?" she teased.

Selara straightened. "I'll have some too," she said, her cheeks reddening.

M brushed her green hair to the side of her face with a wicked smile. "Maybe there's hope for you yet, dear!"

The three sat together, drinking wine. Selara did her best to manage the burning sensation in her mouth and throat. She was feeling a bit light-headed.

"Now we have a little problem here, don't we?" M said, looking directly at Saffron. "This little girl is completely untrained and undisciplined." Selara opened her mouth to speak, but she was cut off. "No, young lady!" she said, pointing her finger at her, mid-swallow. "You can't control Dark *or* Elemental Majik. If you can, then prove it!" M challenged.

"I can make a fire serpent," slurred Selara under her breath.

M rolled her eyes. "Seriously? Really?" She shook her head in disgust.

Selara knew M was right. She was always a slave rather than a master to the majik. It protected her, but it controlled her. She also knew that every day she was losing more and more of herself.

"Well, I can't teach you how to control Elemental Majik. But I can teach you how to use and control Dark Majik. But we don't have much time," M stood up and began to pace, thinking. "Daemon is amassing an army, and he intends to wipe out what little's left of Elemental Majik. So move as fast as you can, and don't come back until you've learned everything an Elemental Fire Queen should know. And then I'll teach you everything a Dark Majik Queen can do. Then we'll go dancing with Daemon!" She winked, taking another swig from the bottle.

chapter xii

Rule 12: Never let Elemental and Dark Majik humans marry

The Keep bristled with news and gossip. Everyone raved about Sara, the Wind Elemental who flew into the Keep and used her powers to stop the epic battle between Tamara and Selara. Most of the gossip revolved around the unexpected, but not altogether surprising, wedding announcement of Jonrah and Tamara. Servants made sly remarks about Jonrah being too scared to refuse Tamara. The minstrel Binoche, a celebrity in his own right after Selara's kiss, had a new ballad called "The Storm Princess." Two outcast Night Birds frequented the common area for the first time in years. It was whispered that they were bonded with Selara and Alan. Speculation mounted about the arrival of the old Earth Elemental along with his good-natured Ogre friend. Selara herself was cloistered by the wizard Saffron and not allowed to communicate with anyone for the coming weeks.

Talon and Seanna, overjoyed with their son's betrothal, ignored the lurid gossip about Jonrah marrying his stepsister. Jonrah never thought of Tamara as a sister, and everyone in the castle knew that. They knew their marriage was inevitable. With Selara whisked away by Saffron, Tamara didn't have to have the difficult conversation. She was glad to dodge it.

Far away to the west, a secret meeting between the leaders of the militant Oman Nomaji was at a crossroads. The hooded stranger, Cambrian, relayed the news about Selara and Sara. He explained the vicious firefight between Selara and Tamara, and the unimaginable power of Sara's green lightning storm. The majority decided that both sisters needed to die, but not everyone was comfortable with the decision.

"She's only a child," argued Bon.

"A child who can bring green lightning down at will. A child who will make the Nomaji slaves for her entertainment. You heard what the Seer told us," argued Rayne. "You don't need a Seer to tell you what will happen when she turns."

"*If* she turns," countered Bon.

"She *will* turn. Or have you forgotten? Sara's a Dark Elemental like her sister. You saw the green lightning yourself. Something must be done before the two of them tear this kingdom apart. Our spies in the Keep will tell us when that little storm witch is most vulnerable."

Just outside the tent, Rayne's daughter listened. She shook her head. *There must be another way,* she thought.

The Nomaji always lived in fear of those with Elemental or Dark Majik abilities. Their sons and daughters were often used or manipulated by individuals who abused their majik gifts. There was the Dark Queen and then lesser tyrants who preyed upon the Nomaji. Normal humans were virtually defenceless against majik that could bend people's will or conjure and create deadly soulless creatures to attack and intimidate.

The Oman Nomaji were starting to fight back. They knew that all those who practised majik were vulnerable to the arrow or the dagger. If the majik mortals were caught unawares, they could not protect themselves and would die like any other human being. But if they were aware of the danger, they were virtually impossible to kill. The Nomaji became masters of stealth, and they used their creativity to create weapons that worked independently of Majik. The leaders of the Oman Nomaji wanted a future where Majik didn't tip the scales of their freedom or their independence.

Grog felt out of place at the Keep. He was unclear as to where he would live and how he would fill his days. Since Whig brought him back from the Second Realm, he had a purpose and a quest. Now, with no immediate threat or places to go, he was unsettled. He politely declined an offer of his own chamber in the castle, being used to sleeping out in the open or in extremely Spartan conditions. Sara found him sitting in the street quietly watching people going about their day. Those passing by eyed him curiously.

"What are you doing here?" Sara asked. *He looks so sad.*

"Grog sitting," said Grog.

"Let's go for a walk."

Grog rose up slowly, and Sara grabbed onto his pinky finger. The contrast between the petite Sara and the massive muscular Ogre was a magnet for every passerby.

"Let's get out of here!" Sara said, looking up at Grog.

The two followed the streets down to the dock, and Sara gave the ferryman his fee as they boarded the barge. He took it reluctantly, knowing who Sara was, but relented. Grog breathed in the air from the lake and stared out at the multi-coloured buildings laid out neatly in the distance. Deep green and gold fields lay just beyond the lake. Sara could see that Grog was happier here. Soon Sara and Grog stepped onto the road. The sun was high, and the cricket voices sung in the noonday heat.

"Everyone says there's a war coming. Will you fight with us?" asked Sara.

"Only if war comes to Grog," Grog said, walking.

"Whig says no one wants war. We only fight to keep the people we love safe or to save our own lives."

As they came to a bend in the road, they spotted an old man doing his best to jack up his wagon and put on the wheel that lay despondently on the dusty road. The man's shirt was soaked with sweat; he wasn't having much luck. The old farm horse was growing restless hitched to the wagon. Looking up, the man saw Grog approaching. He quickly retreated to the other side of the wagon.

"Farm Man need help!" Sara bellowed, doing her best Grog impression.

Grog turned his head, raised his thick eyebrows, and gave her a crooked smile. He lumbered to the wagon. The horse gave a quick concerned neigh.

"Don't worry, he's not hungry!" Sara shouted to the farmer, who reluctantly came out of hiding.

Grog picked up the corner of the wagon easily, and the farmer tentatively lifted the wheel and slid it back on the axle. Grabbing his mallet, he hammered a new pin into place. Grog lowered the wagon.

"Thank you so much! I was hoping someone would come along. My name's Silas. Who are you two?"

"Grog," said Grog.

"My name's Sara, and I'm pleased to meet you!" she said, politely shaking his hand.

Silas tried to shake Grog's hand but ended up shaking finger.

"We don't see many Ogres in this part of the kingdom. What brings you to the Keep-Lands?" he said, swatting a bloodsucker on his neck.

"Friends," said Grog.

"My wife and I live alone just over the ridge. Will you come and have the Meal at Midday with us? It's the least I can do after you helped me with the wagon." Silas groaned as he straightened up. "Things have been tough for us since our son passed on."

"Of course, we'll come," said Sara.

Grog boosted Sara onto the wagon bench beside the farmer. Looking awkwardly at the tiny wagon, Grog decided to walk beside them.

"Your friend is a man of few words, isn't he?"

"I guess you could say he gets to the point very quickly," said Sara, smiling at Grog.

The wagon creaked slowly up the road. The horse, sensing home, picked up the pace towards the weathered buildings clustered together. The smell of dung and sweet grass hung in the air. Grog breathed deeply and smiled.

Sara could see Grog relax. He loved the open country far away from the bustle of the Keep. Sara had an idea. "With just you and your wife running the farm, I'll bet you could use some help. My friend here could help you around the farm. What do you think, Grog?"

"Yes," said Grog.

"We couldn't pay you. But we can feed you," said Silas. The farmer looked him up and down, wondering if he'd spoken too soon. He imagined how much food Grog could eat.

Sara noted the concern on the farmer's face.

"Don't worry, I'll talk to my father, and he'll make sure you're well supplied." Relief showed on Silas' face.

"We have a guest room off the side building where you can sleep. It used to be Kan's room. Of course, I'll have to run it by Sylvia first."

Sara was beaming. She knew Grog would be happier here than at the Keep. He loved animals and hard work. The farm would give him something to do.

"Sylvia!" said Silas. "Come out and meet our new friends!"

The door opened to the farmhouse, and a blind woman with a white apron came walking out, tentatively feeling for the handrail. "Hello!" she said. She shook Sara's hand and then shook Grog's hand. "You are a big one, aren't you? Can I touch your face? I want to see what you look like."

Sara gave a worried side-glance at Grog. He nodded.

Sylvia ran her fingers gently over Grog's face. "What a handsome man you are!" Sara stifled a giggle and tried to look serious. Grog beamed and gave her his best smile.

"His name's Grog, and he'd like to help us on the farm. What do you think?" asked Silas.

"We can use all the help we can get," Sylvia said.

Sara looked around. The buildings were in disrepair and the fields unproductive. "It looks like you haven't had much rain."

"Yes, it's been a dry year, but I'm sure things will turn around soon," said Silas.

"I'm positive they will!"

They ate the Meal at Midday on benches outside, and when they were finished, Silas offered to drive Sara back to the Keep.

"I won't need a ride," she said as she began to lift into the air.

"You can fly!" he said, his jaw dropping.

"Flying Girl," Grog added matter-of-factly.

"I can do a lot more than that," she said. Sara rose up above the fields, and thick clouds materialised. They circled the farm slowly as dark shadows enveloped the buildings. There was a low rumble, and rain pelted down.

"Well, thank the Gods. You're a Rainmaker," he said, looking up at her tiny form. "My great grandfather talked about Rainmakers, but I never thought I'd live to see one." Silas took his hat off and let the rain splash his face. He laughed.

Sylvia reached out and took Grog's arm. He led her to Silas, and the three of them let the rain cool them down in the noonday heat. Silas grinned from ear to ear.

"I've never seen anything like it," he said with tears of joy.

Sara waved and flew in the direction of the Keep. Silas, Sylvia and Grog waved back to her far below. The rain lasted well past supper.

Deep in the bowels of the fortress, Selara followed the wizard down a winding staircase to the old dungeon. There was a strange circular room with thousands of tiny candles perched like a ghostly army on several tables. Saffron told her that these candles would help her learn to control and focus her powers. Her task was to light and to extinguish the candles one at a time as she sat quietly in the centre. For Selara, it was like trying to thread a needle with a thick rope. Selara sat on a large cushion, unable to manifest a single spark. "Firk!" she said in frustration. She re-adjusted herself, hoping it would help.

She imagined a fiery thread that she could use to touch the wick of one candle. Exhausted, she screamed and sent out a fiery blast — vaporising a small army of candle soldiers. Nothing was left but a scorched table with a few waxy stains. She was upset for losing control, while at the same time impressed that she had eliminated the little army completely. *There goes rule number two again,* she chortled. "Rule number two: Don't lose control and vaporise Saffron's candles or he will never let you out of his dungeon." She laughed out loud. Still laughing, she extended her finger and a thin beam of fire reached out, leaving a single candle burning in the half-light.

She couldn't believe her eyes. She marvelled at the tiny dancing flame. *It could not be this easy,* she thought. Selara smiled. She was delighted with herself. She realised that she needed to let her powers happen naturally rather than trying to force them. *Only nine hundred and ninety-nine to go.*

By the time the moon travelled through the night and the sun rose, Selara sat in a galaxy of flickering candles. She wove threads of fire like a spider. She moved them from flame to flame, lighting and extinguishing them with the dexterity of a fiery tailor. She was having fun. She let go of all her worries and embraced the moment.

When the old wizard opened the heavy door, he was taken aback. A thin blanket of fire floated in the darkness, woven from thousands of glistening threads extending from Selara's slender fingers to every candle in the room. He stood in the stairway enraptured by the symphony of fire. The room suddenly went black, and laughter bubbled from the darkness. Selara had never laughed so much in her life.

She wields the power to destroy, but even more fascinating is her power to create, he pondered.

Selara stood on stiff legs and embraced the old wizard. He stood rigidly, not accustomed to open and overt displays of affection. Her young energy rekindled something inside him that had been dead for a very long time: hope.

Her woven blanket of fire gave Saffron another idea. He had servants bring buckets and buckets of fine white sand into the circle room. Selara's new, more challenging assignment was to melt the sand into glass. It would take an incredible amount of power coupled with fine control. Back in the village, when she subdued the green flames, her footsteps turned the sand to glass, but this time she would control it.

After Saffron and the servants left, Selara pondered how to proceed. She sat quietly in the middle of the room and thought about how she felt in the white-hot fire at Old Mill Village. She decided to put herself into a light trance. She breathed deeply and rhythmically. *Firk, this is hard,* she thought. After a time, her hands began to glow orange, then red, and then bright white. She touched one finger to the sand and it melted into a clear translucent syrup. She picked up the small glowing ball and squeezed it in the palm of her hand. The translucent ball felt like warm clay. She smiled at the memory of Jonrah's hot coal trick. *If he could see me now!* She let her mind drift, and the image of Fletcher soaring with joy in the early evening filled her thoughts. She wandered out of her trance and opened her hand. Lying there in the palm of her hand was an exquisite figurine glistening in the torchlight. It was a Night Bird in full flight. She picked it up gingerly and examined it carefully. She thought that Sara might like it. She smiled.

Selara worked through the night, making gifts of glass for all the special people in her life. Sometimes the glass was so fragile it shattered, but she'd re-melt it and try again. She created an intricate glass serpent for Saffron and a beautiful vase of glass flowers for her mother. She was finishing a crystal ball with colours swirling in the middle for Jonrah when she thought about Tamara. Selara paused. She should hate Tamara for attacking her so viciously, but she knew that love could cause people to go to impossible extremes — hadn't her own parents risked her life by sending her into the past to save her? She knew that Tamara was badly injured in their firefight. She hoped that someone helped her afterwards, but knew Tamara was too stubborn to ask. The entire fight was caused by a misunderstanding. *How was I to know that Jonrah was my brother?* she rationalised. Selara re-focused and began weaving an exquisite glass tiara decorated with inter-woven flames. It was the most delicate and beautiful piece yet. She placed it gently on a wooden table with all of the other gifts.

When Saffron saw what she had created, he was awestruck. The control of her Elemental Majik was beyond anything he had ever witnessed. He held up his fire serpent, nodding and smiling. Selara could see he had her grandfather's book in his hand. He called the servants to deliver the gifts while he re-set the room for training in battle majik.

When Tamara heard that Selara made the gift for her, she wept. It was the most beautiful thing she'd ever seen. She couldn't understand how anyone could forgive her for what she'd done. She sat down in front of her mirror, placed the tiara on her head, and uncovered it for a brief and guilty second. She felt like a queen. The tiara was stunning, resting on her golden curls. From this day forth, I'm a new person. I'll never lose my temper like that again, she promised herself.

As the weeks passed, Selara performed more and more wonders with Elemental Majik. She studied her grandfather's book with Saffron's help. He chose the immediately useful spells. Selara was very adept at remembering what she read. At times, it felt like she'd used these spells all her life. Saffron speculated that Selara was an old soul, possibly a great sorcerer in a previous life.

After many weeks of hard work, Selara was ready to work with M. She wasn't looking forward to it. She was anxious. Day after day as she focussed on her Elemental Fire Majik, she could feel a part of her was unsettled. She sensed it was the Dark Majik within her. It paced like a wild beast in the mental cage she'd built for it. Rule number two was evaporating. Soon this darkness would break free, and she would have to face it. It frightened her. All her life this majik possessed her without warning and changed her into something that she didn't recognize. It only manifested when she was in pain or in danger. When it did appear, she was not in control of Greenwald or Nova. They were the judge and jury. They protected her at all costs, but sometimes the cost was the death of an unfortunate creature.

Selara vaguely remembered chanting and speaking to Dark Majik creatures, but it was as if the speaker was someone else, not her. Her deepest fear was becoming permanently possessed and consumed by Dark Majik. She lay in bed, dreaming of a hungry green animal unleashed upon an unsuspecting world.

It was a moonlit night when Selara made her way down the winding trail through the woods to M's cottage. All of the barriers were gone, and the way was lit by tiny, twinkling green stars like slivers of emerald littering the winding path. Fletcher floated silently ahead of Selara, scanning the trees protectively. Fletcher read Selara's thoughts about this portion of her training, and he was anxious and on edge. Selara's voice rippled in his thoughts. *Don't worry, it will be alright,* she thought — trying to convince herself and Fletcher at the same time. The path opened onto the familiar meadow and a sliver of dim light stretched across the ground as M opened the door. The green dragon was nowhere to be seen. Selara gave a worried glance back at Fletcher and whispered a goodbye into his thoughts as he pressed his wings into the night breeze and went back to Winn.

M smiled and embraced her. Her demeanour was more subdued. "How's my favourite Elemental?" she asked. She stepped back. "Show me what you can do!"

Selara immediately sent a thin shaft of fire into the night sky. She sent subsequent shafts of fire that intertwined into intricate designs, lighting up the sky.

"Bravo!" M said sarcastically "but–"

Selara let a bolt of fire go like an arrow, cutting a perfect hole through the nearest tree. She sent out several more arrows of fire, and all of the surrounding trees bore tiny perfect holes drilled through them. Wisps of smoke rose from the bark.

"Lovely but –" M froze mid-sentence. She couldn't move.

"Unbind," Selara said, smiling, and M took a deep breath.

"It seems you've learned a thing or two," she said, still trying to catch her breath. "Surely Saffron didn't teach you that spell?"

"My grandfather's book."

She sensed that M was not her usual self. Something was bothering her.

"While you're staying with me, it's important for you to focus. There is not much time before your skills will be needed."

Selara nodded without a word, steeling herself to face the thing that she feared the most.

The two entered the little cottage. The atmosphere didn't seem as warm and inviting as it was during her first visit. Things seemed cold and intense, and even the roaring fire didn't warm her.

"Saffron speaks very highly of you. He says you have unlimited potential as a Fire Elemental — but in this place, none of that matters. You are here to harness the Dark Majik that is flowing through you." M turned to tend the fire, but Selara felt her worry.

"Is everything okay?"

"Of course, it is," M said absently as she poked at the coals in the fire. Selara didn't believe her. They spent a quiet uncomfortable evening until it was time for bed.

Selara tossed and turned in her bedroll, feeling she was being watched by malevolent eyes. Morning came too quickly, and the two ate silently, lost in thought.

After breakfast, M led Selara outside into the clearing in front of the cottage. "You can only access Dark Majik when you're in danger or enraged. I'm going to focus on enraged because that's what I do best!" she said with an evil grin, brushing a wisp of green hair away from her eyes.

"But I'm feeling fine. It's a beautiful day. This isn't going to work."

"Oh, it's going to work. I guarantee it," she said. "Remember dear, this is not personal, it's Dark Majik training."

"What do you mean?" asked Selara, her smile fading quickly.

"You'll see. By the way, how's that hunk of a brother of yours?"

"What?" asked Selara, seeing M's demeanour change.

"That cowardly hunk of a brother. I'm surprised he didn't take you when he had the chance."

"Stop it!" said Selara, the colour rushing to her cheeks.

"You secretly wanted him too, didn't you?" purred M. The grass around Selara's feet began to smoulder and smoke. "I'll bet he was so jealous when you kissed that minstrel boy, wasn't he? But he wouldn't do anything about it because he is just a coward like your daddy!"

"Firk!" said Selara, screaming and throwing a flaming ball directly at M while Greenwald slithered up from the ground and advanced on her.

M deflected the green ball of fire and walked slowly towards Selara, ignoring the serpent that stood frozen. "Good," she murmured. A strange chant formed on her lips, and the serpent disappeared. Selara was a statue frozen in place. "Now focus," said M. "Control your rage!"

Selara was a wild animal, collared by a huntress. The state she was in was normally brief, but M was prolonging it. The spell was a steel trap, and M wasn't letting her out.

"Control it," she hissed. "Clear your mind and focus on your rage!"

Selara shut her eyes tightly and screamed in pain. This was torture. She was drowning in a sea of boiling rage. Green acid burned through every cell of Selara's body. Through sheer will power, she forced herself to relax, to float calmly in the seething green ocean. When she opened her eyes, she saw M's smirking face.

"That was fun!" "M" said. "Now let's talk about your mother!"

M was relentless, incredibly cruel and creative. Just when Selara thought there was nothing that M could possibly say or do to trigger her rage, she found another way. When the sun sank low, Selara was beyond exhausted, but she was gradually becoming stronger than the green monster that had been her master and her protector for so many years.

Back in the Keep, Alan opened his satchel. The circlet lay sparkling before him. Saffron told him in secret that he was not to present it to Selara until she completed her majik training. Saffron said that it would be disastrous if she wore the circlet before she was ready. She could be possessed by Dark or rogue Elemental forces, and no one would be safe.

In his dreams the night before, a Wraith visited and told him that Selara was in grave danger. It said that she must wear the circlet soon, or Daemon would become the ruler of the kingdom and all would be lost. Alan woke up from his fitful sleep and took the satchel out from its hiding place. He found the circlet, glowing and pulsing with power. Saffron could not be found, and each night the Wraith in his dreams became more and more insistent. It told him that when the circlet came close to her, it would glow brightly. In this way, she could be found with the help of a bonded Night Bird.

Alan decided he couldn't wait. He needed to give the circlet to Winn, so she could search for her. He would have given it to Selara's Bond-Mate Fletcher, but he was seeking help from the Clan. Alan reached out to Winn in his mind, and soon she fluttered onto his window ledge. "You must take this circlet to Selara as quickly as possible," he said.

Where is she?

"No one knows, but when you come closer to her, the circlet will glow brighter."

I'll try, she said, taking the circlet.

"This is very important. Do not rest until Selara wears it," said Alan.

Winn nodded, holding the circlet in her beak. She rose into the wind and began to circle above the Keep and spiral outwards, checking for any changes in the circlet.

Daemon sat in his candle-lit room and poured over a three-dimensional model of the kingdom. Tiny soldiers and Daemon Wolves were spread across the landscape. There were rivers, mountains and a white castle on a lake on the far side of the kingdom, but that wasn't where he focused his attention. He was examining the tree line at the edge of the Southern Mountains above the Valley of the Skulls. Blood rushed to his face as he pounded his fists on the table. "Firk!" he said out loud. "The Night Birds are no longer neutral! Two have bonded with Elementals — unacceptable! Another has my precious circlet." Did they think this betrayal would go unpunished? He smashed his drinking cup against the wall. The tiny squadron of soldiers fell down.

He re-focused on the tiny soldiers and lined them up, methodically. There were three groups of men. His plan depended on his archers. One group would flush out the birds and burn their forest homes while the archers cut the birds down as they took to the air. He would decimate the Clan before they joined their Elemental friends.

The makers of arrows worked tirelessly for days, creating large bundles to be carried by horseback to their attack positions. Many were concerned that their work would bring judgement upon them. Some of the workers disappeared quietly into the night, fearing retribution from the Gods and the Night Birds themselves.

As the sun rose over the tangled tree realm of the Night Birds, the mood was sombre. The Elder Bird Seraphim had succumbed to his years. An elaborate resting place of woven branches was being prepared, and plans for selecting a new leader were underway. Birds from the Clan gathered in the circular meeting place and began their complicated and time-consuming debates to determine a suitable leader. Flank watched the proceedings deep in thought. He was haunted by what the Elder Bird had said to him.

Soon the forest was filled with the rich tones of the Night Bird funeral dirge. While the proceedings were taking place, the normally watchful birds were unaware of the preparations going on around them. Armed parties carefully remained concealed, posing as migrating Nomaji hunting parties, moving mostly under the cover of darkness in small groups so as not to alarm the birds. After days of preparations, the attack force was ready.

The Night Birds were still in the process of determining their leadership when a fiery arrow plunged into a dead tree at the edge of the Clan boundary. Another and another followed until the dead wood burned violently. The Night Birds were in complete disarray as random arrows skewered unsuspecting birds where they perched. Green fire consumed the dry basket homes in seconds like an angry serpent. Gavel readied himself to launch into the air. Before he could move, he felt an arrow pierce his chest.

A curtain of fire surrounded the Clan territory as hundreds of arrows rained down on the birds and their families. Warrior Birds took to the air, but they were killed instantly by the archers. Dart managed to weave through the hail of arrows and tear into a group of archers, slashing their flesh without mercy. He was dispatched by a second group of archers set back from the first.

As the smoke rose into the sky, it had the unintended effect of blinding the archers. The targets were now obscured, and groups of birds escaped in droves through the thickening clouds of smoke. The archers fired blindly, missing most of the fleeing birds. As the fires raged, almost half of the Clan managed to escape.

There was no thought for revenge or counter-attack as clouds of Night

Birds and their chicks took to the air. It was a forced mass migration with no destination. They flew as one swarming, frightened mass until they descended far away into the mountain ledges above a lush green valley far to the north.

Flank watched the prophecy unfold in front of him. Hundreds of years of labour and tradition were destroyed overnight. As the smoke thickened and more and more birds escaped, Flank sprang up as well, concealing himself in the billowing black clouds. He flew in the direction of the Keep with the rest of the scattered birds. He needed to find his daughter Winn.

Fletcher knew that something was wrong. He felt an overwhelming, inexplicable heaviness. Clouds of smoke were moving slowly across the kingdom, and Fletcher followed them to their source. From a distance, he saw that the lands of the Night Birds were a fiery inferno. Armies of men around the flames were cutting a firebreak while others moved in with swords and arrows, killing any remaining birds. Fletcher seethed with anger but kept his distance — not willing to be one more casualty of the horrible massacre.

Far away in the Keep, men carried large timbers through the breezy underground into the castle courtyard. Every nook, cranny, and hidden hallway was used to help fortify the castle defences. Makeshift buildings grew like honeycombs of a wooden beehive, an ark anticipating the storm.

Livestock pens were organised, and sacks of grain were piled high inside the fortress. This would be the last stand for all of them. Daemon had been slowly squeezing the life out of the kingdom, and he was preparing his final victory. He rode hard now to meet with his commanders and prepare for the last battle. Without warning, a powerful green light exploded in his mind, causing him to fall from his horse. *What in the world was that?* he asked himself. He stood up and dusted himself off. There had been an unprecedented surge of Dark Majik. He had to find the source. He didn't want anything to

interfere with his war. He rode quickly in the direction of the distur-
bance.

190

chapter xiii

Rule 13: Never use time incantations

Nestled in the deep green folds of the Keep farmlands, Grog stretched out in the hay. He was uncomfortable in the fancy room that Silas offered him. He enjoyed the cold, the smells, and the sounds of the outdoors. The hayloft was the perfect place for Grog. The animals came to know him and waited expectantly for the squeaking of the floorboards and the footsteps down the giant ladder that Grog built to hold his weight. Grog busied himself feeding the chickens, horse, and cows. He enjoyed the early morning attacks by the old bull when he sent the cows out to graze. It kept his reflexes sharp. He was careful not to hurt him.

Silas and Sylvia were making preparations to leave the farm and retreat to the protection of the Keep. The king's messengers were insistent. The people from all of the surrounding lands must return to the castle for safety. Grog, no matter how capable he was in battle, couldn't protect them from the coming army.

There was a steady stream of families on the road in the past few days. They packed everything they could on overloaded wagons and navigated the potholes and muddy stretches towards the Keep.

Sara kept her promise, providing enough rain to turn the fields of parched brown to vibrant green. The downside of the bountiful rain was the muddy roads where the farmers' wagons now slipped and bounced. Not one of them complained. They welcomed the relief from the unseasonably dry summer.

Grog busied himself packing up the wagon with everything that Silas and his wife Sylvia found important.

"We're so happy to have you here," said Sylvia, putting a hand on Grog's shoulder.

"Grog help!" he said, grateful for the opportunity to be useful.

"You've been such a blessing," she said. "It's such a shame to have to leave the farm now that the crops are doing so much better, thanks to you and your friend."

Grog nodded and busied himself loading the last of the crates onto the wagon. The cattle and livestock left the night before, driven by the neighbours along with their animals. Large makeshift stables and barns sprung up inside the walls of the Keep and were bursting with the herds normally roaming the countryside. There was no point leaving the livestock to starve or be eaten by Daemon's forces. The Keep swelled to ten times its regular population, and life was chaotic. An army of guards and servants worked tirelessly to keep order. Elementals used their majik to help with construction.

Soon Grog, Sylvia, and Silas were on their way. "Goodbye, house!" said Silas, giving one last glance at his meagre farm. "I surely hope you're still here when we come back!" The heavily weighted wagon squeaked and squealed down the road towards the Keep. It joined the small sea of Nomaji and Elementals alike.

Grog walked alongside the wagon. The people left a wide berth around him. He'd donned his battle-gear in case of an early attack on the road. He absently ran his fingers along the handle of his sword through force of habit. He was a formidable adversary, but Grog had no interest in fighting if he didn't have to. He had found a new purpose. He found his place at the farm. He was good at it, and others appreciated his help. As he remembered his battle with Daemon-Wolves, a crooked smile formed on his lips.

Smoke rose from new ovens and fire grills. The cobblestone streets were crowded with new people, pets, and livestock. Commerce in the Keep tripled, and merchants were flourishing. A small army of bakers, cooks, carpenters, physicians, security, and majik practitioners worked hard to provide the needed goods and services. Although these were danger-ous and uncertain times, a feeling of excitement buzzed throughout the castle. The people had hope, for the first time since the old king, that their world would change. The Peace Princess was here, and she would bring prosperity and justice back to the kingdom. The people were tired of petty tyrants. They wanted their voices heard and their lives valued.

Talon enlisted the help of Jonrah and Tamara to help with the resettle-ment of the refugees. They also led the work crews creating makeshift hospitals for the possible wounded and setting up massive tables for mess halls and working areas.

Jonrah looked at Tamara and smiled. She was helping direct the steady stream of people. She spent the days solving the millions of tiny problems springing up from building a city within a city. He had never seen her this way. Tamara had always been more concerned about what she was wearing or what the local gossip in the castle was. She took on the new responsibilities with a surprising energy and purpose. He won-dered if her firefight with Selara had burned off the last of her temper.

Jonrah was relieved and grateful that his majik was able to heal her. Her injuries had been so severe that he was frightened his abilities would not be enough. He knew deep down that he would have given his life for her, so she could be herself again.

Tamara turned to him and gave him a wink. He smiled back at her. Things had changed. They were both different. The fight somehow brought them closer. She promised herself that she would be a different person, and Jonrah could see that it was true.

Shortly after Silas and Sylvia were settled into the encampment, Grog was approached by Talon, Whig, and Alan. Talon brought Whig and Alan along because he knew they were close to Grog. Grog was just stacking the last crate for Silas when he turned and saw the three walking towards him from the crowd.

"Glass Man!" said Grog.

"No, Grog!" screeched Alan. Too late. Grog locked him in a friendly bear hug.

"Put him down! You big oaf!" said Whig. "We have an important mission!"

Grog released Glass Man and turned to Mouse Man.

"We need you to convince the Ogres not to fight for Daemon," said Talon.

"Ogres no listen," replied Grog.

"You have to make them listen. We have no quarrel with them. We need you to convince them that Daemon doesn't care about them and only uses them for his own interests," said Talon.

"He's not going to understand all that," said Whig. "Grog, listen! Daemon killed your family. Stop Daemon from killing your friends. Talk to the Ogres."

"Grog try," said Grog with a furrowed brow.

"We'll have horses and provisions ready for you this afternoon," said Talon, already moving to his next concern. Among the collection of his concerns was how Selara was doing with her training. There had been no news for weeks. Everyone received her amazing glass gifts, so it was easy to assume that she had mastered fine control of her Elemental Majik, but he was unaware of who was helping her master her Dark Majik. He had his suspicions, but he tried not to think about it.

When the sun reached the top of the sky, the motley group left through the main gate, boarded the ferry, and rode together past deserted farms and fields. Alan would have preferred to have Winn join them, but her mission to find Selara was far too important. Regardless, Alan was glad to have Whig and Grog riding beside him. He owed Grog his life. If it hadn't been for Grog, he would have been torn apart by Daemon-Wolves. Even though Whig was almost one hundred years old, he was a wise and resourceful companion. *He didn't seem a day over ninety,* Alan joked to himself.

Alan, Whig, and Grog wound their way through the countryside and to the almost impenetrable tree line towards the village of the Ogres, a village deep in a rugged forest. Years before, when they had declared their independence and left the Dark Keep, they carved out a pastoral oasis for themselves out of rock and wood. They used their massive strength to move mountains of rock and reclaim the fertile soil beneath.

The Ogres appointed a queen whose responsibility was to keep everyone safe, healthy, and productive. Mosiah was the third queen since the establishment of the village. She was young and had not yet chosen a life mate. After the death of the first queen, something had happened to the Ogres that no one could explain. They had always been fiercely independent, but day by day they became more docile and their attitudes towards Daemon softened. Mosiah realised this but did not understand why. It was as if the entire village was bewitched.

The journey was long and monotonous, but Grog enjoyed the company of Glass Man and Mouse Man. He had died saving one of them, and the other had brought him back to life from the Second Realm. Grog had liked being reunited with his wife and daughter, but as he was returning to life, his wife told him to stop Daemon and his evil from poisoning the land and its people. It made leaving them that much easier.

The human villages they passed were mostly empty, but a few remained populated with Daemon loyalists. They shouted and jeered at the three of them as they passed but kept a wide berth. Grog was not a creature that anyone wanted to quarrel with. Fortunately, no Marauders or Daemon-Wolves confronted them as they were all pressed into the service for the impending war. The smell of smoke drifted from the smouldering fires in the Clan territories. It was a grim reminder of Daemon's evil work.

"Winn told me what Daemon did to the Clan villages," said Alan. "Daemon has no idea of how dangerous those birds can be."

"You reap what you sow!" Whig said. "When the True Queen is ready, Daemon'll have more to worry about than angry Night Birds!"

The darkness of the forest grew more and more intense as the path closed around them. The trees stopped abruptly as if cut off by a giant sword. A wide clearing opened up before them. Alan marvelled at the massive walls encircling the Ogre village. The dwellings reflected their strength. What they lacked in adornment, they made up in size. Several warriors looked at them suspiciously as they approached, but when they recognized Grog, they relaxed and greeted him with bear hugs and friendly cuffs to the head. Alan and Whig smiled. They hadn't seen this side of Grog. He motioned them to come forward.

The guards tied up the horses and sent the party through the entrance. As they passed the stone gates, Alan's jaw dropped. This was not what he expected. The village looked like a bustling anthill, teeming with life. Artisans, bakers, potters, and blacksmiths busied themselves in the afternoon sun. Ogre children ran laughing in the streets. There were vendors with baskets of fruit and vegetables, and all manner of goods lined in front of large stone buildings rising up to frame the circular village streets. *I could never have imagined this in my wildest dreams,* thought Alan. *Most humans would never believe that Ogres were capable of this kind of industry.* The Ogres always seemed slow and lumbering to him, without the capacity for this kind of sophistication. He felt sheepish for having thought that way.

"Home," said Grog, opening his arms wide.

"Grog, this is the most beautiful village I have ever seen!" said Alan.

Grog gave him a crooked smile, nodding.

"We don't have time to sight-see," insisted Whig agitated. "We have to speak with the queen."

Most of the Ogres went about their business, but some stared at the three of them walking, not used to seeing Hu-mans in the village.

"Why are the Ogres so loyal to Daemon?" asked Alan. "They've supported him for as long as anyone can remember. Isn't it true that he was vicious and cruel to them? Isn't it true that he killed your whole family, Grog?"

"Yes, Daemon evil," said Grog.

"Then I don't understand. Maybe he has used his majik to bewitch them."

"Actually, you can't bewitch an Ogre," said Whig. "They are immune to Dark Majik because they were originally created through it."

"I wonder what hold Daemon has over them?" said Alan.

After Grog convinced the warriors to let them pass, they entered a massive stone building in the centre of the village. The Queen met them. Mosiah was happy to see Grog. He hugged her warmly before lovingly cuffing her on the head. She did the same to him. *I'll never get used to that*, thought Whig. They moved into the main palace and sat down to talk to Mosiah.

"There's a war coming, and King Talon asks that you do not fight for Daemon."

Mosiah paused for a moment, thinking. She replied thickly, "We serve Daemon in all things."

Whig looked at her curiously. Something was wrong with her. He picked up the mug of water, sniffing it. "Wait!" said Whig to Alan and Grog. "There's something wrong with this water."

Alan and Grog put down their mugs.

"I can smell it." Looking at Mosiah, he asked, "Where does this water come from?"

"From our village well." She pointed in the direction of the centre courtyard. The group walked down the spiral path to the well bordered by ornately carved stones.

"I think this is the problem," said Whig. "Bewitchment Majik won't work on Ogres, but potions will."

"But how?" asked Alan. "What's the source?"

"Your answer's most likely hidden at the bottom of that well. It's hundreds of feet deep! How are we possibly going to get down there?" asked Whig.

"Leave that to me," said Alan.

"Glass Man," nodded Grog.

Grog stood in front of Alan while he stripped off his clothes. Before any of the Ogres could intervene, he dove into the well. Before long, a round metal ball with curved markings bobbed to the surface. Whig snatched it up in a piece of cloth and looked at it thoughtfully. Alan rematerialised, dripping wet. He dressed.

"This orb is what's kept the Ogres loyal for so long." Whig handed the glistening ball over to Grog, who crushed it with a rock. Green liquid oozed from the torn metal, soaked up by the protective cloth. "Don't touch that liquid," warned Whig.

The Ogre queen had the remnants carefully collected and taken away into the forest for disposal.

Whig passed his hands over the water in the well. The earth shook slightly. Whig felt the grains in the sand and opened them. Whig drew the potion out of the well and into the surrounding earth to let it dissipate far away from the groundwater. "In a few days, I think their loyalty to Daemon will have ended," he said. "But now we have to get back to the Keep!"

"Take Grog and go back. I think I'd better check the rest of the village wells on the way back," said Alan.

Grog gave Mosiah a huge hug. They touched foreheads. Mosiah looked deeply into Grog's eyes. He gave her a crooked smile. "When war has passed," he said softly.

Whig smiled and shook his head. *Life is full of surprises*, he thought.

The three of them left together, but Alan soon headed in another direction towards the villages of Daemon loyalists.

M could see that Selara was taking control of the Dark Majik forces that possessed her for so long, but M sensed that something or someone was fighting back. She didn't share this with Selara because she didn't want it to disturb her training.

Selara was feeling strong. M had forced her to control the twisted rage that had been her life-long companion. She was now ready to tackle the teleportation spell. M demonstrated it, disappearing and reappearing several feet away. M, preventing the spell from working, made Selara practise the incantation until she perfected it. When she felt comfortable, Selara spoke the incantation and disappeared. But she did not reappear. M was immediately concerned.

Selara found herself standing in front of a large stone monolith. Green mist swirled and stars sparkled around her. Circular stone benches surrounded the monolith. Selara looked around. *I've seen this place before.*

I'm in my childhood nightmare, she thought.

The mists parted, and a tall middle-aged woman stepped forward. Selara recognized her from her nightmares. She was the woman in her window. The woman paced slowly around the stone pathway, never taking her eyes off Selara.

"Who are you, and what's this place?" asked Selara.

The tall woman smiled, barely containing her excitement. "I've been waiting for this moment for a very long time."

"I've never met you before — how can you possibly know me?"

"I was there when you appeared at the Battle of Albright. The wizards used you to distract me long enough to spring their trap. But they made a mistake. We were joined. Their spells became entwined. You became my way back. I only needed to wait. But then you poisoned yourself. You were such a stupid little girl. If that Earth Elemental hadn't saved you, we wouldn't be meeting and I'd be trapped here for eternity. I guess I owe him a debt of gratitude. As soon as you used the teleportation spell, I brought you here to me. Do you like this place? I hope so, because it'll be your home for a very, very long time."

The regal woman, beautiful and dangerous, paced while she spoke. A chilling realisation crept into Selara's mind as she put the pieces together — she'd never faced danger alone. She'd always had help, and this strange woman was somehow responsible. All of her years growing up, she'd had a secret protector.

"Now you'll help free me, so I can once again return to my rightful place as Queen. After all, you're the very reason that I'm trapped here." A chill ran through Selara at the coldness in her voice. "And now it's time for you to pay for my protection. You've had a good life — a life much longer than it would have been if not for me. You'll give your earthly body to me, so I can live again and take my rightful place as ruler of your kingdom. You see, you're already destined to be Queen, so there'll be no arguments. No one'll suspect the Dark Queen has returned. I'll enjoy ruining your pristine reputation. I'll make sure everyone you love grows to hate and despise you. Sweet Selara will be responsible for murdering every wizard she meets. Sweet Selara will be responsible for the death of her half-brother. And besides, you don't know the first thing about what it takes to be a Queen, but I do. Your body shall be mine, and your spirit shall remain here inhabiting my body forever," she said with a flourish.

"Firk, No!" screamed Selara. "I didn't ask for your protection — I don't owe you anything. You're a monster!" Selara looked around helplessly for a way out.

"You would have died ten times over had I not saved you. Your Elemental powers are limited and weak compared to the power of Dark Majik. You owe me!"

Selara knew she was trapped. She didn't know how to re-materialise. The prospect of being stranded here for eternity terrified her. But worse than that she feared for her friends and family who would become the Dark Queen's first victims, trusting that the Selara they knew and loved wouldn't hurt them or abuse them. She felt groggy. She was losing herself in the seductive green mist — this liquid reality. She felt her body changing. She raised her hand. She looked in horror. One of her fingers was missing. She touched her cheeks. They felt unfamiliar. She looked down. She was taller.

Selara found herself drifting. The Dark Queen smiled looking at the smooth skin of her own hands. An evil grin crept onto her face.

As if in a trance, Selara was forgetting who she was. Just as she was about to lose herself completely, she felt another presence enter the green reality. It was M, her long hair flowing in the unnatural wind, her eyes focussed on the regal woman in the room.

"Do not interfere with the transformation!" screamed the Dark Queen.

Selara briefly saw her hand change back — all of her fingers intact.

"You are messing with the wrong lady! She is *my* student, and her body does not belong to you."

Selara felt some of her strength returning, but she found it harder and harder to remember herself. Her fingertips glowed slightly, the only true light in the vast green sea.

M's hands burned a bright green and a massive serpent emerged from them, coiling around her body, ready to spring. The Dark Queen rubbed her palms together, and a seven-headed hydra formed. Sharp green sparks flew as the two creatures snapped and parried. "She's mine!" the Dark Queen spat, distracted from the transformation. "I kept that little brat safe until she was old enough for me to take her!" Her voice became shrill and desperate. "You know the heart of Dark Majik. You know we take what we desire from those too weak to keep it."

"I think that you have underestimated this girl. She is more than capable of keeping what you desire," said M, smiling.

"Don't be ridiculous. She's just a weak Elemental with limited majik. When I possess her body, she'll be magnificent and everyone'll fear and worship her."

Meanwhile, unnoticed by the two combatants, tiny flames burned on Selara's fingertips — dim red candles in a green storm, buffeted by the swirling wind. She felt her grandparent's hands on her shoulders, and then a soft voice in her mind, *You're the child of two rivers, take your love into the world and heal it.* Selara's palms grew warm in the cold green mists. A warm light slowly transformed her.

Almost imperceptibly, a tiny orange flame wrapped itself around Selara's ankle and slowly twisted around her body. A second flame, bright green and surging, rose up her opposite ankle. The two massive fire serpents stretched to their full height and stood glowing majestically in the green mist. They focussed on the Dark Queen. Unexpectedly, a third creature appeared behind the two serpents, its massive head towering above, its scales green and sparkling. It stood protectively above Selara, waiting patiently for her instructions.

"Who summoned the dragon?" the Dark Queen screamed over the howling whine of the green wind. ". . . and how did that horrid Elemental serpent enter this domain? Who summoned the dragon? What's happening? This is impossible! I possess her! Who summoned the dragon?" she demanded stamping her feet and sending a ball of fire into the mists in frustration.

She jerked her head around and looked accusingly at M, who had a bewildered look on her face. M paused, and a wicked grin formed on her lips. "I guess she's the Dark Princess of Peace after all. I always liked this one."

"No, she's an abomination! That Elemental creature's an abomination!"

Nova spat sparks in response. Selara's eyes were white-hot coals. Her entire body was glowing. She felt a unified strength she had never experienced before. The mists shifted. The orange and green serpents were pulsing fiery rivers, glaring at the Dark Queen with malice.

"No! The girl is a common Elemental — her Dark Majik comes from me!" The Queen was confused. Her heart started beating quickly in panic.

The green serpent at the Battle of Albright had not been an accident, or an illusion, or even borrowed majik from the Queen herself. The serpents had not come from entwined spells. Somehow both serpents came from this Elemental.

"So it's true. She never needed your help. You just *assumed* it was all you." M laughed.

Selara was now glowing so brightly that the two women shielded their eyes. Nova and Greenwald attacked in unison, but the Dark Queen's body resisted the fiery fangs. A twisted smile formed on the grinning skull as her gaping wounds healed instantly. Nova and Greenwald tore at her flesh. The smug grin vanished from M's face as she realised what the Dark Queen had done to herself. She was impervious to physical attack. She had committed the unspeakable sacrifice that twisted her very soul. That was why the wizards needed to trap her, because her body could not be destroyed. Strips of flesh were torn from her then re-attached themselves, making her whole over and over again. M turned away as the Queen's face was torn off completely, leaving her exposed skull. Her flesh obediently regrew, the torn pieces knitting themselves together while being slashed relentlessly by the two serpents.

Selara remembered what Jonrah had told her about the dangers of the time spell when it was used without an anchor. She had memorised the spell from her grandfather's book against Saffron's wishes. The spell was extremely dangerous and only used as a last resort. She could cast the spell directly at the Dark Queen without being drawn into it.

M watched in horror as the Dark Queen advanced on Selara like a half-dead thing, dying and then being brought to life over and over again, reforming as the serpents did their best to protect Selara. *The pain must be beyond imagination*, thought M.

Without warning, the dragon bellowed, and Nova and Greenwald drew back. The dragon bathed the Dark Queen in green fire, leaving a charred body, then bit her in half. The two pieces fell to the temple stones with an unpleasant slosh. Silence. M and Selara looked at each other and breathed a sigh of relief. But the two scorched halves of her body reattach themselves. As the Queen's flesh healed and re-grew, Selara felt she had no choice.

She began the forbidden time incantation, focusing on the Dark Queen. Looking more human than corpse, the Queen stood before Selara. "You can't kill me, so don't even try. Soon you'll live in this body, and there's nothing you and your creatures can do to stop…" The Queen stopped mid-sentence, listening to what Selara was saying. She recognized the words. She knew what Selara was attempting to do. "Wait. Stop. You'll kill us all!"

It was too late. The mists swirled quickly around the Dark Queen, consuming her. She vanished. Multiple queens appeared like soap bubbles, standing before Selara. Some wore distinguished outfits while others were horribly disfigured. All of them were bitter, angry, and screaming at her. In the chaos, M muttered the word *paradox* as she closed her eyes and braced herself. The green world howled and imploded upon itself, tossing Selara and M into a sea of darkness.

Soft clouds moved slowly in a purple sky. There was a ringing in Selara's ears. Selara looked up to see her grandparents standing over her, smiling. They were young and energetic. Ceeka perched gently on Grandmother's shoulder. Selara felt a love deeper and stronger than she had ever felt before. Grandmother spoke in her mind. *We are so proud of you, Selara! And it's so good to see you if only for this brief moment.*

"I know this place," murmured Selara, warm tears running down her face.

"You're almost ready. But there's one more task that you must complete. It won't be easy, and we can't help you." Her grandfather looked suddenly sad.

"Don't fret, child," Ceeka was now speaking. "My brethren and your people need you now more than ever."

At that, the three of them turned and walked away from her into the mists.

"No, come back!" she pleaded. "Let me stay here." As they faded, Selara felt a deep peace and then a heavy darkness enveloped her completely.

When she woke up, her head was aching. She tried to move, but her hands and feet were bound tightly. Her head pounded, and she couldn't remember a thing. A tall, sneering man looked down at her maliciously. "I have a special fate waiting for you — little princess!" He slapped her face hard, and she cried out.

High in the trees, hidden from Daemon's war party, Winn watched helplessly as Selara was struck over and over again. The small circlet glowed brightly in her beak.

"I see you have forgotten who you are — that's such a pity," sneered Daemon. "So helpless, — I wish I had more time to play with you, but I have work to do. By the time you remember who you are, it will be too late." He slapped her once more before he approached his commander.

His words were for the benefit of Dane and the men close by. The truth was that he could have killed her instantly and ended any possibility of her challenging him, but something made him hesitate. Whether it was her beauty, her vulnerability, or a long-forgotten kinship with a family who'd forgotten him. He couldn't be certain. He only knew that her death could not be by his hand, and he could not stay and watch it happen.

Selara had no idea who this man was, or what he was saying.

"The people of the village will now see you burned at the stake like a common witch, and any thoughts of defying me will go up in smoke." He laughed mercilessly. "I'd love to stay and watch, but I have a war to wage." He leaned in close and spoke quietly to Dane. "Bring what's left of her to me when it's done."

High in the trees, three Night Bird Brethren, their faces red with clay, watched Daemon return to his horse.

Dane was taken aback. *Why not just kill her now?* he thought. Dane nodded, perplexed and reluctantly gathered his squadron together while Daemon rode off, lost in his thoughts. Dane scanned the trees nervously.

Winn followed the group cautiously as the Marauders tossed Selara on the back of a horse and began their journey through the woods towards Circle Village.

Alan entrusted Winn to bring the circlet to Selara, but now she was too late. The group travelled through the day, flanked by Winn and the gliding Brethren. Villagers cheered the procession. They spat on Selara and cursed her.

Tears streamed down her face. Selara's body ached. She was beaten and bruised. When they reached the stockade, a soldier cut her ropes and tossed her unceremoniously into a dirty cell. She sat despondent, rubbing her chafed wrists. The sunlight from the tiny windows was the only light.

No matter how hard she tried, she couldn't remember what happened to her or who she was. All she knew was that she would die here. They told her she was to be burned to death at the stake. She had no idea why.

Winn held the circlet in her beak. It was still glowing. She flew up and hung it securely in the highest branches of a tree just outside of the village, and then flew down to the prison, perching by the small windows, looking down at the crumpled and dispirited girl. Something terrible had happened to her. Her tremendous powers were gone, and she sat there staring listlessly. Winn watched Selara helplessly, wishing she could bond with her and help her regain her memory. A short time later, there was the jingling of keys, and a large man grabbed and dragged her out of the cell into the blazing sun.

Watching the Elemental being brought out, Dane noticed more and more Night Birds collecting on the rooftops and in the trees. He felt a hundred eyes on him. Judging. Condemning. He gulped. Even more unnerving was that every one of these birds had stained their heads with red clay. This was not normal behaviour for any creature. *What was worse than angry Night Birds?* he asked himself. *Crazy Night Birds!*

In his mind, he could still smell the burnt feathers and the smoke from the terrible Night Bird massacre. Even though he was simply following orders, the death of so many innocent creatures still weighed heavily on him. There was also the very real threat that this girl would suddenly remember who she was and incinerate them all. He quietly cursed Daemon for not dealing with this quickly.

Soldiers continued to pile wood around the burning post. They dragged Selara to the post and bound her to it. The noisy crowd tormented her, but a young hooded figure slipped through the crowd, her face stained red. She carried a water sack. She gently lifted the spout to Selara's parched lips. The crowd jeered and laughed at her, but her determined brown eyes remained focussed on Selara.

Selara drank deeply and said, "Thank you."

The girl smiled and whispered, "Don't be afraid, the Brethren are here for you." Selara stared at her blankly, not knowing who the Brethren were.

Several more hooded figures dispersed themselves into the crowd as silent as death, their faces stained red. The strange men and women stood stoically, unaffected by the noise, focussed only on Selara. Bystanders gave the strangers worried looks. Dane's men were too busy building the fire to notice that they were surrounded.

When the soldiers took their torches and lit the dry kindling, the Night Birds closed in. Smoke lifted and swirled as the flames crept steadily towards Selara. The smoke and heat was unbearable. Blisters formed on her feet. She cried out in pain.

The cloaked bystanders tore off their hoods to reveal their stained faces. They rushed the soldiers with sharp daggers, their Bond Mates slashing and attacking them from above. Dane suddenly felt a searing pain in his back.

High in the trees, Winn watched. She stared at Selara. She didn't care about the swarming Night Birds or their Bond Mates. She only cared about the girl in the flames. Overcome with grief and despair, she snatched up the circlet and dove fearlessly towards Selara. *This beautiful woman would die wearing the crown that was her birthright*, she thought.

An old woman shrieked upon seeing the massive black bird swooping down into the flames. "Her Familiar's trying to save her!"

An archer had just enough time to let an arrow fly before one of the

Brethren cut him down. By now Winn was black lightning, and the arrow easily missed its mark.

In the confusion, Commander Dane spotted the circlet in one of the birds' mouths. *It's that damn Night Bird,* he thought. Holding his bleeding side, he shouted to his men to save the circlet before the flames destroyed it, but there was no one left to carry out his orders. The Bond Mates had dispatched them all efficiently.

Winn swooped directly into the searing blast. She flapped her wings hard and gently placed the circlet on the unconscious girl's head. *It is done,* thought Winn.

Suddenly, above the crackling fire, there was a high-pitched humming. From out of the flames grew two glistening serpents winding protectively around the glowing girl. Her eyes shot open. Without warning, a voice spoke in every mind of every creature assembled. The voice said, *Stand back!* The villagers panicked and scattered. The Brethren stood like ghosts unaffected by the smoke, the panic, or the noise. The bodies of dead and dying soldiers lay strewn around them.

In desperation, Commander Dane pulled a green bottle out of his vest and threw it into the inferno as he retreated to the horses. An eerie glow surrounded the fire. It brightened slowly into a massive fire serpent with seven heads. Its eyes fixed on Selara. Selara looked at the hydra unconcerned, knowing it would never harm her. The serpent changed alliances quickly. Rather than attacking Selara and the Brethren, the hydra turned away from her and began attacking the retreating villagers and consuming the buildings.

Selara spoke softly to her fiery protectors. The two of them vanished without a trace. Winn flew down from her perch and stood on the ground before her with head bowed low in respect. The remaining Night Birds settled on the shoulders of their stoic Bond-Mates. The robed figures dropped to one knee, their heads bowed. Selara stood naked before them, stained with soot, her unprotected clothing completely incinerated. She felt self-conscious and vulnerable, but under the present circumstances, she was past caring.

One of the Brethren presented her with a robe and sandals, which she gladly received, dressing quickly. The circlet shone brilliantly on her head. She pulled her hair back and knotted it. She coughed. *I smell like a campfire,* she thought. She surveyed the Brethren. *They have all bonded.* "Thank you!" she said, addressing the birds and the humans alike. She squared her shoulders and stood up as straight as she could.

"Together we have much work to do." She tried her best to act like a leader, but she still felt like a fraud. They needed her to be the Princess of Peace, and she wasn't sure what that looked like. She adjusted the ill-fitting robe. Her head was aching, very much like after drinking M's wine. Yet she remembered everything. All of her training, the Dark Queen, M coming to her rescue, and getting to meet her grandparents and Ceeka once again. She felt balanced. She had faced down the forces inside her, and she felt reborn. She worried about what happened to M. Selara didn't see her in the Second Realm, so she must still be alive.

"You'll need food and water for the journey," said an old man stepping forward. "We'll bring you what you need."

She recognized Barnard from Old Mill Village.

Seeing every Night Bird resting on the shoulder of their Bond Mate, Winn felt uncomfortable. She decided it would be proper to stand in for Fletcher. She flew up and perched gently on Selara's shoulder.

You love Fletcher very much, don't you? spoke a voice directly into Winn's mind. Winn was taken by surprise and almost lost her balance. She hadn't even noticed that she was understanding Selara while she addressed the Brethren and Night Birds. This was not Alan speaking, it was Selara.

How? replied Winn.

"It seems the circlet allows me to speak with you even though we're not bonded," said Selara. "You saved my life, and I will forever be indebted to you! I grew up with Fletcher and the two of us are bonded."

Winn became suddenly embarrassed. "I know. I was sent by the Elder Bird to kill him for bonding with you, but then I accidentally bonded with Alan. I am just as guilty as Fletcher. "You love Alan!" Selara teased.

"No! He's a Hu-man," she said, giving Selara a light cuff with her wing.

Selara laughed.

Bernard came back to Selara with a journey bag with a waterskin and food. Selara slung the bag over her shoulder and began walking, followed silently by the Brethren. She realised that every one of the Brethren and their birds would give their lives to protect her. *But they're so creepy*, she thought. She found their strange silent manner and their red stained faces, unnerving. She was glad they were on her side. She did owe them a debt of gratitude for keeping her safe until her memory returned.

She observed that some of the human Brethren were a mixture of Elementals and Nomaji. They were a formidable and diverse group. Their Night Birds were all outcasts from Fletcher and Winn's Clan, probably bonded years before Daemon began his rampage. She wondered how they remained undetected for so long.

In a strange way, the Brethren made her feel somewhat normal as she didn't know of any other humans who had bonded with Night Birds except Alan. She had heard a lot about Alan, but strangely their paths had never crossed. She was told it was he who risked his life to steal the circlet for her. *He must be very brave, sneaking into Daemon's castle by himself,* she thought. She herself didn't feel very brave. Many people depended on her now, but the mastery of her powers was new and she was still very insecure.

The spell she used on the Dark Queen backfired, and for a horrifying moment, she created a small army of very angry Dark Queens from different time rivers. Somehow they all arrived at that particular moment. She assumed that they couldn't occupy the same place and time. *Why is there only one of me, but so many of her? Had all of the time-rivers converged so that many of my selves sent many Dark Queens back in time over and over again?* Thinking about it made her head hurt even more. She was afraid she'd make even more mistakes. She re-adjusted her robe. She worried that the Brethren would support her even if she wasn't a worthy leader. Whether she wanted it or not, she was the leader of a group of zealots and their Night Birds dedicated to fulfilling her every whim and desire. She wasn't absolutely sure who was the most dangerous, them or her.

chapter xiv

Rule 14: Never wear the wraith circlet unless it chooses you

Pip and Dane took to the forest after the total disaster at the village. He was wounded and bleeding, dispirited and defeated. The Elementals had a whole different play book than regular mortals. They could die, come back to life, control other people's majik, fly, and melt into the ground. They had all manner of unnatural powers. He knew Daemon made a huge mistake not killing the Fire Elemental immediately. If he were in charge, things would have been different. She had the help of some weird and clandestine Night Bird cult. He shuddered remembering the red clay faces. He tightened the makeshift bandage around his ribs. He had had enough. He didn't care if he lived or died. However, he knew with certainty that he was not going to die fighting for Daemon.

They rode for an entire night through dense forest with no particular destination when strange things began happening. He stopped to rest and change his bandages when hundreds of tiny green fire snakes surrounded them. If they wanted to burn him to death, he didn't care. But they didn't strike. After a time, they retreated back into the forest from whence they came. *That was weird!* he thought. Travelling on foot, leading Pip, he heard a huge roar. A massive fire dragon stood in front of him, threateningly. He threw up his hands and said, "Kill me now, monster. But make it quick."

The dragon looked at him, confused and vanished.

A beautiful woman in a flimsy housecoat appeared in its place. "Good evening, handsome! Do you want to have some fun?"

Dane had heard about the Dark Witch although no one had seen her in many years. The tales of her beauty didn't do her justice.

"Look, I'm tired, and I just want to rest," he said.

"I have everything you could possibly desire!"

"Aren't you a little cold? Where are your clothes?"

"What do you mean? Can't you see my beautiful dress and my golden sandals?"

"No, but I'm not complaining."

"Oh my God!" she said, covering herself up as best as she could. "Turn around, I command you!"

"If you want. Sure." Dane turned around while M bolted back to the cottage.

After a short time, she heard a knock at the door. She opened it to find Dane standing there holding his side. M tightened her robe.

"So you're immune to my spells?" she asked.

"Grew up around Dark Majik. Don't think it affects me anymore."

M found this exciting. There was nothing like free will to help with chaos and unpredictability. "Are you a soldier?" she purred.

"Not anymore."

"Let's see if you're immune to healing majik," she said. She reached out and tentatively removed his blood-soaked bandages. M placed her left hand over Dane's seeping wound.

He clenched his teeth and flinched. Sudden relief washed over him as the pain disappeared along with his gaping wound. However, he watched in horror as it re-appeared on M.

She took in a sharp breath, her eyes never leaving his. Fresh blood dripped from her side and down the length of her robe. A wicked smile bowed her lips, and the wound gradually disappeared from her body.

"I guess I'll have to get this washed now," she said nonchalantly looking at the bloodstains on her housecoat. "Now let's get you out of those disgusting clothes!" She drew Dane into the cottage where a cheery fire crackled inside her river stone fireplace. An unopened bottle of wine with two empty glasses sat on the table.

Dane disrobed. He groaned. He was stiff and aching. His muscular body was a road map of healed battle-scars. Weapons, straps and worn leather fell to the floor. He was too exhausted to care about modesty.

"Well, since you're no longer a soldier, I might have some other work for you to do around here." Her cat's eyes assessing him. "For room and board, of course!"

Dane looked around the tiny cottage. "There's only one bed."

"Exactly," she answered smiling as she shut the cottage door.

Daemon's forces marched steadily on the Keep Lands. He sent emissaries to collect the Ogres. They returned with bent shields and broken swords. For some reason, the stupid Ogres no longer did as they were told. But he wouldn't need the Ogres. He could win this war with only his army and the Marauders. When they laid siege to the Keep and breached its walls, he would send in his hordes of Daemon-Wolves to kill everyone in the castle: men, women, children and any other creature that opposed him. He was confident from Oag's information that there were not enough Elementals left to give his forces much resistance. Their champion should be reduced to ashes by now. *Where the firk is Dane?* he asked himself.

How theatrical would it be to parade the fire wench's head on the end of a spear in front of her father! He could only savour that image because he didn't trust the Elementals. They might somehow bring her back to life if they found the rest of her body. Maybe he should have brought her out and had her burned in front of the Keep. But that too was too risky. A rock could turn into an Elemental and save her, or a water Elemental could come out of nowhere and douse the flames. Her death needed to be both ironic and permanent. *Let's see those Elementals raise the dead from ashes!* he thought.

Talon and Seanna worked hard to prepare for Daemon's onslaught. No one knew the whereabouts of Selara, and there was no word from Alan. They needed to win the war without her. The Keep was a steady hive of activity. Every form of watercraft was brought in and tied up safely. The people from the farms and industries around the castle settled safely inside. They had gathered enough food and provisions to last for months if necessary.

Daemon's army assembled on the horizon, bristling with weapons. He could see the Marauders carrying long boats with siege ladders. The plan was to attack from all sides and overwhelm the Keep. Then he could capture the King and the Queen along with the remaining Elementals and make sure they didn't escape like before. They would suffer. His Daemon-Wolves would clean up what was left. As deadly as they were, they were only animals and could be easily deceived. He had to make sure that didn't happen.

Battering rams and siege hammers were at the ready. Daemon watched the steady stream of soldiers and equipment from a rise at the rim of the valley. *Everything's going exactly as planned,* he thought.

In contrast to the Keep, the Dark Castle was virtually empty, except for a few Nomaji villagers. Every creature and warrior had been pressed into service. Oag was left alone in his tower room. Daemon's hubris caused him to believe Oag was useless now that victory was all but assured.

High in his tower room, Oag watched a celestial chess game played out in his mind. The pieces moved slowly into place. Oag neglected to give Daemon vital information that would have changed his battle tactics. If Daemon knew the true number of Elementals still alive, he wouldn't have attacked the Keep in an all-out assault. Oag took great satisfaction in giving Daemon only selective information. Dae-mon's cruelty and arrogance would lead to his downfall. *Oag, the God of Thought, the lowly, despised and abused servant of Daemon, will be the dagger in his heart!* Oag congratulated himself on his wonderfully poetic words.

Oag neglected to tell Daemon that Alan, the Water Elemental, had found the potion enchantment in the Ogre well, negating Daemon control of the Ogres. Oag also neglected to inform him that Elemental children were showing their talents at younger ages and some Elementals were manifesting new and greater powers.

Attacking the Night Birds and destroying their Clan homes was a grave tactical mistake that Daemon made all by himself. He had also ignored the growing threat of the Brethren and the Oman Nomaji. Daemon's cruelty and paranoia made his handling of Selara his biggest mistake. Oag had predicted that Selara would regain her memory before she was burned to death, and he was right. *Clever Oag,* thought Oag, munching on another unfortunate sparrow. Oag watched his celestial chess match with anticipation. He sprinkled more seeds by his window. The Queen was about to enter the game.

Tamara gathered a group of Fire Elementals together while Jonrah organised a squadron of Wind Elementals. They spread out around the main walls behind low stone barriers encircling the Keep. An army of archers joined them. The Wizards of Albright joined the group the night before and offered their services to Talon. They were stationed on the east wall.

It was early morning and eerily silent. The valley held its breath.

The first sign of attack was long, dark boats moving like menacing insects towards the dark silent waters of the lake. Each boat held ten men carrying their weight in weaponry, supported by shield bearers and archers. They moved slowly and methodically like menacing centipedes. Bard, Daemon's newly appointed commander, led the first wave of forces since Dane was nowhere to be found and was presumed dead. Bard knew the likelihood of success with the black boat assault was minimal at best, but he didn't care. He was a street-thug-turned-commander who had no respect for the men under his command. He would have preferred if Daemon stopped toying with these traitors and just send in the Daemon-Wolves. They could swim in the lake and scale the castle walls. He had seen what they were capable of. He considered the boat tactic a waste of time.

The boats rushed forward quickly in unison, steadily closing in from all sides on the silent lake. As the boats came into range, a supporting volley of arrows flew like deadly bees high into the air, intended for the Keep warriors around the perimeter of the castle. Jonrah's Wind Elementals worked quickly, creating powerful air currents sending the arrows back randomly from whence they came. The boat-soldiers huddled under their shields as their own arrows pelted down like lethal rain. Another whirlwind caught their shields and tore them from their hands, sending them flying hundreds of feet into the air, making the soldiers vulnerable to the Elemental archers. The boat-carrying advance on all sides was facing the same difficulties, but some boats were able to land with their shield-bearers intact. They circled the castle and unpacked the battering rams.

Then unexpectedly, a massive green flame serpent appeared on shore, weaving its way through the advancing troops, and headed into the water towards the Keep from another direction. Tamara spotted it before any of her companions.

"Don't let it reach the main gate!" she screamed. The green scales popped and sparked while the serpent weaved and glided silently over the dark water. Tamara's eyes went white hot and steam rose up around her as her powers reached their peak. The Fire Elementals around her stepped back to watch a white glowing serpent of fire quickly target the advancing creature. Hot white fangs sunk deep into the dark serpent, and the lake bubbled and steamed as the two serpents wrapped around each other in a struggle to the death.

On the far side of the castle, a small group of soldiers were now battering the door of the east gate. Only it wasn't the east gate. The wizards had created an illusion. The soldiers were actually hammering feverishly at a stone wall.

Back in the lake, several more Elemental serpents joined Tamara's. In a few moments, they surrounded the perimeter of the castle. Three more Dark serpents wound their way towards the Keep and clashed with the defenders. The ground troops waited as the lake twisted and turned in a steaming mass of flame and sulphur gases.

Flank surveyed the battlefield, gliding high in the air. The soldiers, serpents, and boats resembled toys powered by children playing at war. In his memory, Flank heard the tortured screams of his fallen comrades dying at the hands of these very same soldiers now spread out around the Keep. He wanted to tear the offending men to pieces. He didn't see their families, or their humanity — only their dark, despicable deeds, following the orders of a vindictive mad man.

Simultaneously, hundreds of Night Birds came out of nowhere, attacking the archers and overwhelming the Dark Army. They moved like feathered reapers, dark shadows fueled by anger and Blood Revenge. They twisted and turned, snapping bones and gouging at eyes. They were as vicious and ferocious as Daemon-Wolves. The birds targeted the archers specifically, assuming that every one of them was directly responsible for the destruction of their Clan Village and the slaughter of so many innocent Night Birds. The Clan Code of Revenge was deeply ingrained in their culture, and the soldiers were now paying the price for their loyalty to Daemon. The archers and ground troops turned and ran, but the birds continued to attack like a murderous hailstorm, killing and disembowelling.

Out of the forest and into the clearing, Grog lumbered along with the warriors of the Ogre village. He saw the smoke in the distance. *Friends need help,* he thought. As he and his comrades drew closer, Daemon's soldiers winched and loaded the catapults. The siege soldiers were so concentrated on their equipment that they failed to notice the small army of Ogres behind them until it was too late. Not willing to engage in hand-to-hand combat with the powerful creatures, the siege soldiers fled. Grog and three of his friends tipped over the nearest catapult, watching it tear to pieces when the force of the tip sprang the trigger. Grog was amused. The Ogre army smashed the remaining catapults and flanked the third wave of soldiers.

The entire battle plan was in disarray. Daemon hadn't anticipated the Night Bird attack or the Ogre warriors changing allegiances. He was furious as he watched Wind and Fire Elementals using their powers against his men. *Where are they all coming from?* he asked himself. *Some of them are even children! Where was that fool Dane?* He realised Oag's treachery. As soon as the battle was over, Oag must die horribly! Daemon still had one last hope of victory. He had held back two of his most devastating weapons: an increased army of Daemon-Wolves in the hundreds and a small Fire Army. None of the Fire Army soldiers could be injured or killed with Nomaji weapons. He had gambled; his powers were depleted.

He sat on his horse as powerless as any Nomaji, trusting that his last move would win the war. It would be one combined and final bloody assault. He imagined the powerful creatures killing everyone and everything on the battlefield before attacking the Keep.

His soldiers and creatures of war were collateral damage now.

Far away in Daemon's castle, Oag uttered one word, "Checkmate."

Daemon-Wolves spread out on the edge of the beautiful valley like a dark curtain.

On the horizon, a small hooded figure walked slowly, leading what appeared to be a group of acolytes. A Night Bird glided softly beside her. The figure was oblivious to the killing mass of teeth and claws that lay before her.

Selara remembered the very first time she had ever seen a Daemon-Wolf. Jonrah decapitated it as it leapt to attack them. He used his majik to trick them into attacking an illusion. She smiled at the memory. Selara marvelled at how innocent she was when she first returned. Time and tragedy had transformed her.

The walking party stopped. The circlet glowed as Selara spoke to all of the Dark creatures at once. She gave them a choice: Leave this place and retreat to the mountains or be put to death. There was confusion among the ranks, but slowly, a small group of Daemon-Wolves separated from the larger group and headed east towards the mountains, following a new alpha leader.

The remaining alpha male turned his head and growled. He glared at Selara. Several of the beasts around him gathered to attack. Before they could move, green and orange serpents sprung up from the ground and encircled Selara. They towered over the malevolent creatures and launched tongues of fire at them. The acolytes went down collectively on one knee and made the Sign of the Holy Night Bird followed by a new sign that Selara had never seen before, the Sign of Serpent. The alpha male's eyes widened in fear. Because he was the Alpha, he had no choice but to attack or be demoted and lose his status. He sprang at Selara. She nodded to the serpents. In the blink of an eye, he was reduced to ashes.

Both serpents did something they had never done before: they paused and turned their fiery faces to look at Selara. The power relationship flipped. They would no longer choose when and what they would kill. Through all of her work with Saffron and M, Selara was no longer the young victim who needed protecting, she was the master who wielded the power of Dark and Elemental Majik together with authority.

She nodded. Nova and Greenwald exploded onto the battlefield. Daemon-Wolves attacked the serpents ferociously, their numbers overwhelming the fiery creatures. Greenwald and Nova disappeared under the snarling mass. For the first time, Selara was concerned about her charges. She was responsible for them. Ever since Saffron had decapitated Greenwald, she knew they could be hurt in battle. Greenwald returned unharmed, but he needed time to heal. If the Daemon-Wolves somehow dispatched the two of them, Selara and the Brethren would be vastly outnumbered. She was not confident in her ability to dispatch them all.

Three of the wolves realised that the robed group was undefended. They advanced quickly on the nearest Brethren. Selara moved into her battle stance and was ready to attack, but there was no need. In seconds, snapping, slashing birds overwhelmed the Daemon-Wolves. The Daemon-Wolves were blinded and cut to pieces trying to fend off the united flock. They struggled in vain to protect themselves. The birds were enraptured in the Blood Lust and consumed the wolves where they fell. The Brethren looked on dispassionately. The young woman who gave Selara water, smiled sadistically.

Selara looked away from the carnage. *At least Greenwald and Nova didn't leave such a mess*, she thought.

Even though Winn experienced the Blood Lust as well, her bonding with Alan had expanded her thinking and she realised that she could choose to be enraptured or resist it. She chose to remain with Selara.

As her fire serpents continued to struggle with the sheer numbers of Daemon-Wolves, Selara decided to help them. She manifested the fire dragon when she was threatened by the Dark Queen, but she didn't know how she did it. The dragon just appeared. She focussed on trying to manifest him now. She struggled unsuccessfully. When she was ready to give up, she remembered her dragon song. She had sung it at M's cottage. She chanted it now, with confidence. The air shimmered around the Daemon-Wolf kill circle. It was like a door opened out of thin air and a huge, shimmering green dragon stepped through. The dragon stopped and waited for Selara's command. The Daemon-Wolves, so preoccupied, didn't notice the massive fire dragon.

How do I talk to this thing? she thought. *I don't even know what the words to this dragon song mean. The circlet didn't seem to work on the dragon.* Miraculously, the words she needed filled her mind. They were the words in the old language. They came from a place deep in her soul. She sang the words now, and the dragon didn't hesitate.

With an earth-shattering roar, it spit green flames over the circle of Daemon-Wolves, incinerating most of them and leaving scorched fur, bone, and ash. Nova and Greenwald exploded from the kill circle like a fiery tornado. The dragon worked in concert with the serpents, consuming any trace of the Daemon-Wolves. The creatures writhed and howled as the tongues of fire spread over them. The Daemon-Wolves evaporated in the fiery ripples of a rising tide, purifying and vaporising every vile creature in its wake, sending them back to where they came.

Selara really wished she didn't have to kill them all, but at least she'd given them a choice. Several Daemon-Wolves left the battle at her request. She wondered what would happen to them now. As deadly and brutal as they were, they were still living, breathing creatures who didn't choose to live this way.

The Brethren chanted a prayer of thanks, celebrating the power of the Dark Princess of Peace. Selara felt embarrassed. She was a fraud. Yes, she could wield powerful majik, but she was not a goddess or the Princess of Peace. She was just plain Selara.

On a faraway peak, Daemon lurched in a spasm of pain and disbelief, feeling the abrupt death of his creatures spawned by his twisted majik. He shook and vomited. His whole body burned in green acid. His powers were depleted. He no longer cared about the ashes, or the Fire Army, or even the battle. He turned his horse and galloped off to the Dark Castle, abandoning his war and his forces.

Selara walked through the steaming field of ash, unconcerned with the still smoking remains of the Daemon-Wolves. The Marauders on the edge of the blanket of fire watched in fear as the hooded group crossed the smoky field towards them. Many of the ground troops tried to run away. The remaining Dark Commanders threw jars of green liquid in the direction of the figures in desperation, spawning a new army of fiery green beings. The reptilian soldiers oriented on the silent figure of Selara. They were flaming nightmares, fully armed with weapons of fire.

As the Fire Army approached the group, an ancient chant rose up in the battlefield, and the entire Army of Fire turned as one, directly on the remainder of Daemon's soldiers. The air wavered, and a massive fiery dragon joined them. Selara continued her march with the sombre Brethren matching her, step for step.

A horn sounded from the castle as the lookout saw Daemon's forces joined by the mysterious green army. It was Saffron who first spotted the hooded figure in the centre of the enchanted army. He realised the spectral soldiers were not intent on attacking the Keep. They were striking down what was left of Daemon's warriors. Selara had returned. His prize student was now using Daemon's majik against him.

The fiery soldiers showed no remorse and no mercy. Daemon's soldiers fought valiantly, but their weapons passed through the bodies of the enchanted army with no effect. Meanwhile the reptilian fiery swords cut them to pieces, cauterising their dismembered limbs where they fell.

Fletcher knew exactly who was responsible for the defection of the Fire Army, and now directed the new wave of Night Birds to flank the soldiers who were trapped between reptilian fire and the wrath of the Night Birds. Daemon's army quickly lost the will to fight and scattered in a disorganised, panicked, hopeless retreat.

The Night Birds were fueled by blood revenge, and the remaining Elementals wanted to erase all loyalty to Daemon from their world forever.

Selara's voice rose up above the battlefield. The word "Stop!" echoed in every language and into the mind of every creature. The battlefield went silent; every man, woman, bird, and creature stood still. Selara told everyone to sit down. She shivered. *So much mindless violence*, she thought. The green fire army vanished in a wisp of smoke along with the dragon. The Brethren gathered around her protectively. Selara felt a strange comfort having them close as she faced the multitude. From high above, Fletcher swooped down and landed gently on her shoulder. She smiled at him and pressed her forehead into his feathers as the entire Brethren went down in unison on one knee and made the Holy Sign of the Night Bird. Selara gathered up her courage and spoke to every mind directly.

"For far too long, our world has been torn by war and bloodshed, but this ends today," said Selara, her voice echoing throughout the valley.

There was a collective gasp as two enormous fiery serpents rose up behind her, twisting together in one unified fiery column. One head green, and the other head orange. They were tall and majestic with eyes smouldering. They quietly surveyed the motley collection of mortal creatures sitting motionless on the battlefield. Seeing Selara standing there with her two serpents and a Night Bird on her shoulder sent rippling murmurs throughout the battlefield and along the castle walls.

Saffron wiped tears from his eyes. He was witnessing the prophecy come true. The Peace Princess had indeed returned, only this time she was no longer a child. She was a True Queen.

Jonrah swelled with pride seeing his sister wielding her full powers. He put his arm around Tamara and held her tightly. She had tears in her eyes.

"Without your courage, she wouldn't be here to end this war. You are as much a part of this as she is. I'm proud of you son!" Talon put his hand on Jonrah's shoulder.

Jonrah nodded thanking his father. In the high tower Seanna watched her daughter. She was proud of her accomplishment but knew this peace was fragile and her work was just beginning.

"Go find your families and your loved ones. Tomorrow will be a new day of peace, and there is much to do," commanded Selara. *There were so many unnecessary deaths here.* The fiery column disappeared, and Selara stepped over the bodies of dead and dismembered men and various creatures. Tears threatened to escape her eyes. She had been too late to stop the war and felt responsible for the dead. Everyone around Selara, including the Ogres and Dark creatures, moved out of her way, bowing to her as she passed. The circlet glowed brightly on her head, and Winn and Fletcher flew silently by her side.

When she reached the barge, she was met by Talon and Seanna. There were tears in their eyes. While Selara was speaking, news came that Sara was murdered. With the war raging, an assassin somehow entered the Keep and took Sara's life. Her parents informed her that Whig found her. He took her body into the forest. Seanna knew what Whig intended to do, and she was terrified for both Sara and Whig. If he made a mistake or faltered because of his age, Sara would remain in the ground forever. She was not sure if Whig had the strength to perform this kind of majik.

Before the grieving family arrived, Whig stood before Sara's body and gently kissed her forehead. He took off a necklace with a blue stone that he kept around his neck, and placed it around Sara's. Her face pale and her lips blue, she reminded him so much of little Selara after she died from the poison berries. *A life for a life,* he said. The mound where Sara lay began to liquefy. Her body disappeared slowly into the earth. Whig placed his palms on the ground and began humming. His mind connected with life in the forest. He saw the sun splashed onto the leaves and its energy travelled through miles of cells, into deep roots, and through his hands. The forest reached out to embrace Sara. Long root tendrils wrapped around her skin and the life energy of every tree, plant, and blade of grass poured into her cells. Whig was in ecstasy, connected to all the life that sprang from his beloved earth. He smiled and continued to concentrate. As he felt the last of his life force leaving his body, he decided to leave a sign for Selara. He stood up and turned to stone.

When the party arrived in the forest, only the lonely stone figure of Whig marked where Sara had been buried. When Selara saw the stone figure and the pink writhing ball laying at his feet, she burst into tears. She remembered Earth Mob when she first met Whig. She inwardly wondered if the circlet allowed her to speak to worms. She picked up Earth Mob, smiled, and told them to go home. She set it on the ground, and the pink writhing ball melted into the soil. Stone Whig looked down where Sara lay, keeping a silent vigil. Overcome with emotion, she sobbed, praying that the Earth Majik would work. Seanna bent down and held her.

Mourners lit candles around the mound, and Seanna, Selara, Talon, Jonrah, and Tamara kept a constant vigil. They were joined by a group of the sombre hooded people and their Night Birds. Seanna and Talon looked at each other, wondering who they were.

The question on all of their minds was why. Who murdered Sara? Why would they do such a thing? Sara was just a child. She wouldn't harm a single soul.

In the Second Realm, Sara sat silently on a mountain, watching the purple sunset. Whig sat beside her. "Why did you die for me?" she asked. Whig turned to her and smiled. *He seems younger and full of energy*, she thought.

"I have lived a long life, Sara. It has been my honour to know you and to give you back your life. Do you remember the little girl I told you about? She was your big sister who travelled back in time with your grandparents. I met her when I was just a boy. I had no idea who she was or what she would become. I brought her back from the dead as well."

"But I'm still here," said Sara.

"Not for long," replied Whig. The two gazed over the hazy mountains and watched the purple sun begin to disappear along the horizon. "Well, you'd better get going," said Whig. Sara stood up and gave him a warm hug.

"What happens now?" she asked, but Whig only smiled. Sara found it hard to breathe. She looked at her hands; her body was fading.

Early in the morning, the mound began to crumble. Seanna held her breath as a delicate hand broke through the surface. She rushed to the mound before anyone could move and began digging desperately.

Sara sat up and coughed, held tightly in Seanna's arms. The Brethren began singing a song of thanks. Sara smiled at her mother. She was calm.

"I met Whig and I had the chance to say goodbye." She looked down at herself, seeing the bloodstain on her muddy dress where the dagger pierced her heart. "I'm a mess," she said, scraping off the moist earth.

Everyone laughed. Her family hugged her tightly. Talon bent to pick her up, but she insisted on walking. Everyone cried and celebrated. Even the Brethren were smiling.

The Keep was electric with a wild feast lasting far into the night. The streets filled with people. Dark and Elemental practitioners celebrated together. Street vendors worked overtime, the smell of cooking permeating the streets. In the castle dining room, Talon and Seanna sat at a table with honoured guests.

Two strangers walked arm in arm into the room, causing a fluttering of whispers. The stunning woman, with shimmering green hair and a gorgeous glistening dress hugging her voluptuous body, smiled at her companion, a muscular man sporting a swirling black moustache and an iridescent black silk suit.

"What's she doing here?" Seanna spat, livid. "That man has terrorised the people of this kingdom for years. They have no right—"

"These are new days. We have to learn to forgive and forget," said Talon.

"Just keep that wench away from me!" said Seanna storming off.

Minerva smiled wickedly, loving the stir she and her companion created.

"I love your dress!" laughed Selara as she approached them from the table.

Selara was able to see past Minerva's glamour spell.

"Well, one must make do with what one has!" She gushed, "Thank you for lifting the curse, by the way!"

"I can't take credit for that! Daemon exhausted every shred of majik he had and the curse went with it."

Dane was doing everything he could not to make eye contact with Selara. One of the Brethren standing near Selara eyed him suspiciously along with a particularly large Night Bird. They had become Selara's unofficial bodyguards and never let her out of their sight. They knew that Dane had tried to kill her more than once, and they weren't taking any chances.

"Commander Dane! How's retirement treating you?" teased Selara.

"Just fine," he said nervously, looking around the room.

"Dane and I are a couple now. We are both making up for lost time!" Minerva purred, playing with Dane's moustache. "It appears Master Dane is immune to Dark Majik, and I find that enchanting."

"Enjoy yourselves," said Selara, smiling.

"Please say hello to your mother for me," Minerva said slyly.

The muscular Brethren acolyte gave Dane a threatening sign running his finger along his throat.

Selara smiled, pretending not to notice, continuing to mingle. She waved at Tamara and Jonrah. Tamara wore the glass tiara she made for her. It matched perfectly with her flowing orange dress. She smiled back. Their difficult conversation never happened. No words were ever needed. Tamara was the perfect match for Jonrah and Selara had long forgiven her.

The next day, Selara went out by herself against the emphatic protests of the Brethren. She took Storm and rode deep into Daemon's old territory. She found him when the day was fading. He was in his planning room, a crumpled wreck, completely consumed by dark thoughts. All of his castle creatures and helpers had left him. They were no longer controlled by the fear that had kept him in power. He slumped despondently in his chair, completely deflated. He could not even muster the strength to climb the stairs and kill Oag. Selara looked at him now more with pity than hatred. He looked up at her through sunken eyes.

"I know a place where you can heal," she said, placing a small stone in his trembling hand. Selara concentrated and began an incantation, and for a moment even the walls around them seemed to melt. Daemon vanished.

Ninety years into the past, Daemon collapsed to the ground as Jonrah, Selara, and Fletcher simultaneously vanished into the present.

Grandmother and Grandfather walked towards the crumpled body of Daemon.

"It looks like she did it!" grinned Grandfather. The two of them lifted Daemon onto his feet. He shuffled along with them towards the farmhouse. "We have a lot to talk about, Grandson."

Ninety years ahead in the future, Selara walked to the castle window and peered out at the twinkling stars of a new age. "Good bye, brother," she said sadly.

Most of the Daemon-Wolves had been incinerated by Selara, but other Dark creatures still survived, now homeless and without purpose. They gathered together at Daemon's castle. They chose a leader, a creature they could trust and would always determine the truth and conduct himself honourably. Oag was the new ruler of Daemon's lands.

Selara returned to the Dark Castle five days after her coronation. Oag, in anticipation, had the castle cleaned and decorated for her arrival. He fussed and shuffled about, making sure everything was perfect.

He met her at the city gates with her delegation. She was as beautiful as he remembered. Oag knew he was a very underwhelming creature to look at, but Selara treated him with the utmost respect. She no longer looked at him with the fear and revulsion of her younger self. She now understood the value of his ability and his vast knowledge. She also understood it was his courage that had turned the tide of the war.

In the entry hall, she presented him with a crystal crown that she made herself. She told him it was clear because nothing could be hidden from him. Oag bowed low, and she placed the crown on his head. The motley crew of mortals and immortals cheered. Oag vowed to rule with justice and truth rather than fear.

Selara had a busy week rebuilding the broken kingdom. She sent workers to help the Night Birds develop a new Clan Forest. She sent a fully recovered Sara to put out fires on the battlefields and beyond. Selara found very little time for herself.

Grog found Silas and Sylvia, and helped them re-settle. Grog loved farm life, but he needed to make a special trip to the Ogre village. The remaining Ogre warriors returned to their settlement and pledged their allegiance to King Oag.

One evening, Fletcher insisted on Selara coming with him for a walk beyond the Keep Lake. Fletcher was persistent and told her he had found something she had to see. She reluctantly agreed, feeling exhausted.

They followed a winding path through the forest, then without warning, Fletcher abruptly disappeared. He began to call for help through their bond.

Where are you? she asked him, upset.

Not much further. Hurry!

Selara rushed up the path to find a bonfire burning in a cosy forest opening. There was a large beautifully woven bench with a round opening so that two people could climb into it at once. It was held securely with rope between two trees. A picnic was laid out on a woven table adorned with lit candles. Bottles of wine, a picnic basket and a leather satchel hung from a tree by the rushing creek. A little clear pool of water poured out in front of the bonfire and then wove itself around the trees to the waterfall. The scene was beautiful, surreal, and completely unexpected. Selara looked around in astonishment.

"Okay, Fletcher! What's going on here?" she shouted into the trees. Fletcher could not be seen or heard, and he blocked her from his mind. She walked curiously around the campsite. She wondered about the satchel hanging from the tree, and looked inside. There were clothes and sandals in the bag, large enough for a man. *Not for me, I guess.*

Then miraculously, a figure rose quickly out of the pool. It was like glass at first, and then became solid.

"Winn, what's wrong? What happened?" Alan shouted, looking around. When he spotted a shocked young woman standing directly in front of him, he realised he was naked in front of the Queen. "I am so sorry!" he said, doing his best to cover up. "It's that damn Night Bird!"

Selara turned her head and tossed him the bag. She was smiling.

"It looks like there are two scheming Night Birds who decided they would introduce us. I guess they felt we should spend some time together," giggled Selara.

"I am going to wring her little neck!" said Alan, shivering through clenched teeth, doing his best to put his clothes on.

"Come by the fire. You must be freezing," she offered.

Alan dressed hastily and rushed to the warmth of the fire, his teeth chattering. He couldn't help but be reminded of the night he and Winn had first met.

They climbed into the bench basket, and Selara pulled a large thick blanket around the two of them. She could feel her heart beating faster. They huddled close, swinging slowly and feeling a bit awkward. The awkwardness eased as they both became warm and cosy, sipping wine and sampling the contents of their picnic basket.

"My name's Alan by the way. We've never officially met," he smiled, offering her his hand. She shook it meeting his eyes.

"My name is Selara, and I'm pleased to meet you," she said, smiling.

"I wonder if those two match-making Night Birds have got it all wrong," Alan said, looking deep into her bewitching green eyes.

"What do you mean?" asked Selara.

"What possible business could a Fire Elemental have with a Water Elemental?"

"Lean a little closer and find out!" She winked.